Nicola Pearson is a new recruit to the Federal Bank in Sydney, hired to devise a new system to manage the trading risks of the bank. It is the mid-90s and she has to prove herself professionally and intellectually to win over the dealers, especially their boss Tom Forrester. He has recently returned from a three-year stint in London to run the Federal Bank's financial trading operations.

Nicola has been left in the lurch by her ex-husband and does not trust men, lacking confidence in her judgment of them although she is confident of her workforce skills. She lives quietly, keeping her private life to herself and worrying over a secret.

Tom is also divorced, following a marriage experience which left him very disillusioned. The world sees him as living in the fast lane and Nicola is not his usual 'type' but something about her calls to him.

He gradually recognises she is bottling up a secret. Does he hold the key to relieving her worries and changing her life?

TRADING SECRETS

LOUISA VALENTINE

Trading Secrets

Copyright © Louisa Valentine 2021

Published by Louise Wilson, South Melbourne, 2021

www.louisewilson.com.au

ISBN 978-0-6450741-3-0 (digital)

ISBN 978-0-6450741-4-7 (print)

Cover design by Bookcoverology

Cataloguing in-publication data is available from the National Library of Australia.

CHAPTER ONE

Nicola Pearson fanned herself with the hand clutching her notepapers, deftly used her right hand to punch the number code into the security keypad and took a deep, steadying breath to control her pulse. *You can do this.* She sucked in another deep breath. *You can do it.*

She possessed supreme confidence in her work skills. Being capable banished an amazing number of inner insecurities. But recovery from her marriage to David meant that regaining belief in herself as a woman remained a work-in-progress, continually challenged by the man's world she inhabited at work.

The door clicked open. She'd known what to expect but the testosterone 'hit' was palpable. Legions of screen jockeys, the big swinging dicks of the finance world, manned the wall-to-wall desks crammed with computer screens. Summoning every ounce of the confidence she needed to face this challenge, Nicola stepped into the enormous noisy space as the door slammed shut behind her.

As trading positions with Asia gained or lost thousands of dollars, disembodied yowls of rage, whoops of joy or frustrated expletives inflated the general buzz of the crowded room. Traders in Singapore and Hong Kong, three hours behind Sydney at this time of year, were preparing for their lunch break by squaring off their books in Sydney's financial markets.

Everyone else was waiting for London markets to open, eleven hours behind Sydney.

During this mid-afternoon lull in the daily frenzy of a trading floor, its occupants needed a diversion, and she was it. Nicola, a woman on a mission, determinedly ignored the ogling dealers as she marched past them.

She sized up the nature of her likely opposition by scanning the overall environment. Unlike her last job at the Grosvenor Bank, the signs here were positive. This trading room, at least, seemed under control. Desks were relatively tidy. Floors were free of paper rubbish and clutter. There were no black lace knickers or G-strings stretched across any computer screens here. Someone in authority undoubtedly discouraged this particular gang of young bucks from displaying their trophy symbols. She breathed a silent *Phew*. In the sexist world she inhabited, it was a small but promising sign that their boss might, just might, show her a bit of respect.

'Well … hull-*oh* there!' Mr. Hot Shot himself could hardly wait to attract her attention. He swivelled towards her, lunged forward on his chair and leered at her.

She took an instant dislike to the lascivious tone of his voice. Like wolf whistles in the street, cocky one-liners of this nature were best ignored. She glanced at him and kept on walking.

His eyes narrowed with annoyance before he tried again to engage. 'Looking for Tom Forrester, babe?'

'Babe' had the ring of a deliberate sexist taunt. Her skin crawled in disgust. *In your dreams, buddy. I'm not your babe, and never likely to be.*

'That's right.' To avoid giving him any hint of encouragement she didn't break step. She had no intention of being sucked in as one of the boys, a tit-for-tat player in the suggestive banter infecting trading rooms like these, full of guys. Let them think she was uppity. She had to establish some above-the-fray respect if she had any hope of succeeding in her new role. And it was crucially important to her that she did succeed.

'Over there.' He jerked his thumb towards the corner office.

His screen tag put a name to his face. John Wrigley. She made a mental note to be careful of him in the future. He exemplified why these men were not her kind of people, although her job meant she had to work with them. Not that she was sure that *any* men were her kind of people. She murmured 'Thanks' as she passed. Good manners were timeless and never went astray.

John's directions weren't needed. She already knew Tom's office would be in the prime corner position. No-one wasted panoramic views over the finest harbour in the world on underlings.

The dealers closest to her quarry's office had been alerted by Mr Hot Shot Wrigley. A female target was approaching. They nudged each other and snickered. New women in the trading room were a welcome distraction from perpetual enslavement to the flickering screens. Who was this chick, and what was she doing there? Who could be first to score?

Head held high as she ran this gauntlet, she reached the corner office dead on time for her appointment. He should be expecting her but she tapped on the open door out of common courtesy and eyed the lion's den.

Tom Forrester, head of the Federal Bank's financial markets division, was tilted back on his swivel chair, phone jammed against one ear, barking staccato instructions into the handpiece. Tom Forrester. Foreign exchange dealer extraordinaire. Financial strategist without equal. Negotiator par excellence. Master of all he surveyed. Her likely foe as the strongest force standing between her and the task she had been hired to design and implement.

Alerted by her knock, Tom's gaze zeroed in on her as he continued to listen to the conversation at the other end of his line. Blatantly he gave her a silent but comprehensive once-over.

Nicola's fragile self-confidence as a woman took a hit. Her throat went dry and she swallowed nervously. A secret corner of her brain had been hoping that this particular man would be different. He was higher up the pecking order, supposedly more career-wise than the men lined up outside his door. It was tough surviving in such a macho workplace. She could almost read those carnal thoughts of his, running like a ticker-tape, and she was tired of men's one-track minds.

Body language is everything. Don't give him the advantage. She stiffened her spine and stood taller. She wouldn't crumble, be defeated. Two could play Tom's game. What was good for the gander was also good for the goose.

Challenging his roving eyes with boldly appraising eyes of her own, she stepped forward into his office. As she neared him, a shock of recognition zapped her brain as she registered the colour of his penetrating eyes. Deep midnight blue. It was uncanny. She'd only ever seen that precise shade and colour intensity on one other person, the most important person in her world. Nicola hesitated for a second as a shiver of apprehension sprinted down her spine.

She shook off that eerie sense of connection, recovered her equilibrium and cast her eyes over the rest of him, half hidden behind the barricade of his massive desk. What a man! Seated before her was the complete physical opposite of her old boss at Grosvenor Bank, Richard Bourke. Birko had warned her to expect a forceful character, a man to be reckoned with. Why hadn't Birko also warned her that Tom Forrester fitted every media stereotype for a top-league international banker?

He packed a visual punch, scrambling her insides. For a moment she succumbed guiltily to the same sexist attitudes which troubled her in reverse, soaking up his physical appearance. His height above the desk indicated he'd look down on most other men. His dark, almost black hair was cropped close to his skull. With his straight nose and strong jawline of classic film star quality, he'd be every woman's first choice for the James Bond role. His business shirt gleamed white and fitted snugly to his torso. No sign of flabbiness thickened his middle, the curse of desk-bound men. His suntanned complexion indicated hours spent on the corporate entertainment circuit, perhaps aboard a yacht on Sydney Harbour, or thwacking golf balls round one of the famous sand-belt courses in Melbourne. Nicola guessed his age as mid-thirties. Like the trading room outside, his office positively reeked of testosterone.

She wrenched her brain into gear. Remember you're through with men. They're selfish. They let you down. Don't let this man's good looks and powerful aura derail you, Nicola. Stay focused, girl.

He slammed down the phone and stood for the introductions. Yes, his height fitted her estimations, perhaps six foot three. Stretching across his intimidating desk, he extended his hand for the obligatory handshake as he said, 'Tom Forrester. You must be Nicola Pearson. I've heard all about you.'

Nicola kept an iron control over her expression. Trying to put a new player on the defensive was the classic approach in business. At least he hadn't sounded sexist, just business-like. What had he heard about her work? Good or bad? Nicola didn't take his bait. Who cared what he'd heard? She simply smiled and offered her hand. 'Hello Tom, that's right, I *am* Nicola Pearson.'

Their hands met. A spark of electricity shot through her hand and wrist and zinged its way to her heart. The charge was almost painful, like the zap when you touch a car door sometimes. Her counterpart visibly flinched, then he released his grip. Hastily she stepped back.

'Sparks flying already, Nicola?'

She might have taken this as sexist repartee except that, momentarily, Tom Forrester had looked stunned, caught off balance. He'd dropped his bantering tone. She decided to take his words literally, as if they forecast workplace struggles ahead of them.

He recovered masterfully, clearly an expert at handling awkward moments. 'It's as hot as Hades outside today. Dries out the skin.' He rubbed his hands together as he advanced a plausible excuse for the sparks. 'So does the air conditioning in this trading room.' He waved a hand towards the control unit on the wall.

She raised a puzzled eyebrow at him and he said, 'We need to counter the heat generated by the technology. Dehydration builds up a charge of static electricity.'

This was turning into a memorable day. Supercharged in every way. First, his eyes. Now this bodily crackle between them. She nodded her acceptance of his quick-witted explanation and said, 'Hope it's not a sign of things to come, Tom. Shocks, that is.'

He stared at her for a moment. It was a thoughtful stare. 'Quite. Let's get on with our meeting.'

They both took their seats, warily facing each other across the desk's expanse. Apart from the papers he'd been flicking through during his telephone call, his desk top was amazingly neat and tidy for a trading manager. Nicola wondered, did that mean he employed an efficient personal assistant, or was he a self-disciplined type with a well-ordered brain? She'd soon have an idea.

Tom seized the conversational initiative. 'I hear from the Chief that you've been hired for a special project.' He sounded blasé, as if her project was low down on his list of priorities. She'd wait and see what he said next.

'I've been flat strap this week, finalising a major deal, with no time to focus my full attention elsewhere. That last phone call was part of it.'

Why do men feel the need to big-note themselves? Nicola made an effort to keep a dead-pan expression on her face and leave the conversational ball in his court.

It worked and he said, 'I know this project involves risk management, hence your request for a meeting with me.' He fiddled with a pen on his desk as he watched her. 'I'm waiting to hear about it.' He leaned forward in his chair. 'Direct from the filly's mouth, you might say.'

How quickly he'd slipped back into macho-mode. She didn't simper in response. She rolled her eyes at his put-down, the kind too often used by men to keep women in their place. No filly was she. What an image! Immature, flighty and prancing. She had a job to do, and she must mark out her territory and stamp her authority. Her colleagues must learn to see past a female body to a brain, where she knew she stood on firm ground. She'd start by training him. Culture change started from top management. Deliberately, she said nothing and gazed at him steadily. Let him extricate himself.

His next remark adopted a more objective and conciliatory approach, proving he was no fool. 'Sorry. I picked the wrong metaphor. Half way through it I realised I could hardly say 'horse'.' His appreciative glances indicated the flirtatious direction of his thoughts had resumed. 'Let's start again. Would you like to explain your special project and how it will impact on my area?'

Nicola awarded him a few marks for at least realising his error, acknowledged his apology with a nod and replied in her most dignified and formal manner. 'Most certainly. That's why I made this appointment. To outline the project', she paused, 'and to gain your co-operation.' There was no 'hopefully' about it. She fully intended that Tom Forrester would co-operate, sooner rather than later.

He slipped into the usual impatient, abbreviated communication style acquired by all who inhabit trading rooms. 'Fire away.'

Her confidence level rose: her firmness and refusal to play games between the sexes had successfully shifted Tom into business mode. She knew from her experience of the fast-paced world of a money market trading environment that she couldn't waffle on. Traders had famously short concentration spans. She'd have to get to the point of this meeting as fast as possible, but first she needed to stroke his ego. Men *and* women responded better to the carrot than the stick.

'You, probably better than most people, know that the Federal Bank leads the way in global risk management systems. Your input was integral to the development of some of them. The global limits system in particular.'

'That's right, to control the credit exposures of the dealers to other banks.' As if gratified at her recognition of his role, his chest puffed up a little.

Nicola still needed to prove she knew more than the basics where his territory was concerned. She expanded on his statement, adding her contribution. 'And to control the limits on their trading risks as well. All those derivatives trades, built upon a foundation of spot deals, forward deals, swaps and options, and incorporating interest rate risks.'

Tom's eyes lit up. 'Now you're talking my language.' He swung back on his chair, the picture of manly confidence. 'Sometimes it goes against the grain, being hamstrung by bureaucracy. The boys chafe at the bit sometimes, being reined in, but the system works pretty well overall. We've never experienced a problem with a rogue trader, or an unsustainable loss on an adverse trading position.'

Nicola congratulated herself that her game-plan was working, so far. After a somewhat shaky start, her softly-

softly approach was taking her forward. Macho-man was conceding the logic of the situation, which would help when she got to the tricky bit.

'I'd like you to know, Tom, that the strength of the Federal Bank's management team was one of the reasons I accepted the offer to work here.'

'Good. Then you do understand we have to take risks, but in a prudent fashion.'

'Of course, I understand completely.' She paused as she reached the crux of the matter. 'I'm glad you think that prudence is the essence of it all, Tom, because that *is* my job, to develop a system controlling a bit more of your trading activity.'

'You've got to be kidding. You!'

Nicola had been expecting disbelief but never allowed scornful remarks like that to disconcert her where her job was concerned. 'Well, Tom, that wasn't exactly a vote of confidence, but yes, me.'

A glimmer of remorse chased across his face. She seized her opportunity to make him squirm a little more. 'When I first came into this room you declared you'd heard all about me. Why act so surprised now? What exactly did you hear?'

He backed off. 'Not much. The Chief informed me he'd hired a specialist analyst to upgrade our management information and control systems. He mentioned it was a woman, with a big reputation in her field, but I didn't catch the name. As I said, I've been busy.'

That predictable 'busy' excuse, so often trotted out to

cover an awkward moment, still hadn't explained his surprise. She waited impatiently for him to fill the ongoing silence.

He watched her impassive face for a moment and continued. 'I assumed my area would be an integral part of any upgrade. But I didn't expect the project manager would be someone like you.'

'And what *exactly* do you mean by that last comment?' She fixed him with her sternest gaze.

'Well, er …,' Tom faltered.

Nicola could almost read his mind. She'd already given him plenty of clues that she took offence at deprecation. For all he knew, she could be one of those placard-bearing women's lib types, and he could be heading down an express route to charges of sexual discrimination or harassment. She wasn't a strident feminist, but it was almost funny to watch him struggling to climb out of the hole he'd dug for himself.

A second later a broad and genuine grin lit up his face. 'Someone so electric.'

Nicola burst out laughing. He'd extricated himself in a way she'd not expected. It seemed a keen sense of humour lurked behind all his machismo. Recalling their initial handshake, she couldn't resist the chance to reciprocate his innuendo. 'You are too. Remember?'

Tom grinned at her again. 'Touché. Okay, Okay, point taken. What exactly is it that you plan to do with me?'

Humour was one thing, but she'd never been good at

the double-entendre game. Nicola must get this back on track, even if she'd almost lost her way when side-swiped by the impact of Tom Forrester's unexpectedly devastating grins. They changed his forceful image completely. Was he Dr Jekyll? Or Mr Hyde? He was the most charismatic man she'd ever met.

She smiled sweetly at him, all innocence, as she resumed her appeal to his ego. 'I plan to spend quite a bit of time with you. We'll have to work pretty closely, because I'll need your assistance. I understand the basics of the derivatives trades undertaken here, but I'll need you to explain to me some of the finer points.'

A third grin lit his face. 'It will be my pleasure, ma'am.'

His suggestive drawl prompted a frown of annoyance from Nicola. Was he stupid?

He proved to have a brain after all by backing off again. 'So that's the area you'll be concentrating on. Good, it's long overdue. I don't mean here specifically, in this bank. I reckon we do a pretty good job controlling our dealers. Mainly because our management staff understand the trades. No, I mean generally, in the wider market. The market's gone crazy.'

'That it has.' Damn. Her response was insufficient. Everything about his words and body language demonstrated a one-track mind where she was concerned. She needed to re-programme the mindset of Mr Thomas Forrester by providing more proof of her professional credentials. 'It's obvious that GRB International in

London went belly-up in 1993 because its top management didn't have a clue what their derivatives trader was up to. One employee ultimately brought down the whole bank. That was a couple of years ago yet the control systems remain problematic.'

'Yep. I'd just arrived in London when it happened.' He looked at her with the glimmerings of respect. 'So, you *do* know a thing or two about the crazy world inhabited by dealers?'

'I do, especially the systems which attempt to control them.' She teased him a little. 'It's self-evident, don't you think? Would they have hired an amateur for this job?'

Tom's eyes betrayed a hint of amusement.

Nicola ignored that flicker. Her passion for her cause took her over. 'The Federal Bank's proposed system is badly needed in the broader financial market place. If I can design this new system effectively, we'll be able to sell it to other banks, as happened with the earlier approaches taken to risk management.'

He sat up straighter in his chair, paying more attention now. 'You're trying to turn your cost centre of the bank into a profit centre?'

'Maybe,' came her guarded reply, 'but first things first. A workable system.'

'Our special protective shield, eh?'

She smiled her agreement. 'And, in your role, you know full well that the project carries significance well beyond these four walls. Maintaining confidence in our banks is important for the welfare and security of the entire community.'

A surge of adrenaline flooded her body with this thought of the intellectual challenges ahead of her, and the enormity of her task. The design of the system didn't bother her. That was the easy part. The real challenge was to convince a large group of sceptical, resistant and head-strong men to accept it and adopt it. If she failed, her contract with this bank would be terminated, turning her world upside down. Again.

Nicola curbed her enthusiasm, aware that the man sitting opposite was studying her closely, like an exhibit in a freak show. She stopped talking. She waited. She watched his demeanour change, watched him relinquish, for now, his game of predatory man versus subservient woman. His eyes signalled a careful, intelligent assessment of one human being by another. Apprehensively, she waited for his response. Had she gained his respect and backing?

The seconds ticked by. Eventually he said quietly 'I do know. Right, Nicola, it's a deal. I'm your man in the team working on this project.'

Your man. Those words resounded inside her head. There was no time for any more men in her life. David had cured her of that. The rat. She had no interest in finding a replacement rat. She wasn't going to count on any man ever again. Her circle of trust did not extend beyond herself and a few close family members and friends. Counting on her rewarding work was far more reliable and preferable as her life strategy. And necessary. She needed to work. She had responsibilities beyond these walls.

Nicola forgot, for a moment, that time is of the essence in a trading environment. Once a decision is made you move on. No daydreaming, no mucking around. Her brief reverie was interrupted by the tapping of a pen flicking against the desktop and Tom's distinctly masculine voice. 'Are we done for now, Nicola? Gotta go, need to call someone urgently, following up on that last call.'

'Yep'. She gathered her papers and stood up.

Tom sprang from his chair and strode around his desk. Up close he was even more dominant. His eyes locked on hers as he extended his hand again. 'Thanks for dropping by to fill me in. See you soon.' His baritone voice hinted subtly at something more than routine business.

Nicola braced herself for the zap. No sparks flew this time when her hand encountered the firm pressure of his strong, warm flesh and bone.

Tom's voice, and his touch, triggered a few wayward thoughts. Eons ago, before she'd banished all thoughts of romance from her mind, she *would* have welcomed attention from a hot-blooded male like Tom.

She stamped on these thoughts. In her best professional manner she said, 'Thanks for your time today. I'll ring in the morning to set up our next appointment.'

He gave her hand a slight squeeze before releasing it.

'It's been my pleasure. I can tell already that the next few months are going to take us to some stimulating new places.'

'They'll be a challenge for us both, I'm sure.'

He grinned at her. With a devilish twinkle in his eyes.

CHAPTER TWO

Directly across the harbour from his office, near the tip of McMahons Point, Tom lolled on the balcony of his luxury apartment. Beer in hand, he chilled out as the dusk faded into night and the city lights sparkled reflectively across the harbour. He loved this time of day. In this place. It was one of the reasons he'd returned from his three-year posting in London. Daylight saving meant he could occasionally be home from the office in time to savour it. He'd been alone every night in this eyrie, with no females sharing his brand-new bed. Better not let the fellas at work find that out. They'd think he was losing his touch. Not that he cared what they thought.

A suburban train rumbled its way across the Bridge. A police siren wailed in the distance. Across the bay, at Luna Park, young people screamed with ecstasy as the Wild Mouse hurtled them along its roller-coaster track. The rigging on the yachts bobbing way below him in Lavender Bay clanked rhythmically. In London he'd missed these unmistakable sounds of Sydney Harbour.

Tiny beads of perspiration dotted his forehead. His damp T-shirt stuck to the back of his chair. Sydney in February was an enervating place, its humidity at its height, but his apparent lethargy was deceptive. A stirring of restless energy had him on edge.

His mind flicked to that woman today. Nicola. Her sudden appearance in his office had floored him. The Chief had informed him that the new risk management specialist was a woman but age-wise he'd expected an old boiler, not the proverbial young chick, to use the inelegant jargon he'd overheard being bandied around in the trading room after she left.

His gut reaction had told him one thing ... the Chief's new hire was quite a knockout. As the meeting progressed, his more-considered reaction had been to admire a professional operator, who certainly acted as if a brain operated inside her head. Not too young ... maybe late twenties. He could see why the Chief had brought her on board. His newest recruit was definitely going to be an asset to the Federal Bank.

As a person she seemed far too self-contained. A bit up-tight maybe, but feisty. Something about her bearing and expression hinted that a lot lurked beneath the surface. She even had the makings of a sense of humour, a quality that appealed to him.

Nicola Pearson and her mysteriously seductive powers

intrigued him. Why, he didn't understand. Great style, true. Slim, elegant. But definitely not his usual type. The 'gentlemen prefer blondes' maxim had guided him to date and he'd ended up with Catherine. His ex-wife. She was the reason he restricted himself to sexual relationships these days, guarding himself against falling in love, even with blondes.

Nicola didn't have long, shiny, toss-it-around blonde hair like Catherine, although her mass of wild curls was well cut and held a certain appeal. Her glossy lipstick was entirely up his alley. He hadn't been able to take his eyes off her mouth when she talked.

Catherine's brand of female behaviour was missing too … the kind that had once sucked him in, like the vortex of a whirlpool, before he'd learned to distrust the power of those innocent-looking swirls and eddies. Nicola had made no attempt to flaunt herself sexually at him. She used intellect as her weapon of choice. That keep-your-distance manner of hers indicated one very proper lady, nothing like Catherine. Yet those expressive iron-grey eyes of hers would reel any man in. The way she used her hands mesmerised him. She held her head high, like a queen. All in all, this was one classy lady. He couldn't wait to get to know her better.

Man, she was wasted in a high-rise office. Working on this risk-management stuff she'd never see the light of day. She'd be head down, tail up at her computer, concentrating, writing proposals, working fourteen hours a day. Starting early. Getting home late.

It puzzled him. Why wasn't she like Catherine, sitting in her local café, sipping on her latté and idly turning the pages of some women's rag full of tips on how to keep your man happy in bed? That's what classy women did these days, didn't they? Hell, with her current job, Nicola would barely recognise her own bedroom, let alone some guy's bachelor pad.

Earlier, while waiting for the London market to open, he'd stood by his office window idly watching the bulk of his co-workers leaving for home. He'd seen Nicola sprinting across the city square below, heading with the crowd of 9-5 office workers towards the transport hub at Wynyard. He'd thought 'Well, I'll be darned; she *does* have time for a life. She's in a hurry. That sure is someone who can't wait to get wherever she's going. Lucky bloke.'

Lucky? Who was he kidding? She wasn't his type in the looks department, she had dark curly hair for God's sake, and he wasn't used to someone as challenging as her. She had gravitas, a sense of purpose. Just like his mother had. He almost dropped his beer as that thought popped into his head. No. She was nothing like his mother … apart from displaying a particular type of seriousness. But he sure was tired of bimbos like Catherine, he didn't trust them, and in the matter of sex appeal there's no doubt Nicola possessed the mysterious X-factor. As she hadn't given *him* the come-on, was he losing *his* sex appeal? He chased away that uncomfortable thought with another swig of his beer.

CHAPTER THREE

Nicola sighed. And sighed again. It was one of her little idiosyncrasies. She did it without even realising, when she was ill at ease and pondering a course of action. Even in her school days her friends had teased her about it.

She'd spent the last hour thinking about that meeting with Tom Forrester. A sparring partner of his ilk was unexpected. Birko was a pussy cat by comparison. Tom was the type to see straight through her acts of bravado in the workplace and penetrate her thin veneer of self-assurance.

Even if she'd acquitted herself quite well in the meeting today, a man with such a penetrating eye as Tom would shortly see her limitations when it came to handling the opposite sex. She'd have to tread carefully to keep her project on track.

Nicola sighed yet again, shut down her computer,

grabbed her briefcase and rushed out from work. If she hurried, she should make Milsons Point in time.

Catching a taxi wasn't an option. The traffic was too heavy. The approaches to the Harbour Bridge would be a veritable car park. She'd never make it in time.

The North Shore train rumbled in overhead as she negotiated the ticket barrier at Wynyard Station. There was no time to scan the destination indicator board, but no need to worry. Every train crossing the harbour stopped at the station on the northern end of the Bridge.

She raced up the steps to No 4 Platform and jumped into the carriage, heart pounding, as the automatic doors closed.

Milsons Point station was the hub of a small village-like community, but idling her way past the shops was an indulgence for another day. She rushed headlong from the train and was the last parent to arrive at the long day-care centre, barely making the cut-off time for collection.

The supervisor chastised her. 'Just in time, Nikki. Don't do this too often.'

Nicola shrugged off the Nikki tag. She'd trained most people to call her by her full name, as she preferred, and Nicola was more dignified than Nikki in the professional workplace. But there was no need to make an issue, here, of the natural Australian penchant for shortening every-one's name.

'I know, Jenny, I know, sorry, sorry, sorry. It was my first day grappling with the new project. There was a meeting which disoriented me, far more than any meeting during my old job at Grosvenor Bank. I won't cut it so fine tomorrow.'

'You need a backup resource.'

'Agreed. And I've found one, and hired her, as from Monday. Stephanie Johnson. A uni student. She needs the money, and this job will still give her plenty of time to study.'

'Will she pick up Thea every day?'

'She will, to take the pressure off me on the days when I can't get away at the exact right moment. I'll introduce you both next Monday when I'll fill in the permission forms authorising her as a pick-up person.'

As Nicola spoke, a curly-headed tot ran in from the playroom and two chubby arms clutched at her skirts. An eager little face looked up and a piping little voice greeted her. 'Mummy, mummy.'

Nicola's beaming smile mirrored the smile on her daughter's upturned face. She bent over, swung Thea up into her arms, gave her a big squeeze and planted smooching kisses on both cheeks.

'Hello sweetheart, Mummy's missed you up to here today.' She patted the curls atop Thea's head to indicate the level and make the child squirm and giggle. 'I miss you like that every day. I bet you had fun though, as you always do.'

She deposited the child back on the ground. Thea held out her paint-splattered hands to demonstrate the highlight of that day's fun. 'Pain Mummy picsha.'

'Did you darling? Clever girl. I'll have a look in your

bag when we get home. We can put your picture on the fridge door. It's time to go home now. Let's say goodbye to Jenny.'

'See y'moro.'

'Good girl. Wave bye-bye. Off we go.' Nicola grabbed her collapsible stroller from its parking bay and slipped Thea into it.

It was a short walk home to Kirribilli, the suburb on the eastern side of Milsons Point station. Around the corner from her apartment was the Australian Prime Minister's Sydney residence, its headland vantage point providing spectacular views of everything famous about Sydney. Nicola's modest flat in no way compared, trading the outlook for a few extra square metres of floor space, where Thea had some room to play when they were at home together.

Nicola pushed the stroller along the uneven pavement, fanning herself in the February heat. The Harbour Bridge towered above, its sandstone pylons supporting its soaring iron arch and span. If she didn't have Thea to consider, she could easily walk to and from work, across that Bridge, like hundreds of her fellow commuters. Directly across from her, at this narrowest part of the Harbour, the ferry hub at Circular Quay bustled with peak hour activity. If the timetable for her wharf offered a better service, she could catch the ferry.

But her daily routine revolved around Thea. Trains were frequent and meant she could avoid the traffic-jam hassle of taking her car each day, and the expense of a city car park, freeing up more money for Thea's child care needs.

She chose this suburb to cut short her commuting time and lengthen her daily time with Thea. Kirribilli was an expensive place to live, but it was worth it. For Thea's sake.

Nicola unlocked the front door and manoeuvred the stroller safely inside.

'Here we are darling, home again. Let's get you out of that contraption now. It's hap-hap-happy hour.' After several years as a single parent in the full-time workforce, Nicola's end-of-day routine was down pat.

As the safety buckle clicked off, Thea pushed and wriggled and levered herself up so she could climb out. Nicola tickled Thea as she helped her from the stroller. The responding giggle signified high spirits. Good. Some nights Thea was pulling at her hair, whingeing, too tired for anything but a cuddle.

'First of all, let's put your painting of Mummy on the fridge.'

Nicola retrieved Thea's pint-sized backpack from the carry compartment under the stroller. The cute pack was an integral part of their daily routine. Thea observed that her Mummy carried a bag when they went out, and so must Thea, even if she preferred to drag hers along the floor by one grimy strap.

Holding up said bag by said strap, Nicola withdrew the piece of paper covered with random lines and splotches of paint. 'Oh, I like it. You drew lots of squiggles to show Mummy's curly hair.'

Nicola rearranged the fridge magnets to accommodate the new piece of artwork and Thea beamed with pleasure as her grubby hands roamed across her precious masterpiece, crumpling it and accidentally ripping a small piece off one corner.

'Oops, careful. Let's leave it there and look for that Playschool DVD you were watching last night.' Fifteen minutes of TV per day wouldn't turn her child into a zombie. It gave both of them some breathing space after a long and busy day.

Bright images flashed up on the TV screen and bouncy music filled the kitchen. 'Narnas,' Thea responded gleefully, indicating one of her favourite songs in the show. Nicola plonked her in the high chair and scrubbed at the sticky little hands and fingers with a wipe. The remnants of paint would have to wait until bath time.

'While you watch, Mummy's going to cook our dinner.' Nicola knew her soothing voice was all that Thea needed. She didn't care what was on offer. Some children were picky about their food but Thea, a human garbage bin, would eat almost anything thanks to her mother's strict training regime. As a younger child Thea had quickly learned to eat the food on her plate because if she fussed and threw it on the floor, her evening meal disappeared into the kitchen bin, leaving only her milk.

If truth be told, Nicola didn't need to stress herself about cooking after work, as Thea ate well at the long day care centre. The centre's chef served freshly-cooked hot meals for lunch, with fruit and milk as morning and afternoon snacks. Nicola and Thea's evening meal always featured simple fare.

While Nicola diced the veggies, Thea sat with her in the kitchen in her high chair, eyes glued to the screen. Distracted from any hunger pangs, she could escape for a few minutes into another world as she wound down from her busy day playing with the other toddlers. Nicola poured a small quantity of tap water into a melamine cup and Thea slurped it down so she could then bang her empty cup on the tray of the high chair, revelling in its satisfying drumming sound.

Within fifteen to twenty minutes of unlocking the front door Nicola said, 'Right, Missy Moo, here comes your dinner. The people at Playschool are going off to their houses to have their dinner too. Let's say night-night to them.'

As the screen went dark, Nicola's careful timing minimised potential wails of protest and tantrums. Thea banged her spoon in gleeful anticipation as the bowl was set before her, dipped in her spoon and rather erratically aimed its brimming contents for her mouth. 'Mmmm.' Thea licked her lips in appreciation. It was another game they played together. How loud could the Mmmms be? Each tried to outdo the other.

'Good girl. Eat up. You'll grow big and strong, like Mummy.'

Nicola didn't eat with the child. It was too early.

Besides, eating would distract her from concentrating on every new sign of development in the rapidly-expanding vocabulary of her small daughter, one of the many miracles of childhood. Instead, Nicola saved some of the vegetables to eat later, by herself, usually adding some chicken or a lamb chop for extra nutrition. Her hectic schedule meant she wasn't as well-fed as Thea between the hours of nine and five.

'Now your milk. My, oh my, you're drinking it fast tonight. Have you got hollow legs?'

'Ollo leg.' Thea giggled as she lifted her legs and examined her toes, searching for milk running out the bottom.

The meal over, Nicola lifted Thea out of her high chair and she ran straight to the bathroom. Bath time signified relaxation and play-time, with lots of splashing as Thea poured bathwater into and out of containers of all shapes and sizes.

Tonight, extracting Thea from the bathtub involved a tussle of wills. Nicola pulled out the plug and let the water drain away before Thea would give up her splashing fun. Nicola swathed the wet body in a Blinky Bill towel, cuddled and tickled her as she was dried, snapped into her just-in-case-of-accidents night-time nappy and clad in her pyjamas.

'Now for your teeth. Lean over, sweetheart.' Thea obligingly stood tippy-toed on her plastic stool and leaned over the hand basin. She liked the flavour of the child-friendly toothpaste and tried to grab the toothbrush to lick the paste off the brush before it made contact with her teeth. 'No darling, Mummy has to brush your teeth for you. We have to make sure we brush them all properly.'

Nicola picked up the battered copy of Mem Fox's invaluable 'Time for Bed' book to complete their bedtime ritual. As she reached the final page and read out its closing *goodnight*, Thea yawned and snuggled into her pillow, happy in her trust that she'd be safe when her Mummy turned off the light. Thea's deep-blue eyes were drooping as Nicola bent down for the last goodnight kiss.

Thea, her precious child. Almost, but not quite, the image of her mother. Her eyes were different. As Nicola gazed lovingly at her adorable daughter, smiling at the last flutter of Thea's eyes before sleep claimed her, she recalled the undeniable surprise earlier that day, the jolt when she matched Tom Forrester's deep midnight blue eyes to the exact shade and colour intensity as Thea's.

How extraordinary it was. She'd never met anyone with eyes matching Thea's before today. Meeting Tom had been strangely disorienting. His overall oomph and undeniable charm did not entirely explain his attraction. Subliminally she'd registered a weird and unexpected connection, but the stress of the meeting meant her mind didn't roam free. This afternoon she'd not consciously pondered the matter of his eye colour.

Tonight she did. Thea did not share her mother's grey eyes or David's rather run-of-the-mill blue eyes. Tom's eyes had come as a shock.

The strange coincidence of the eye colour brought her a painful jolt of unwelcome memories. She wondered what her ex-husband was doing in far-off PNG, the country where they'd lived together before their marriage foundered. It was a while since she'd thought of David, who'd walked out three years ago, leaving her in the lurch. He'd never met Thea and retained no ongoing contact with Nicola. Life most definitely didn't go according to plan.

Her earlier buoyant mood slipped into melancholia. Rather than watch her usual TV programmes, she gave herself up to nostalgia. Pouring herself a glass of Sauvignon Blanc, she grilled some chicken to go with her vegetables and selected some music. The soundtrack of her favourite movie *Sleepless in Seattle* kept her company as she ate.

Nicola absorbed the timeless lyrics of the Jimmy Durante tracks from the movie, sipped on her wine and firmly counted her blessings. 'I've got Thea. She's my reason for living. She makes me happy. I make her happy. I have a good job which pays the rent and the bills. What more could I want?'

Tom couldn't resist his crazy itch to know more about Nicola. As the bell chimed eight on the distant clock tower, he punched the button to reach his old mate Birko, his counterpart at the Grosvenor Bank. A family man, a bit harassed, his hair thinning and his waistline thickening, Birko didn't fit the physical stereotype for his macho workforce role but mentally he still fired on all cylinders.

'G'day Birko. Top of the morning to you. Everything okay in your world?'

'Yeah Tom, everything's fine.'

'Sarah and the kids still as gorgeous as when I saw them a few weeks back?'

'Driving me mad, but I wouldn't be without them. What's up?'

Tom decided to play down his curiosity about Nicola, to see what Birko would volunteer. Even Tom's rivals grudgingly admitted that an ability to check and cross-check, make independent assessments, was one of the reasons for Tom's success.

'A bit of human resources research, mate. Tell me, what's the story with Nicola Pearson? I hear she worked for your outfit before she came here.'

Birko chuckled. 'I was expecting this call.'

'Yeah, well, she was in my office yesterday. I want to know why she's been hired. Is she up to it?'

'You mean, did your boss hire her as a display piece?'

'The thought did cross my mind. She *is* pretty stunning.'

'Have no fear, she's up there with the best and brightest. I know you've only been back in town for a matter of weeks, so I'll excuse your lack of market savvy. She's got an economics degree from Sydney Uni with a major in maths and stats. She worked overseas in some Third World country, I forget which, and when she and her husband split she came back home.'

'How long ago was that? Recently?' Tom wanted to test the depth of Nicola's experience.

'It was while you were busily making a name for yourself in London, mate. Maybe three years ago, maybe a bit less.'

'And that's when she joined Grosvenor Bank?'

'Right. She joined us then, assigned to the risk management area. She started off writing papers on the topic of country risk analysis. I've seen them quoted in the Fin Review. And the FT in London. Didn't you see any of those?'

'Nah, Birko, must have missed them. I was always on a plane to Europe or the States when I was in London, then stuck in meetings in some new city. There were so many briefing notes to read before meetings I didn't always catch the papers. With so many stories every day, I didn't register all of them. And registered even less the names of those who wrote them.'

'Yeah, life's tough mate. Anyway, back to Nicola Pearson. The country risk thing meant she wrote our Board papers supporting our international lending proposals.'

'Sounds impressive.'

'Right, but there's more. About a year ago the powers-that-be moved her into the trading risk assessment area, which employs a lot of maths freaks. They do a lot of financial modelling work, and mutter about Black Scholes and other mysterious formulae. It's all beyond me, I'm a simple barrow boy at heart, I like to trade, but they all sound as if they understand what they're doing.'

Tom hoped Birko would confirm his assessment: 'So she's not just a pretty face. She's done well for herself, in a relatively short period of time.'

'Bloody well, I'd say. She's smart, but she's worked hard over the last few years.'

'She's the conscientious type, you mean?'

'Yeah, Tom, she's one serious lady, if you can forget about how you'd like to take her home to bed.'

Tom gave a relieved chuckle. 'So she had the same

effect on you, then? When she worked at your shop, I mean.' There was a reason he was friends with Birko. Unlike many of their colleagues, they both treated women as people, not objects, even if spontaneous feelings of unexpected desire took some suppressing at times. Like now, with Nicola.

Birko replied, 'On any bloke, I'd say. Never tried chatting her up myself. I'm more than happy with Sarah.'

That's right, Tom mused. Birko and Sarah were the perfect couple. He thought again. Birko was Nicola's old boss, and Sarah was Birko's wife, so Nicola and Sarah had more than likely met and might even be friends. Birko might know a lot more about Nicola's private life than Tom had anticipated when he made the call. He delved further.

'Divorced, eh. Yesterday I saw her leaving our building early, with all the nine to fivers. She was in a hell of a hurry. Looked like she was rushing off to meet someone important to her.'

'I think she'd have been going to collect her kid. I know nothing about her love life, but I know for a fact that she has a daughter. Her pregnancy ran its course in the early part of her time here.'

Tom's canvassing of future possibilities with the intriguing Ms Pearson came to a screeching halt. His visions of blissful adventures in the bedroom evaporated in a microsecond. A child! That put a whole new complexion on things. This meant 'end of story' where

Nicola was concerned. Catherine had seen to that. He gasped. 'Christ, Birko, how old is this kid?'

'Around two, maybe a bit more. The divorce must have come through while Nicola was on maternity leave. I vaguely remember Sarah telling me.'

'You mean some bloke got her pregnant and then left her holding the baby?'

'Dunno. Maybe she ditched him.'

'So how does she manage to do this complex job of hers with a kid in tow?'

'She seems to manage. Some days when she worked here she looked pretty tired, but don't we all? When my kids were babies they kept Sarah and me awake half the night.'

'Yeah, but how does she juggle child care and our ridiculous working hours?'

'Probably by leaving work a bit early and working at home at night to make up time. Maybe by employing a nanny.'

In the face of all this unwanted news, Tom gritted his teeth. 'Well, Birko, it's good to have that background briefing. Now I know to avoid her like the plague.' He could scarcely believe his own words. There had been a time when a mother and child was exactly what he'd wanted in his life.

'What!' came the startled reply. 'I thought you were tired of all the empty-headed beauty pageant queens and looking for a smart woman to settle down with. Nicola is both beautiful and smart. Not that I'm match-making.

She's altogether different from your usual taste in women.'

Tom recalled the years he'd wasted with Catherine, repressed the pang in his heart and let his head rule. 'Women with children are most definitely off my list. They score zero as candidates for any kind of permanent relationship.' Even to his own ears, that sounded a bit too adamant.

'Why's that, exactly?' came the cautious response.

Tom shot back. 'Too many complications. All that endless hassle over babysitting problems and ex-husbands and access rights and financial support payments.' He paused while he mentally reviewed all the other disadvantages accompanying single women with children, decided there were too many, gave up in disgust and added 'Etcetera, etcetera, etcetera.'

'Jeez, mate, why do you say that?'

Tom retorted acerbically, 'I've seen it all before. With our mates. It's hard going for all concerned. Especially the kids. Ongoing arguing and tension and to-ing and fro-ing. And the whole stepdad thing. I wouldn't want to be one of those.'

'Those what?

'A step-father. Count me out.'

'Okay, Okay, I hear you loud and clear. You've made your point. Remember, not every step-family is like that. And I thought you liked kids. You seem to like ours.'

An involuntary sigh escaped Tom as he pictured his friend's lifestyle. It's what he had wanted with Catherine.

'They're great, your kids. But you've got Sarah and a stable family life.'

Friendly reassurance seeped down the phone line. 'Hey there, buddy. Not every woman is like Catherine. You're well rid of her.'

That was true. He was well rid of Catherine. He hadn't thought of her for a while now … until yesterday. And today.

Catherine. The wife he'd thought he loved, until she showed herself in her true colours. Yellow. For cowardice. Orange. For deceitfulness.

Catherine. The woman too scared to have children. Because it might ruin her figure. The woman who didn't even like children, when push came to shove. The woman too cowardly to admit this before they married. The wife who, behind his back while he was at work, went on the prowl for another fella, one like her who did *not* want kids. The woman who'd cleaned out the house while he was at work, leaving him to come home to an empty shell. The woman who'd killed his trust in women.

Children were off his agenda now, because the first requirement was to find a decent, stable woman to be their mother. Birko had found Sarah at university, before they all joined the career treadmill. Where would he find such a woman, in his high-pressure job, working the unsociable hours he did, earning the obscene amount of money he did? Thanks to Catherine he'd learned the hard way that his trendy job and the colour of his Amex card made him a magnet for the wrong kind of woman.

CHAPTER FIVE

Nicola arrived at the small conference room ten minutes ahead of the scheduled meeting time for her task-force. It always paid to be prepared. She'd emailed the agenda to those attending, and her Power-Point demonstration was ready to go. She'd made it as interesting as she could, and fast-paced, to keep everyone awake at an after-lunch meeting on a hot summer's day. Her carefully structured dot points would keep the salient facts in focus, once question time began.

Nicola glanced at herself one more time in the reflective glass panels framing the doorway. Lipstick on straight? Yes. Her peripheral vision flicked over her suit collar and across her shoulders. Any stray hairs? No. Everything else in order? Yes. This wasn't the time to make an ill-groomed impression. She needed the full professional attention of the men who'd soon crowd the room.

She needed this first group meeting to go according to

plan. Her task, to progress the Chief's objectives of making this the best-managed bank in the country, didn't mean the staff would co-operate with her. Nicola hoped she'd lined up Tom Forrester well enough that his influence as her big gun would sway the others. Was Tom going to stick to his pledge of last Thursday and back her? Would he become her key ally, someone at work she could trust to keep his promises?

As she had at the Grosvenor Bank, she badly needed to prove herself in this new workplace. It made up for her nagging sense of failure on the relationship front. While she mightn't be a good judge of men, she possessed full confidence in her ability to suss out flaws in logic and tell when the numbers didn't add up.

Nicola had worked her way round the rest of her target group on Friday, on a meeting and greeting basis, trying to set them at ease. It was important to ward off the various prejudices which they otherwise may have brought with them to a meeting with a stranger of either sex. Men gave even more grudging acceptance to the idea that a woman might be their peer.

The female strategy of hiding an iron fist inside a velvet glove worked best for her. Feminine charm often lulled the opposite sex into underestimating a woman's ability, and often led to men telling you something they'd never think of divulging to a male colleague. Nicola had found that the softly-softly approach usually achieved far more than full frontal aggression, as long as she combined it with a logical line of argument.

Even so, it was daunting to face a room full of virtual strangers and begin the process of gaining their commitment to her project. She'd made a good start with Tom and now she had to find the right words to inspire this larger group.

The seats filled up as the men filed into the room. Her internal butterflies slowed their fluttering when she saw Tom appear in the doorway. His public support, if he kept his promise, would contribute immeasurably to winning the co-operation and respect of the lesser lights sizing her up, especially that awful man John Wrigley. Preliminary meetings with other executives had swiftly convinced her that Tom was the acknowledged brainpower behind the operation of this section of the bank. Somehow, she needed to persuade the other men present that Tom was in full intellectual support of her work. Then they'd follow their leader. She was banking on that outcome.

She rapped on her lectern and smiled at everyone. 'Good afternoon gentlemen. You all know who I am, and why I'm here, you all know each other, and we're all busy people.' She surveyed the room. She'd started with the right sentiments. Heads were nodding. Traders were impatient people. For them, time was of the essence.

'I'd like to go straight to the first item of business on the agenda circulated ahead of this meeting.' She brought up the first image on screen, setting out the agenda. 'I'm going to work through my preliminary ideas and then throw the meeting open to a discussion of the various forms of derivatives trades.' She paused and waited for a few nods of acquiescence from her audience. 'I'm especially keen for you to alert me to any that I've failed to identify on my first run through the existing policy documents, position sheets and accounting records.' She was deliberately setting them a challenge, to prove that her basic facts were wrong. It might make these macho men pay better attention to her. 'At later meetings we'll deal with the risk profiles inherent in these trades, and eventually the management controls which I'll be suggesting as part of my policy paper.'

There, she'd set out her agenda quite clearly and professionally. A generalised low buzz of voices filled the room as she set the PowerPoint display in motion. Facial expressions showed that some attendees were supportive, some were sceptical, and some were outright scornful of her and her task.

That annoying trader John Wrigley had been especially disdainful. He was a sore loser after he'd failed to chat her up a week ago. He'd been 'out' every time she tried to contact him. He hadn't answered her emails. He'd let the door slam in her face. He'd drawled one-word responses to her questions when she finally cornered him in the trading room.

Men like Wrigley would *not* derail her project. Giving him an icy stare, she used the public speaker's trick for overcoming nerves and scanned the room looking for one of the more supportive men. She found Mack, the equities trader, and focused her remarks on him. 'You're probably aware that an earlier generation of management did a lot of work on analysing and controlling risks, back in the eighties. They thought they had it nailed. But then the old guard retired, the new guard abandoned essential training systems, promotional systems changed and people forgot some of the fundamentals. In a way, we're re-inventing the wheel with our new systems.'

Mack nodded. Wrigley snorted with derision. She anticipated endless trouble with him. Jilted and spurned women could carry a grudge but men like him could also be unforgiving of a public slight against a fragile male ego. Never would he miss an opportunity to sneer, never would he stop attempting to undermine her.

Nicola fixed Wrigley with a withering gaze and carried on, unperturbed. 'But we also have some new issues to deal with, as a result of widespread and interlocking computerised trading systems around the world. Fat-finger events, when traders accidentally key in the wrong letter or number, can send the whole world into melt-down. We have to build in suitable checks for the common sense that's so ... er ... uncommon now.'

Tom sat at the back of the room, surveying the scene. This was her first meeting with the group. He'd bide his time and see how she fared. He hoped she wasn't about to make a fool of herself.

She talked the talk and looked professional. The dark

suit, the light-black tights, the heels, the grooming … but she was drop-dead gorgeous and out of place in this bull-ring environment. He'd even overheard Wrigley say to Mack, sitting alongside him, 'We'd all like to take *her* home. But that stuck-up bitch thinks she's too good for us. Wouldn't I like to show her who's boss?' Tom recalled his recent conversation with Birko. They too were guilty of the secret desire to take Nicola home, proving that Wrigley's opening sentence was normal boys' talk in trading rooms. But Wrigley's following comments to Mack worried him. Wrigley was a creep.

Nicola intrigued Tom. What was she doing messing around in this male-dominated world? What could she hope to know about the intricacies of his particular territory? She'd never been a dealer, so Birko said. What would she know about the decisions he had to make daily?

He spent a few minutes speculating about the world she might inhabit before he gave himself a shake. He'd let his concentration lapse. He must stop thinking about Nicola's other attributes. He reminded himself that she had a kid. She was off-limits. Tuning back in, he realised that Wrigley was trying to cause trouble, already, forcing Nicola to defend her ground.

'The world's moved on,' sneered Wrigley. 'Dealers are too smart these days. The market moves too fast. Bank systems have lost the plot.'

Tom paid attention as she calmly stated her case: 'Don't bet on that, John. Some of the basic rules still apply. It wasn't until that GRB trader took his mandatory five days of leave away from his desk that his secret deals came to light. Once he was no longer there to massage them through the system each day, his complex web of deals began to unravel. He must have been an idiot, because everyone knows about the five-day rule, but then he compounded his problems by running away. Now he's wanted by The Met in London, and by Interpol.'

'Go, Nicola'. Tom cheered her on in his mind. Nicola was capably demonstrating her credentials, but Wrigley was trouble with a capital T, and verging on losing his job. Tom decided it was high time he lent his weight to Nicola's efforts. Last Thursday he'd promised to back her up, and he would. Her project was essential, long overdue and worthy of his endorsement.

His deep baritone voice commanded everyone's attention: 'None of that will happen here. Our traders are already well supervised. And risk management is headed for a complete upgrade because the Chief and I are in full support of the monitoring and management system Nicola's attempting to develop. I, for one, will be working hard to make sure she succeeds. Her systems will provide more protection for me and help me to keep my job. Same goes for all of you. You should all bear that in mind.' He rested his forbidding gaze determinedly on Wrigley.

Wrigley scowled.

'Tom, thank you. I'm glad you're aware of the significance for everyone's jobs … including yours *and* mine.' Nicola's dazzling smile winged his way.

The energy in her smile attracted him like a magnet

and Tom twanged on a hidden string of suppressed excitement. He savoured the thought of the opportunities ahead for testing his mettle against hers … and the opportunities for helping her win through. Ms Pearson would need courage to overcome the many obstacles which would be placed in her path by his chauvinistic and Machiavellian colleagues, especially John Wrigley.

Tom conceded he might have been resistant too, just like John, given different circumstances. If she hadn't injected such a jolt into his jaded outlook on life. And if he hadn't known about that kid. Having that kid somehow made her seem vulnerable, suddenly, in need of protection against the likes of Wrigley. Real men always defended women and children, didn't they?

CHAPTER SIX

Tom was spending another solitary evening, nursing his beer on his balcony and musing. He grimaced as he recalled that he'd caught himself watching the clock today, wishing that 2.30 would come quicker. These meetings with Nicola were turning, too rapidly, into the highlight of his day. Simply being in the same room as her beat all the buzz of the trading room.

That afternoon's task-force meeting with Nicola had been another group affair, like the one last week when she'd dealt effectively with Wrigley. She'd done well today too.

The meetings scheduled for tomorrow and Thursday would be one-on-one consultations, so that Nicola could explore some technical issues with him. These issues needed clarification, as they formed some of the building blocks for her ambitious management plan.

He couldn't wait for tomorrow to come. His brain

might tell him one thing—'Stay away.' He should listen to his brain which was insistently reminding him, 'She's got that kid. She's not your type. You go for blondes, remember. You're asking for trouble, too many complications there, buddy.'

But a desirable and intriguing woman can overturn any man's best-laid plans.

He couldn't quite understand what it was about her that overrode his common sense. Let's face it, she'd never have any time for him as that kid and her job meant she already lacked enough hours in the day.

Was it simply her wry sense of humour exerting a pull on him? The world would be a better place if more people understood the attractiveness of this characteristic.

Her energy definitely appealed to him, her passion for the project. People lit up when driven by a passion. Her knowledge appealed too. The world was at a point where knowledge meant power. Power demonstrated by a woman held all the fascination of a cobra waiting to strike randomly at a target. Her target in these meetings was always the person who thought bluster was more important than brains. He had to give her full marks for knowing how to cut such people down to size with an impressive display of factual knowledge and incisively logical arguments.

He had to admit, she was reeling him in with her beguiling ways. Not that they seemed contrived. She appeared oblivious of her impact on him. There was never the faintest glimmer of coquettish behaviour.

Damn it, she broke all his rules, all his pre-conceived ideas about what he wanted. Did he really know what he wanted? All he knew was that the life he'd been leading held no joy. He knew, because people told him often enough, that he fitted the image of the guy with everything—fancy job, fancy apartment, fancy car, fancy girls dangling on his arm. But that elusive something was missing.

Thea was in bed and asleep, with a light sheet over her because of the heat. Nicola had eaten and was cleaning up the kitchen. Her tired eyes drifted offline. Unbidden, an image of Tom and his intriguing blue eyes danced before her. Her brain kicked in automatically and she silently admonished herself. 'Go away. I don't need you to complicate my life'. Her eyes refocused on the Nifti spray, her sponge cloth and her kitchen bench.

Darn it. What was it about that man?

Nicola gave herself a good talking-to. 'You've got no reason to doubt that Tom Forrester has the same one-track mind as his randy underlings. They're aware of my role, but those young dealers still refer to me as a chick, or a babe. In a way, I suppose it's flattering if they see me as a young thing too, part of their world. But ...,' she trailed off. The weight of the world seemed heavy on her shoulders. Work, work, work. Single parenthood. Responsibility. Loneliness.

CHAPTER SEVEN

Closeted with Tom in his office, Nicola concentrated on giving no discernible signal that his presence in the same room had any impact on her. A flood of awareness warmed her insides but outwardly she stayed coolly professional, focused on their joint task.

It was barely a week since they'd met. Tom might be the embodiment of a man living life in the fast lane, with fast women keeping him extremely fast company, but it was dawning on slow-lane Nicola that she wasn't immune to him. His energy and decisiveness were markedly different to the rest of the management team at the Federal Bank—and at her last job at the Grosvenor Bank. Those grey executives faded into a drab background in comparison with Tom. Those others were always careful to hedge their bets. Always they sat on the fence, waiting to fall into line behind a leader like Tom, never willing to go out on a limb and back their own judgment.

As their session came to a close Nicola said, 'I almost forgot to tell you, Tom. I can't make our project meeting tomorrow. I'm booked to attend a seminar.'

He pushed his rough flow charts across the desk at her as he asked, 'Would that be the one about how to calculate the true net worth of the banks we're dealing with?'

She nodded. 'That's the one. It's relevant to the business at hand. How to figure out the true meaning of their complicated balance sheets. How to recognise the risks which are off balance sheet.' She suppressed an internal self-deprecating grimace. His fast women would sneer at her and her set of interests. But at work he shared this interest so she asked, 'Are you attending as well?' It lifted her spirits to think of spending the day with him.

'No, I planned to, but I can't get away for the whole day.' He let out a heavy breath. 'I'm still working on that billion-dollar deal. Got an appointment with the lawyers tomorrow. A few last-minute hitches with the documentation. One of the other banks in the syndicate is getting cold feet.'

'Of course. I understand completely.' That was true, but her mood had suddenly deflated. She gave him the glass-half-full response, 'It's fortunate I'm currently a bit more flexible with my time than you are. Someone from here needs to attend. We'll meet again on Friday, then?'

'For our usual date, you mean.' His voice carried a teasing note.

A sudden surge of bitter-sweet memory swept over Nicola. Her eyes flicked up from her notes, where she was confirming the time of their next appointment, and she felt the surge of a warm blush. The word 'date' triggered the bitter image of a life firmly in her past. It also triggered a tantalisingly sweet image of a possible real date with this far too attractive man, this master of his domain, seated opposite her.

Tom continued with his bantering tone. 'No, unfortunately our next date will have to be on Monday. I'll be in Melbourne on Friday. Business meeting. My deal, still.'

Nicola made a quick comeback. 'Fine then, Mr Big Time, I'll see you at our regular time on Monday.'

They grinned in unspoken acknowledgment that a cheeky approach often defused a lot of unresolved issues between men and women.

Thursday, 6.30 am. Nicola finished towelling off after her shower. She took particular care to dress for her attendance at the seminar. A black designer-label suit with a graceful skirt line was her traditional suit of armour. Under the jacket she wore a cream silk blouse with a collar ending in a scarf, so that it tied like a man's tie, but lower on the neckline. Apart from her high heels and dark-toned tights, her attire was almost a replica of the dress code of the men.

This was exactly what she intended. The respect of tough-minded and competitive men for the professional reputation of any woman was always grudgingly given and easily lost.

It was her jewellery which set her aside from the men —a gold choker necklace, toning in perfectly with her skin and hair colours, a gold bracelet on her right hand, small onyx earrings, and a gold wristwatch with a broad black band. The only thing missing was her gold wedding ring.

She readied Thea for the day and they had their usual breakfast. Thea, as if sensing her mother's rush and the slight change in routine, squirmed and grizzled in her high chair, sending splashes of milk flying from her cereal bowl. Nicola was forced to keep her distance to avoid soiling her work attire. They set off later than usual for the long-day-care centre, upsetting Nicola's plans to be the first to arrive.

She made the registration desk just in time before the day's seminar session began. Nicola looked forward to the proceedings, secure in her knowledge that she could hold her head high in this company. The first speaker took his place at the microphone. 'Gentlemen', he said, 'the focus of our discussions today will be counterparty credit risk assessment techniques.'

On and on he droned. Nicola found it hard to concentrate, and couldn't avoid comparing him with Tom. Ah, if she were back in the office, the prospect of her daily meeting with Tom would be keeping her awake. Wide awake. Keyed up in mind and body, pulse raised, shivery with anticipation. She scolded herself. Tom shouldn't be entering her thoughts unbidden like this.

Nicola wasn't speaking at today's seminar, she was there to learn, but the morning tea break was welcome. The next speaker by now was aware that amongst the sea of black suits and shiny slip-on shoes was a pair of high heels, and the meeting wasn't entirely comprised of men. 'Ladies and gentlemen', he began. By lunchtime, it was apparent that Nicola was the sole female present that day. 'Lady and gentlemen' began the next speaker and the audience sniggered. Two men sitting near Nicola turned and leered at her.

The final speaker completed the cycle of one-upmanship. 'Lady Nicola and gentlemen', he began, and the audience laughed. Heads turned to where Nicola sat, rather self-consciously acknowledging the speaker's attempt at gallantry.

The men present didn't take long to associate the 'Lady Nicola' in their midst with the name sometimes appearing in the financial press. At the post-seminar drinks session, one predatory type elbowed his way into her discussion group with practised ease, clutching two glasses of champagne, one half empty and one full. He offered the latter to her.

'So you're the famous Nicola Pearson. I've heard the boys at Grosvenor Bank talk about you. Well, well, well. What a surprise package. I've never met a woman before with such an amazing combination of femininity and brainpower.'

Nicola groaned to herself. This oily character had unmistakably downed a few glasses of champagne already. She spoke in icily neutral tones as she accepted the glass. 'Thank you. You're most kind'. Her professional smile was fixed and gracious, but her barricades against the unwanted attention of men were armour-plated. Here was trouble if ever she'd seen it. His chat-up line was new, but his intentions were age-old. He was a drunken version of the odious John Wrigley she contended with at the office.

She turned away from Mr Sleaze to continue the fascinating discussion she'd been enjoying with the man on her right, a visitor from Singapore.

International bankers visiting Sydney had become a part of her world. Counterparty risks were a topic close to the heart of all banks, anxious to avoid the domino effect of one bank going down and taking others with it. Visiting bankers often sought her views over lunch. Sometimes they tried to seek other favours from her, but once the conversation strayed away from professional topics, she froze out any attempt at blatant seduction. How dare they! Most of them wore a wedding ring. Scumbags.

Mr Sleaze ignored the cue. 'How about we get away for a drink, babe, somewhere nice and quiet?'

There was that 'babe' line again. Did men really think this line of chat would work? She replied firmly 'Thanks, but you've been kind enough to get me a fresh drink and there are some colleagues here I should speak to.' He didn't deserve good manners but they came automatically to her.

'Giving me the cold shoulder? Aren't I good enough for you?' He slurred his way through his outburst, drawing unwelcome attention to the two of them. Her peripheral vision picked up a tall, well-built man approaching them, a man she instinctively knew she could trust.

'Nicola, I've been looking for you. We have an issue back at the office.'

With relief she turned towards the welcome sound of Tom's voice and beamed at him. Where had he sprung from? He said he'd be tied up with lawyers and documentation. Happily she accepted Tom's hand on her elbow. She turned to the slurry man and made curt apologies. 'Sorry. Duty calls.'

As Tom steered her away towards the exit, her skirt brushed against his trouser leg. Being this close to him for the first time was as good as she'd feared … and gave her the shivers, in an exciting, trembly way. Suppressing them firmly she murmured as they walked, 'What are you doing here, Tom? I didn't expect to see you.'

'I finished early, and thought I might be lucky and catch the chairman's summary of the day's proceedings.' Nicola nodded her acceptance of what sounded like a plausible explanation. Conference organisers, by that time of day, permitted almost anyone to walk in and join the party, if they looked the part of a delegate.

When they reached the other side of the room, well away from Mr Sleaze, Tom let go of Nicola's elbow. It left her strangely forsaken. Physical closeness with him felt good. She caught his eye. 'I hate to say it, but thanks for rescuing me.'

He murmured, 'I thought you might be in trouble there. I've seen that creep in action in other places.'

'Thanks for your concern, Tom. As it happens, I can admit to quite a lot of practice at evading creeps, but it *is* nice to get some help.' She smiled her thanks at him.

'If everything is fine by you, we can chat here for a few minutes and then I'll depart, as if we've resolved the work problem, leaving you to carry on here. If you want to get away from that predatory bloke, we can leave together now, as if we're heading back to the office.'

'Actually, it's been a long day, so I was just thinking of leaving.'

'Have you got time for a drink, in the upstairs lounge, away from this mob here?'

Nicola hesitated for a fraction of a second. Stephanie *should* be safely at home with Thea, playing games while they waited for her arrival. It was Stephanie's first solo run picking Thea up, and she'd stay until Nicola got home.

It was still early. She *could* accept Tom's casually-extended invitation. Half an hour would make no differ-ence. The evening meal was pre-prepared.

But when Thea's birth had thrust her into the unex-pected role of single parent, Nicola had decided that she'd devote her attention to being a good mother and a good provider for her child. That scenario didn't encompass socialising after work with handsome men while her baby waited anxiously for her to come home and have some fun.

Tom was far too attractive. Physically. Mentally. He'd tempt her to overstay her time. Dutiful habits, her end of day routine and a mother's love called. 'I'd like to, Tom, but I really have to be home soon.'

'OK, maybe another time. See you on Monday then. Same time, same place.'

Nicola watched him stride away and slowly made her way towards the hotel lobby. She was disappointed with herself. Since David, her strongest instincts were to say 'no' to all men, so greatly was she shackled by her inability to let go of her past. It was a long time since she'd lived the carefree life of a single woman, without responsibilities. And never had someone like Tom come into her life before this. Bit by bit he was creeping under her guard. Her determination to freeze men out of her life and concentrate on work and motherhood was under threat. Tom could easily become a dangerous blow torch, melting her resolve.

Tom walked away, effecting nonchalance, but he was disappointed. He'd been hoping to catch a little relaxation time with Nicola. He'd confirmed the location of the seminar and made sure he got here in time for the end-of-day drinks session.

He'd let that 'having to be home soon' comment pass,

not wanting to admit he knew about the existence of her kid. It would betray his undue interest in her private life. They were still negotiating the path towards a successful professional relationship. No need to rush. Slow and steady might win this particular race.

This woman and her high wall of reserve intrigued him. She oozed sex-appeal, intelligence, self-discipline and focus and an ability to understand his world and be an equal partner in it. He wanted to get to know her better. Much better. Holding her arm, walking by her side, being close to her aroused him. Even in her copycat clothing, her feminine elegance was apparent. Yet when others were in relaxation mode at the end of a long day, she still held herself aloof from anything hinting at normal male-female behaviour. Nicola Pearson was turning out to be an Ice Queen, nothing like the women who'd populated his dating world to date. Why was she like this? Was her guarded behaviour somehow connected with that darned kid?

He was grateful for one slight concession on her part. At least she'd said 'I'd like to.' It offered some hope for future developments. He recalled her jumpy reaction yesterday to his teasing use of the word 'date'. She'd flinched, then blushed, proving she wasn't totally immune to him. Good. He was beginning to think he was losing his touch.

CHAPTER EIGHT

W eekend mornings provided a welcome respite from getting up early and rushing out the door. Thea was still asleep when the door buzzer sounded. Nicola peered at her security screen for the ground floor entrance foyer. 'Delivery,' shouted the young man down below, into the microphone.

Did the monitor screen reveal signs of a uniform, and a parcel? Yes, he held a cone-shaped object wrapped in masses of cellophane and tied with generous lengths of ribbon.

She pressed the button giving access to her building, and stood at her front door to receive the package. It was a large bunch of magnificent red roses, delivered with a broad and knowing smile from the courier, and a card saying 'From your secret admirer, who's hoping for more'.

Nicola was transfixed by the sight of the roses. Then thrilled as she remembered this was Valentine's Day. Then puzzled. The card wasn't addressed to Nicola. Were the roses truly meant for her? Had someone made a mistake with the address? Did they belong next door? Surely not. The other residents of this floor were an old retired couple.

She rushed back to her front door. The courier was about to enter the lift. 'Excuse me, what name do you have on your delivery docket?'

'Er … hold on a minute.' He shoved his foot in the lift door to hold it open, fumbled with his clipboard and consulted it. 'N Pearson, Unit 6.'

'That's me, then. Who sent these roses?'

'Don't know. It doesn't say. Maybe it was a cash sale. Sorry, lady, I don't work in the shop.' The lift started beeping, he jumped inside and the doors clanged shut.

Nicola stared after him. If the roses were indeed meant for her, whoever could have sent them? Who'd want to pamper her like this? They were extra special roses, because they exuded a wonderful perfume. She buried her nose in the flowers and inhaled, savouring the unmistakeable fragrance of the blooms. They weren't hot-house bred for the mass market. Their heads wouldn't wilt and droop sadly by Monday. They'd open into their full glory, and finish their days as scented rose tips in an open bowl in her bedroom, reminding her of this moment.

In her mind she ran through the short list of possible candidates. All the men she knew in her private life were associated with her women friends, as their husbands or their lovers. Surely none of them would bother to spend all this money on her, or stoop so low as to betray one of her friends. No-one at the Grosvenor Bank came to mind. Barely two weeks of employment at the Federal Bank meant it was too soon for anyone there to be interested in her.

Unless it was Tom. Her heart skipped a beat. A burst of undeniable elation lifted her spirits at that fleeting thought, that whimsical notion. Then she sighed. How she wished that were true. At their daily meetings he was burrowing his way under her carefully-constructed defences. She'd known him for a little more than a week and yet she'd missed seeing him on Friday, when he was in Melbourne on business.

Nicola thought again. The facts suggested it couldn't possibly be him. Her phone number was unlisted, and the only people at the Federal Bank with knowledge of her private contact details worked in Human Resources. That information was private and confidential. He couldn't access it, even with his seniority in the bank.

Her mysterious 'secret admirer' most definitely could *not* be him. The delivery docket said N Pearson, not Nicola. The name downstairs on her doorbell. Tom would know that N stood for Nicola. Now that was a creepy thought. Maybe someone who lived nearby was stalking her. No, it couldn't be that. These roses were expensive, she could tell. Surely stalkers didn't spend a fortune such as this.

She relaxed a little, preferring to dream that, by some miracle, it might be Tom. It made her happy to think, today, that the romantic notion of two hearts calling to each other might possibly be true.

Down on her hands and knees, she hunted through the back of her least-used kitchen cupboards to find a vase capable of doing justice to these magnificent blooms. Following all the instructions on the pack she cut the stems to suitable lengths, crushed the stems, sprinkled the preservative into the water and placed the roses into a pleasing arrangement in the vase. She set the vase where she could sit and watch the buds unfurl over the next few days. The card was tucked in at the back, where Thea couldn't easily see or reach it. Nicola wanted to keep this card safe from grubby little hands and a slobbering mouth.

For a moment she day dreamed. About what might be. One day. With someone she trusted and loved. Someone sexy and full of life, like Tom. Someone who loved her *and* Thea. The film *Sleepless in Seattle* came to mind even though she kept telling herself she wasn't interested in another relationship. Her story was too complicated. No man would be interested, once he found out.

Thea ambled into the room, rubbing her sleepy eyes and dragging her ragged comforter Blanky behind her. Nicola swept up her here-and-now treasure in life, gave her a big hug and said 'Gee I love you.'

Tom's balcony was his favourite spot for relaxation. He liked to sit here in the mornings whenever possible, enjoying the sunshine and the fresh air, idly taking in the panorama before him. It was an antidote to his hectic working routine. Anyone else would rave about his view of Sydney and its harbour, but after a while one took it for granted, like today. Flicking aimlessly through the Sydney Morning Herald, he sipped his morning mug of English Breakfast tea.

The extra-large section of Personal Notices in the paper, mostly in celebration of Valentine's Day, grabbed his attention. A cheeky smile of anticipation briefly lit his face as he wondered if the roses had arrived safely. Music filled his living room and impelled Tom to add his baritone contribution to the last few lines of one of Jimmy Durante's timeless songs. Jimmy was right—trying to make someone else happy had certainly put a bounce in his step.

He didn't care two hoots about what the neighbours might think, hearing him singing on his balcony. God, it was good to be alive this morning.

It was a stroke of luck that he'd happened to be driving by Nicola's place yesterday, on his way home from that meeting at BHP Billiton in Melbourne. It was close to six, abnormally early to be back from an interstate business trip but too late to return to work. Exhaustion after a dawn start to a long and gruelling day had set in and he'd driven straight home from his valet park at the airport, via Kirribilli so he could pick up a few things for dinner at the Milsons Point deli.

Out of the corner of his eye he'd spotted Nicola walking along from the train station, pushing her kid in a stroller, accompanied by a young woman. Both were lugging a few shopping bags. She'd looked tired too and he should have bipped his horn, jumped out of the car and helped her, but he was in a line of traffic with absolutely nowhere to park. That's why he was cruising in the first place, looking for a parking spot, and anyway, how was he going to load that baby and stroller into the car? Did that contraption collapse? Even worse, his car lacked one of those special car seats which were compulsory for babies and toddlers.

His glance at the kid had confirmed she was a girl. Pink sneakers. Pink top. Pink flowered sunhat which hid the child's face. He'd instantly wondered if she was as cute as her mother. This morning he was still wondering.

They'd not seen him as he craned his neck to watch them turn into an older-style apartment block. At risk of being accused of stalking, he'd done a rapid U-turn and directed his car along her street. It hadn't been difficult to jam on the brakes and stop, illegally, in a handy 'No Standing' zone almost opposite her building.

He'd been too late to attract their attention. Through their glass front door he'd seen them entering their lift, all three smiling and seeming happy to be home. As the lift doors were closing, Nicola had bent down and tickled her child under the chin and the stroller had wobbled a bit from the delighted squirming response. It was a playful side of Nicola he'd not seen. She looked like she actually enjoyed being a mother. It proved how different she must be from Catherine.

He'd had no idea this was where she lived. He supposed it was because he didn't patronise the train, as she must do, where he'd be bound to see her among the commuters. With a wry grin he admitted to himself that top league bankers were never to be seen dead on public transport. Their image demanded that they drive an expensive car to the office and park same car in an expensive reserved executive space under a marble and glass high-rise building. Nicola was senior enough for a car and car parking component in her salary package. Why didn't she do the same? How could such a stylish woman be so unpretentious?

As the trio had disappeared into the lift yesterday, an idea had popped into his head. Leaving the car engine idling, he'd sprinted over to the building's entrance gate and searched for her unit number on the residents' index panel by the security buzzer. N Pearson, Unit 6.

Ordering the flowers as soon as he got home, he'd given special instructions for their quality, and for delivery next day. Nothing except the name N Pearson and the delivery address was to be included on the docket, with the sender's name and address withheld. The message to be written on the card was carefully dictated, deliberately not using her name.

'N Pearson, Unit 6' was an identity in the public

domain, painted on her letterbox for all the world to see. It was important, to him, to keep this girl guessing. Nicola looked like she needed a little less work and a little more romance in her life.

What could be better for his strangely workaholic colleague than a little mystery romance? He'd gained the distinct impression, when suggesting that drink after last Thursday's seminar, that the real thing might be too confronting for her yet. He'd decided then to try the indirect approach. A subtle approach to wooing might prove difficult for him to sustain, but it would definitely be fun, and tantalising.

Valentine's Day. Normally he paid no attention to such a schmaltzy celebration. But this year it was different. His thoughts were all of her. He wished that tonight he could share a bottle of champagne with her, on his balcony, and a meal sitting at his candle-lit dining table, anticipating the pleasures of his king-sized bed afterwards.

Then he remembered the kid. What chance was there for romance with her around? Was he mad? Did he want to play second-fiddle to some other Dad?

CHAPTER NINE

It was that door buzzer again. Who could this be on a Sunday afternoon? Nicola checked her security screen and activated the speaker. 'Oh, Maddie, great to see you. Come in. Come in.' A press of the button gave Maddie access.

Maddie Campbell burst through the door with a big smile on her face, full of hellos as she followed Nicola into the kitchen and perched herself at the bench. They'd been friends for a year. From the moment of their first meeting at a lunchtime networking group for women, the two had shared a strong sense of camaraderie, although Maddie worked in a legal firm. Neither had warmed to the rather contrived and self-promotional nature of networking and both had soon abandoned the group. However, that single networking session had modestly achieved its objective—a personal connection which had quickly become a genuine friendship. Perfectly relaxed in each other's company, as if they were good sisters, Nicola and Maddie still met up occasionally.

Nicola busied herself with the kettle and cups and scrounged in the cupboard for a biscuit while asking 'Have you had your lunch?'

'Yes, I've eaten, thanks. I was in the area, so I thought I'd drop in. I wanted to see how you're liking the new job and see how you and Thea are doing.' Maddie looked around the kitchen. 'Where is she, by the way?'

'She's having a little nap. Long day care is pretty tiring for her. She catches up a bit on weekends.'

'Poor little mite.' Maddie clucked her sympathy. 'On the bright side, she seems to be thriving whenever I see her. Not that our schedules leave much time for socialising.'

Nicola agreed. 'Now that you're busy with Pete, it's a bit more difficult. You used to drop in sometimes on the way home from work, but now you need to fly home to him.'

'Fly is right. I can't believe I'm so happy.' Maddie's face lit with joy.

'So where is Pete today?' Nicola smiled at her friend, pleased for her good fortune.

'He devoted his energies yesterday and last night to giving me a memorable Valentine's Day.' Maddie blushed and Nicola felt a stab of envy. Maddie glowed from the aftermath of being well-loved by her boyfriend.

'You mean he's recovering?'

'Nah, he needed to go into the office this afternoon to

finish something left incomplete on Friday afternoon, to have it ready for a client meeting tomorrow at 8 am. He'll be raring to go again tonight.' Maddie grinned in anticipation.

Nicola felt like a nun these days. She'd almost forgotten her life as a sensual woman and her mood stayed more buoyant if she focused on the positives, rather than her lack of a sex life. 'These hours we all work in a globalised market—they're ridiculous, aren't they?' *There, that was a safe response and will deflect Maddie from regaling me with her sexual exploits.*

'You're not kidding. Ridiculous hours.' But Maddie was hot on the trail of romance. 'Now tell me, what's happening in *your* love life? You're far too young to be living the life of a nun.'

'Strange you should appear at this time and be so inquisitive. Bring your tea into the sitting room, I've something to show you.' She chuckled. 'You won't believe it.'

Maddie clambered off her stool and followed Nicola.

'See those roses.' Nicola pointed to the vase where the blooms were beginning to open and spread their sweet perfume.

'Well now, they cost someone a pretty penny. Who sent those?'

'That's my problem. I don't know.' Nicola engaged eye-contact with her friend and gave her a lop-sided grin.

Maddie picked up the card tucked into the blooms.

'Problem? A secret admirer? Wow, lucky you. How romantic.'

'Is it? I think I'd rather know where they came from. What if there's a random perv out there?' Nicola rolled her eyes.

'Don't be mad, a random perv wouldn't do this. Wouldn't spend this kind of money.' Maddie examined the card again. 'It just says 'hoping for more'. Let's hope some gorgeous man will soon reveal himself to you.'

Nicola giggled. Maddie said sternly 'Literally.'

They both laughed.

'Aren't there any gorgeous hunks in your life? At the office maybe?'

Nicola wrinkled her brow. 'No-one who knows where I live.'

'Ah hah, so you do know a gorgeous hunk.' Maddie gave her a playful punch on the arm.

'Well … kind of. Someone I've met at work would fit that description.' Nicola grinned. 'Technically-speaking.'

'What's his name?'

'Tom Forrester. He's the head of the Financial Markets Division.'

Maddie whistled. 'Tell me more. I want to know all about him.' Maddie flopped onto the couch, taking care that her mug of tea didn't spill. 'C'mon Nicola, sit down and 'fess up.'

Nicola obeyed her friend and perched on a chair opposite. Her brow wrinkled. 'There's little to tell. We've never dated or anything. I know him through meetings at work.'

'Tell it anyway.'

'He's tall, dark and handsome.' The words prompted Nicola's sudden mischievous grin.

Her friend understood the irony. 'Spare me! I'll take that literally then. What else?'

'Early to mid-thirties, clever, going places.' *His intelligent confidence appeals to me.* 'Seems to have something of a sense of humour.' *And that's the part I really like.*

'Wow. He's not married, is he?'

'I don't know.' Nicola shrugged. 'There's no wedding ring.'

'Good grief, haven't you made it your business to find out, girl?' Maddie's voice rose in disbelief.

'Nope. Who would I ask?'

'I forgot, no girlie gossip swirls around your workaday world.' Maddie frowned her frustration.

'Correct. I work entirely with men.' *And only one of them appeals to me.* 'Not looking for a relationship anyway.' Nicola gave a defiant toss of her head.

'Oh, Nicola, Nicola, you're working with a gorgeous sexy hunk and you're letting him slip through your fingers?' She huffed out her disappointment.

'Maddie, don't sigh like that. I'm kind of *over* being impressed by a display of testosterone. I work all day with men who flaunt it in my face.' *But somehow Tom calls to me.*

'But I can tell by the dreamy expression on your face that you're intrigued.'

'Maybe a little, Tom *is* different from the others, but he sure as hell won't be interested in me once he finds out about Thea. He'll think that she'll cramp his lifestyle. His underlings talk as if he's a bit of a playboy.'

'Maybe not. Playboy or not, some men are pretty good with other men's children.'

Nicola let that point drop. No need to get into the complicated story about exactly who Thea's father was. 'Anyway, he couldn't possibly have sent the roses. He doesn't have my address. Doesn't even know where I live.'

'Darn. That blows apart that theory.' Maddie bit her lip. 'Well, who else could it be?'

'Maybe my old girlfriends at the Grosvenor Bank got together, trying to cheer me up. Maybe that's why the roses were anonymous.' Nicola gave her friend a suspicious look. 'Hey, it wasn't you who sent them, was it? Is that why you've suddenly turned up today, to make sure I got them?'

Maddie laughed. 'You mean you think I've been play-acting my way through the last few minutes?'

'I wouldn't put it past you, my friend, you do love to tease.' Nicola smiled her acceptance that she didn't mind being teased.

'I can assure you that it wasn't me, and I doubt it was a bunch of girls being nice to a friend who needed cheering up. They wouldn't have spent all that money.'

Maddie pointed towards the roses. 'Someone with serious dollars at their disposal sent you those particular blooms.'

'Do you honestly think so? Sometimes I feel like a complete misfit in the world.' All the gaiety of the moment whooshed out of Nicola as reality hit home. 'I'm a workaholic single parent. I can't imagine myself as anyone's secret fantasy.'

'Hey, your balloon has deflated.' Maddie picked up on Nicola's rapid change in mood. 'Is something troubling you?'

'Nothing in particular. I just abandoned a fantasy world and crash-landed back into my real world, so different from yours.'

'We used to confide our problems to each other. We still seem to be able to pick up where we left off. Please tell me.'

'Well, Maddie, maybe it's got something to do with seeing you so carefree and happy with Pete. Once upon a time I thought that's what I shared with David.'

'Are you missing David then?'

'No. I guess I'm grieving for the state of 'togetherness'.

'And I've been coming on too strong about having this Tom fella as a possible partner?'

'It's fine, really it's fine. Don't worry, Maddie. It's just that suddenly I felt so 'alone'. I never saw myself as a candidate for divorce. I'm still shocked that it happened to me. I'm pretty sensitive about the tag *divorcee.*'

'I know you are. But you're in good company. Many marriages end in divorce.'

Nicola grimaced. 'It still hurts. Getting divorced feels like an amputation. Part of you is cut off forever.'

'I never thought about it that way.' Maddie gave a little frown and pursed her lips.

'You suffer the pain of losing someone, and losing a lifestyle, without the benefit of comforting remarks from half the people you used to know. People take sides. Some offer unsolicited criticisms and judgmental comments. Or even worse, some send you inane and tasteless cards celebrating the event.'

'Of course, you're right, that's exactly what many people do.'

'Maybe that's why we're friends.' Nicola smiled her gratitude. 'You didn't know David or me before I returned to Sydney. You took me as you found me and scarcely acknowledged the possibility of a previous life.'

'Right. You're a fascinating person in the here and now.' Maddie spoke firmly, brooking no dissent.

'Thanks, Maddie, I'm so lucky to have you as a friend. I did make a conscious effort to avoid most of the blame game of divorce. I think it's rather ugly, so I mostly kept to myself. You know that lick-your-wounds-in-private syndrome when you've failed at something.'

'You're no failure.'

'Thanks.' Nicola gave an appreciative smile. She brightened. 'At least I don't have to suffer bumping into David on the weekends at the local supermarket.'

'Then that's a plus.'

'Yep, he's still up there in PNG, his tropical paradise, living with his second wife Susie.'

'I'm glad I've never met him, or I might have been forced to be rude to him and enter into all those games that you say people play. As it is, I'm free to be *totally* on your side.' Maddie reached across and high-fived Nicola.

'He's out of sight, out of mind, almost like a dead husband. However, you acquire a certain aura of saintliness as a widow but a certain taint as a divorcee.' Nicola let out a wry laugh.

Maddie smiled. 'You've reminded me of something. I still find it remarkable that a photograph of my sister, standing smiling beside her husband who tragically died of cancer, sits on the chest of drawers beside the bed she now shares with her new lover.'

'See what I mean? Dead is acceptable. Alive is different.' Nicola continued rather wistfully: 'Unlike your sister, I don't have to worry about new lovers. There's been no-one since David. Or before, either, come to think of it.'

'You're kidding, aren't you?'

'Nope. Even if I hankered for the sexual aspect of marriage, and sometimes I do, that's for sure, I don't have the time or the motivation or the trust. My life now revolves around Thea and my job.'

'Rubbish. You're too young and vibrant for that. Didn't you enjoy sex with David?'

Nicola squirmed a little. She wasn't in the habit of discussing her sex life. 'I have to confess that I did.'

'So you're going to swear off sex for the rest of your life?'

'David walking out on me for another woman made me think there must be something wrong with me.'

'Did sparks fly to begin with?'

'You mean, was it magic, the way some people talk? Not really. We were childhood sweethearts. Comfortable with each other.'

'Well, maybe you've yet to meet Mr Right.'

'That's the trouble. I feel as if my judgment is poorly lacking. I made a mistake marrying David and I don't want to make another mistake, because it would affect Thea.'

'Phooey. You got married too young. Marrying your first and only boyfriend is a recipe for disaster. Someone should have taken you aside and talked a bit of sense into you. You'll find someone to suit the fully grown-up, mature Nicola, and when you do, nature will give you all the answers you need.'

'What do you mean by that?'

'You'll be on fire for him. And he for you.'

'You mean like you and Pete?'

Maddie pondered for a moment. 'Yeah, I guess that's what I mean. A chemical explosion. Now stop being so blue. Sometimes I get the feeling that despite having everything going for you, including your looks, your beautiful daughter and your big impressive job, you lack confidence in yourself.'

'At work, not really. With relationships, yes.'

'You deserve nothing but the best. A new love will come your way. Problem is, you don't believe it.'

'I don't believe it will happen with Tom. Whenever I see him in the corridors at work, talking with a woman, that woman always seems to be a blonde. I doubt I'm his type.'

'How do you know? Wait and see what happens. You've been there scarcely two weeks.' She gave Nicola another friendly jab on the arm. 'Did you know your eyes shine when you talk about people or subjects of interest to you?'

'Is that right? I must look like an idiot.' Nicola chewed on her lip.

'You don't, it's fascinating. If you're involved in a project at work that you feel passionate about, I'm sure this Tom fella must have noticed it by now.'

'Sometimes I do notice him watching me with a funny expression on his face, when I'm getting carried away by my arguments. He must think I'm a bit stupid.'

'See what I mean. He's noticed you. And I'm sure it doesn't mean that he thinks you're stupid. The man probably thinks you're amazingly attractive.'

Nicola's gloomy mood rose with the tide of her friend's enthusiasm. The corners of her mouth turned up.

Maddie said 'It looks as if you've been wishing all along that it was Tom who sent you the flowers.' She grinned cheekily.

Nicola's reciprocal grin silently acknowledged the truth of her friend's perceptive remark. 'Thanks Maddie,

you've cheered me up. It's always good to talk. I'm beginning to see that I'm still spending too much time alone,
here, in the evenings. You lose perspective.'

'Right. You've done the same for me in the past.
Before the advent of Pete, I mean. I'm glad I could return
the favour.' Maddie stood up and prepared to leave. 'Since
it seems that I've somehow managed to do my good deed
for the day, I must fly. Pete awaits.' She grinned unrepen-
tantly. 'Give Thea a big kiss from me when she wakes up.
Bye, hon.' With a hug she was gone.

CHAPTER TEN

Tom backed his car into his executive car space in the basement, jumped out, zapped the locking mechanism and strode over to the lift. He wasn't one for Mondayitis. He was always glad to get to his office on Monday mornings, bright and shiny, ready to face the challenges of the world. That was his job and he enjoyed it.

It should have been an express ride, this early in the day, but the lift unobligingly stopped at the foyer level.

The would-be passenger caught him by surprise. It was Nicola. She looked extra sparkling today, radiating an inner source of energy. He liked her resilience in the face of adversity. It pleased him to see the spring in her step as she moved towards the opening door of the lift. Had his roses done the trick?

But when Nicola saw him standing alone in the lift,

she looked as if he was the last person she wanted to see right now. Her face tensed up. His mood deflated.

Tom took a small step to the left to give her room to enter the lift without colliding with him.

'Hi Nicola.'

'Good morning Tom.'

He glanced sideways at her. With her standing so close, he was sorely tempted. Her reaction a few seconds ago told him that he'd made an impact on her. But what had he done for it to be so negative? He itched to grab a quick but belated Valentine's Day kiss—that would soon test out her underlying attitude towards him. After all, plenty of men and women who engaged in above-board and illicit office affairs managed quick kisses, and more, in the lifts of high-rise buildings. Damn it all, he'd done so with Catherine in the weeks leading up to their wedding.

Maybe the ubiquitous security cameras had increased the riskiness of such behaviours. Not to mention multi-million-dollar sexual harassment lawsuits brought by young women against senior executives for trying to steal a kiss.

A kiss wasn't something Tom wished to risk. Not yet, anyway. Nicola's body language was still too tense. She wouldn't be receptive. To him, at this point, although he'd seen her being playful with her daughter, an encouraging sign that she enjoyed physicality. Maybe one day she'd yield up her delectable self to his physical embrace. In the meantime, as he'd already decided, 'slow and steady' might win this particularly important race. Nicola was the prize he sought, and he was worrying less and less that she came with an attachment.

Nicola surreptitiously edged away from him as the lift doors closed. God, why did it have to be him in this lift? His presence, always so formidable, was even more dominating in this confined space. Above average in height she might be but, in a bare feet comparison, he must be a good seven inches taller. His after shave invaded her senses. Her stomach tightened and she grew hot and bothered in places not hot and bothered for a very, very long time. Yesterday's conversation with Maddie had unexpectedly refreshed her awareness of the big gap in her life. Sex.

She wished the lift would speed up and dump her at her floor. No, she didn't—she wished the lift would stall between the floors and leave them hanging in space for the rest of the day. The heat and energy radiating off him was warming her too. She'd love to reach out and touch him. Rub his skin against hers. Find herself wrapped in those strong arms. Hell, what did she want?

Tom recognised her discomfort. It wasn't like Nicola to look like she wanted to run away. Surely she wasn't frightened of him. Using his impressive height and physique to his advantage in business affairs was one thing. Bulls in a bull-ring had nothing on men in the higher echelons of business. But this was different. He was a total gentleman in matters concerning the opposite sex and never forced himself upon any woman. Did she seriously think he might ravage her in the lift? Sure, he might think those tantalising thoughts, but never would he act upon them, uninvited.

Willing his self-control to damp down the arousal surging below his belt-line, he turned his mind to a more achievable goal, a diplomatic attempt to find out whether his 'something special' succeeded in brightening her Valentine's Day weekend. All he could dredge up as an unimaginative prosaic conversation-opener was 'You're an early bird today. It's only just past 7.30.'

'Very. Usually I get here around 8.30. The Chief wants to see me today.'

Tom nodded. The Chief's days started early, like his. A startling thought followed. She had a small kid. How did she manage to organise herself at home when she was required to attend important early meetings at work? Kids needed looking after. She must have some excellent babysitting arrangements in place with that young woman he'd seen with her last Friday. He couldn't ask or he'd reveal his secret, so he resorted to 'How was your weekend?' He tried to sound casual.

'Fine thanks. And yours?'

Her banal response to his trite question provided no

clue about her reaction to his roses. No clue even that they'd arrived safely.

A little subterfuge in the form of an outright lie was in order. 'Perfect, except for the flood of Valentine's Day cards in my letter box when I got back from Melbourne on Friday. I hardly knew which card to open first. Or who to ring and thank, out of the long list of names in my little black book.' She looked at him as if he'd gone bonkers. He did sound a bit crazy. He rushed on. 'It left me in a terrible quandary all weekend, I can tell you. Now that you're here, possibly quaking with nervous embarrassment, should I thank you for any of the cards? Even though we both know you're not in my little black book.'

Tom asked this question in a quirky tone. Even his use of the word 'quaking' was tongue-in-cheek. Although she seemed edgy right now, he'd never seen her quake before anyone, and he knew instinctively that she'd grasped he was teasing her. This had become their style of interaction whenever they strayed from work topics into personal aspects of life.

Nicola gave him credit for his unerring instincts. Quaking might be too strong a word, but she was certainly a bit weak at the knees without a desk providing a protective barrier between them. A sensation reinforced so deliciously after last Thursday's seminar. He'd noticed the impact of his close proximity. Did he understand the reason why?

She found herself hugely, if disturbingly, relieved that Tom had mentioned the receipt of Valentine's Day cards, but nothing in the way of an activity initiated by him, such as dinner with someone special.

'Sorry to disappoint you Tom. I'm sure you have a veritable platoon of ladies swooning at your feet, but I don't follow the crowd.' She softened her rebuff by delivering it in jesting mode with a smile.

'Ouch. That hurt.' He feigned a heartbroken expression.

'I know you're kidding, Mr Big Time. It didn't hurt at all.' The moment of sexual tension was broken. They both laughed.

Tom scanned the indicator light, flashing through the floor numbers. Soon they'd be at her floor. Now running out of time, Tom fished for what he hoped would be a positive response: 'What about you? Did you have a good Valentine's Day? Did you paint the town red?'

A rather coy smile lit her face. 'As a matter of fact, I did. Well, what I mean is, someone painted the town red for me. I received a most unexpected, entirely welcome and extra special surprise gift. Pity it was anonymous, as I'd like to thank the sender.'

'Special, eh? Made you happy? That's great then,

Nicola. Maybe Mr Anonymous will eventually reveal himself to you.'

Reveal himself. The same lewd allusion made by Maddie on the weekend. Nicola's mind instantly conjured up an intimate image of Tom. What would he look like naked? Magnificent, surely. She was now even more hot and bothered, and a slight blush tinged her cheeks.

At least she'd let him know that something, a gift, had arrived at her home, and that it meant a lot to her, without the embarrassment of acknowledging that the gift was a large bunch of red roses which had made her day. Her year. She hadn't embarrassed herself by implying any hope that the sender might have been him.

The ping of the lift saved her from his further suggestive remarks as they reached her floor. The lift doors slid wide. 'This is me.' She slipped back into professional mode. 'See you at our usual meeting this afternoon. We're meeting in my office today.'

'Until then.' He stepped towards the back of the lift, giving her plenty of room to exit.

Tom's deliberate use of the word 'reveal' had made him happy when he noticed the blush. Good. Naked bodies did cross her mind from time to time.

Tom savoured the slight whiff of a subtle floral perfume which lingered after she exited the lift. It brought back memories. Chanel No 19, he was sure. Catherine had used that same perfume, although it didn't smell exactly the same on her. She'd told him that it was designed especially for Coco Chanel, whose birthday was on 19 August, and once women started using that perfume, they became hooked and they never changed to another. That was the company's promotional message and Catherine had swallowed it without question.

Best not to follow that particular memory back into a period of his life he'd rather forget. Catherine's choice of perfume was a deliberate ploy, an ingredient of a personal marketing plan, whereas he was sure that Nicola's choice was instinctive. The choice of perfume might be the same, but the reasoning behind that choice, and the nature of the individuals using it, were totally different. He knew that for a fact because Nicola being a mother proved it.

Catherine was past history. He'd rather focus on the future, especially the immediate future. In particular, what was coming up later that day—another meeting with the highly desirable Ms Nicola Pearson.

'I know I'm your man for the project, Nicola Pearson, and I'd love to try being your man in other ways,' he muttered towards the hurriedly departing figure, still visible through the narrowing gap between the lift doors.

Increasingly, she offered the irresistible allure of Eve's apple to Adam. Buttoned-up or no, she was proving to be exactly what he needed. Exactly what he craved. A lovely looking woman, with a brain, who enjoyed being a mother.

Birko was right. Nicola was nothing like Catherine. Nothing.

Tom was completely bored with Catherine's type, those trend-setting sex symbols of the glamour set, those nail-polished, Perrier-drinking women who were all about 'me'. He was well and truly ready for a woman like Nicola. Life could have meaning with her.

What more could he do to tempt her away from her desk and her daughter-focus and into his life?

CHAPTER ELEVEN

Tom was on his way to lunch with a mate who worked at the Reserve Bank. Passing by the Cenotaph in Martin Place he realised he was on a collision course with Catherine. That was one of the downsides of returning to Sydney. From time to time he was bound to cross paths with her but he hoped it wouldn't happen too often. It reminded him too painfully of what a fool he'd once been, to marry her.

She'd already spotted him, so there was no way to avoid her. She sashayed towards him, purring 'Long time no see. I heard you were back in town. Now why am I unsurprised to find you here, Tom, in this location? Once a banker, always a banker.'

Tom ignored the question, and her final pout of discontent. 'Hello Catherine. Whatever brings you back to the place you hate most? The business end of town.'

'I'm on my way to a bank's charity fund-raising event.'

'Which bank? The Federal Bank?' Was Catherine about to turn up in his building again? That'd be too hard for him to tolerate without objecting.

'No way. At Menzies Bank.' Her hand waved vaguely towards a stately sandstone building.

Tom's slight frown cleared. 'Right! The millionaire factory,' he drawled sardonically. 'Yeah, I guess it's a good choice of venue for raising easy money. No doubt someone's wife persuaded her husband to host a lunch for a good cause, using the bank's executive dining facilities.' He knew Catherine would miss his sarcastic overtones as it would never occur to her to do something for others.

'Probably. Might even have been the wife of Paul's client manager. That's where my invitation came from.'

This amused him. Paul, Catherine's current husband, would be kept busy feeding her hunger for the A-lister social set.

Catherine smoothed her tight-fitting skirt across her shapely bottom. 'How do you like my outfit, Tom? I'm trying to outshine that bitch Sonia Davies. She thinks she's the fashion queen of Sydney.'

Tom declined to admire either Catherine's body or its cladding. He'd learned long ago that she was addicted to men telling her how gorgeous she was. Catherine rarely thought beyond herself and the appearance of things. As a free-loader at charity events, she was totally ignorant of the work involved in organising them. Sonia Davies was performing the equivalent of a full-time job, voluntarily. 'Catherine, have you ever thought that Sonia might be a clever, hard-working and kind-hearted woman under that bubbly socialite veneer of hers?'

'No way. Not her. Sonia spends a fortune on her back. It's all one-upmanship against the rest of us.'

Tom knew Catherine well enough to abandon his line of argument and he changed tack. 'Well, I hope you came with Paul's credit card at the ready, Catherine. There'll be something at this charity function to tempt you, I'm sure. Perhaps an auction for a holiday in Kalamazoo or somewhere equally exotic. By bidding to win, you'll be able to brag about it to all your friends.'

This time Catherine must have recognised he was having a dig at her. 'Still the same old sarcastic Tom. I know you always hated those affairs. You could never wait to leave.'

'It wasn't the charity thing that I disliked. it was those airheads who always seemed to inhabit our table. Those ladies who lunch, preening themselves.'

'They did flock to us, didn't they! I never could understand what they saw in you.'

'You mean all that gushing was for my benefit?'

'Of course, darling boy. Like me at first, they liked the look of that hunky packaging you come in. They thought you might be tempted to a little afternoon delight.'

'You're unbelievable, Catherine.'

'So are you Tom. You were always so boring, darling. Always so responsible. If it hadn't been for the sex, I'd have walked long before I did.'

'And you discussed our sexual relationship with your friends?'

'Naturally. What else was there to say about my life with you? We lived such a boring existence outside the pleasures of the bedroom and your undoubted skills in that department.'

'And did you truly believe I was like that? That I'd even contemplate the thought of sexual interludes with some of your friends?'

'No, I didn't, I knew you darling, but they were ever hopeful. They couldn't believe that someone like you could be so strait-laced at heart, so conventionally principled. They wanted to test you out.'

'Meanwhile you looked for someone else with *all* the tricks but without the same scruples as me. Someone quite happy for a dalliance with someone else's wife. And you found lover boy Paul, who ain't boring, I take it, either inside or outside the bedroom.'

'Right. We have a great time. Not like with you. You were married to the job. He takes me to all the right places.'

'Maybe I've changed.' He wasn't trying to win her back. He had changed and matured over the past three years, for the better he thought.

'And pigs might fly.' She shrugged.

'And have you changed, Catherine? Has Paul been able to tempt you with thoughts of a family life?'

'No way. He's not interested either, thank God. Children are so restricting. They'd cramp our lifestyle way too much.'

'Don't let me cramp your lifestyle now then. Best be on your way, or you'll be late. I've got an appointment too.'

'Meeting a date are you Tom? Anyone I know?'

'Not a date, Catherine. I'm meeting one of the head honchos at the Reserve Bank. He's a mate.'

'Ugh, I remember that insufferable bore. Always rabbiting on about interest rate policy and the like. He's all yours.' She flounced off.

As he hurried away from his past, Tom caught a glimpse of what he hoped lay ahead in his future. Nicola was scurrying ahead of him along Martin Place and she turned into Pitt St before he could catch up with her. Damn. If Nicola had spotted him she'd be bound to get the wrong idea about Catherine. Sometimes this business of having a glamorous ex-wife was damned inconvenient. Nicola was worth ten of the Catherines of this world—at least ten. And that score was bound to rise if he ever breached the barricades of Nicola's defences enough that she'd trust him with her feelings. Feelings! Come to think of it, did he trust his own? Nicola was beginning to turn his world upside down.

Nicola was on her way to a retail outlet which stocked her preferred brand of her guilty addiction, Rocky Road. She wasn't a regular dessert eater, but on the nights after work when Thea was asleep in bed and she needed an extra pick-me-up, she'd cut off a slice and savour a few moments of sensual enjoyment. Nicola was looking forward to this evening's fix of that delicious combination of coconut rough chocolate, squishy marshmallow and crunchy peanuts.

As she hurried along Martin Place towards her destination, she saw Tom talking to an extremely attractive blonde. They were deep in conversation. Nicola suffered an immediate pang of disappointment. Her hunch was true, this was Tom's type of woman. Probably his regular date. They certainly seemed to know each other well. She was patting her behind in a sexually provocative manner. It was of minor consolation that he seemed singularly unimpressed.

Nicola changed direction slightly, to walk on the other side of the Cenotaph. It shielded her from Tom's view. She didn't want to catch his eye or be introduced to his girlfriend.

'Well, what did you expect, girl?' Nicola muttered this to herself. 'I knew from his impact on me that he was bound to be a serial lady killer.'

Her professional experience gave her an advantage over most other women in understanding these men. She knew that in the international money markets, the fastest-paced and most machismo of all banking activities, the players took a certain pride in their ability to attract women in droves.

Of course, stratospheric salary packages and turbo-charged cars aided their every conquest. Dare-devil, risk-taking behaviour added to the magnetic forces which swirled round these men. But it was rare to find one who was truly different, as Tom had seemed over the past few weeks. Mostly the players in this field suffered from hubris, displayed more money than sense, drank too heavily and snorted cocaine.

'In fact,' she lectured herself, 'counting my time in my current role, including my time at the Grosvenor Bank, I've had at least a year to discover that most of these traders are quite immature and boorish. Forget about Tom. He's not debonair, like I thought, he's as bad as all the others. A compulsive flirt, trying to get into my pants.'

She returned to the office, her packet of Rocky Road stuffed into her handbag, decidedly grumpy and out of sorts.

CHAPTER TWELVE

'Welcome, everyone. Let's get the meeting underway.'

Nicola took confident charge of this first meeting held on her territorial patch. Tom noticed that she occupied a position of respect with several other men in the crowd crammed into her office. At least they'd sat quietly waiting for her to start. No turning away to begin side-meetings amongst themselves. Even that snide bastard John Wrigley was silent for a change. Good on Nicola, he had to hand it to her, she was impressive in her role.

'You probably realise that in our separate individual discussions, we've made quite a bit of progress over the last few weeks. I've done a lot of thinking and have come up with an idea for the overall structure of the system. I'd like to run through it.'

A buzz of speculative murmuring broke out as Nicola activated the PowerPoint display on her laptop. The first image appeared on the wall screen behind her, and she began her spiel. 'The component parts of existing control systems should fit in, as you see on this first slide, without the need for any double entry of data. That sets the scene for most of you here today.' She worked through the individual modules for each department, explaining how they fitted into the overall plan. Distillation of the work of each section into its most fundamental elements revealed a skeletal structure upon which everything else depended. At its epi-centre was the central control mechanism, like the brain in the human body.

Twenty minutes or so into her presentation, she turned towards Tom. 'The module I've been working on with you, Tom, is coming along nicely as my next piece in the jigsaw.'

He nodded to prove his ready acceptance of her statement.

Wrigley was less acquiescent. 'Yeah,' he drawled in his insulting fashion, 'it's easy to talk, Nicola. The world is full of 'gunnas'. You know, I'm gunna do this and I'm gunna do that. When are you going to deliver on this magic mix? The one that's no doubt going to tie us suckers to your apron strings for ever more?' His question ended in a sneer.

Tom cheered inwardly as she stood her ground without any outward sign of dismay. 'The programmers are lined up to start in mid-March. Naturally it will take months to set up the dummy runs and iron out all the glitches before we start using live data. I hope we'll be able to start running a parallel system by 1 November, with cut over to the new system on 1 January.'

'Well I, for one, am impressed,' pronounced Tom. 'Your ideas are ingenious. I have no trouble envisaging the point where my control module will fit seamlessly within the overall structure of your proposal.' Some of the men in this room needed straight talk. 'Your analytical brain is showing, Nicola. It's not easy to sort out the baffle coming from the bullshit artists in these markets.' He directed his gaze at Wrigley.

The other men in the room murmured in support of Tom. The meeting drew to its close, and all but Tom drifted back to their respective desks.

She remained standing beside her laptop before the screen at the front of the room, disconnecting her power cord and bundling her papers together. She noticed Tom watching her, gave him a happy thumbs-up sign and got as far as 'Thanks for your show of support' before her mobile rang. Nicola mouthed 'Sorry' and took the call. 'Nicola Pearson speaking.'

She listened for a few seconds before her happy confidence evaporated, replaced by a frown and a startled 'George! This is a surprise.' Then 'I remember, of course.' She frowned. 'So why *are* you ringing me at work?'

Tom watched her face drain of colour as she listened. 'Oh,' was her initial response. Later, enigmatically, 'I see.' Listening intently for a while longer, she said, 'Alright, George, I'll do that. I'll see you tomorrow at 4pm.'

'Is everything alright Nicola?' He'd seen her hand tremble as she disconnected the call.

She answered with one abrupt word. 'Yes.'

But he noticed a silent tear slide from the corner of her eye. She turned away from Tom and surreptitiously brushed it aside before facing him again.

Hell, what was going on here? Hallelujah. Tom was startled. This determined Ice Maiden could melt after all. She wasn't as tough-minded and self-sufficient as she tried to pretend.

He watched as Nicola attempted to redirect her mind back to the job, to put that phone call out of her mind for a few minutes.

She squared her shoulders and said, 'Before I was interrupted, I was trying to say thanks. Some of those men try my patience. I'm glad you see where I'm going with my framework of ideas for your area.' Her voice was flat as she fiddled idly with the items on her desk. She seemed distracted, her mind elsewhere.

He wondered, was this 'George' fellow the 'someone special' in her life? Had George said something to make Nicola realise he wasn't the secret admirer who'd sent the roses? If so, she didn't seem too happy about it. Things seemed to be going wrong where George was concerned. Why was Nicola willing to drop everything to meet him? Who was this guy?

After ten minutes of uncharacteristically aimless discussion, Tom decided enough was enough. She was visibly off-balance, not her controlled self. 'Come on

Nicola, you've looked quite upset ever since you took that call. Let's call it a day. I'll drive you home, if you like.'

His offer was spontaneous, as he knew he'd be driving close to her door, but he suddenly remembered he wasn't supposed to know where she lived. 'Er, where exactly is home?'

Her response was distracted, as if on auto-pilot. 'Kirribilli. It's not far. If you live on the North Shore, that is. At the other end of the Bridge.'

'I happen to know exactly where that is. Before my stint in London I bought an apartment pretty close by.'

'Oh, so I'm not taking you out of your way. In that case, I'd appreciate a ride home.'

'Collect your things, Nicola. I'll meet you by the lift doors at the car park level. Wait for me there. I'll duck back to the trading room, see what's happening and tell the boys I'm heading off a bit early today.'

As Tom pressed the down button on the bank of lifts and as a lift door opened, he heard 'Hold that lift' from Mack, in charge of equities trading, racing across the foyer. He winked at Tom. 'You're not the only one who needed an early mark today.'

The lift indicator pinged at their destination and the two men stepped out, into the basement car park. A small smirk betrayed Mack's line of thought when he saw Nicola standing there.

'You move fast' he murmured admiringly to Tom.

'It's not what you think, Mack, it's a family emergency.'

'Yeah, mate, right!' Then Mack looked closer at Nicola, tense and white-faced and not at all like her normal self. 'Yeah, mate, you're right.'

Nicola followed Tom across to his car, but she scarcely noticed its shiny silver sleekness. Sinking into her seat she absorbed the comfort of a favourite leather armchair and began to unwind a little, savouring a reassuring sense of being looked after.

Nicola wasn't focused on Tom at this moment. All she could think of was the need to get away from this place, to get home as soon as possible. She was grateful for Tom's offer because it would mean a faster trip home. That call from George Woodard had revived painful memories.

But as they buckled up and the engine roared to life, Nicola's source of tension began to change. Sitting so close to Tom as they negotiated the traffic and entered the flow heading towards the Bridge, her mind shifted gear. He was acting calm and kind, not pressing her to talk, allowing her the space to be silent.

He was making a habit of turning into her rescuer. A role as 'Sir Galahad' seemed out of character with her initial impression of him. Then he'd been tough and relentless, while showing unmistakable signs of being a sexual conqueror out of hours.

Nicola absorbed his sexual aura right now. Shivering at his physical closeness, even more today than that day in the lift, she was determined he wouldn't see the signs. Her sixth sense told her that involvement with Tom would be powerful and overwhelming and would derail her from her current wobbly track.

Nicola disengaged herself from this train of thought by remembering she should pay attention to giving the directions to her home. 'Take the first turn left off the Bridge, Tom, but then go hard left, not straight ahead.'

He raised his eyebrows slightly and smiled wryly at her, like a long-suffering husband would. All that was missing from his response was the 'Yes, dear'. She remembered that look.

'Sorry, I forgot. You know the way to Kirribilli. If you live in the area you probably shop at that fabulous deli near Milsons Point Station.' She was beginning to prattle, saying the first thing that came into her head. She must stop.

'Occasionally. Not regularly, because I eat out a lot.'

The vision of Tom eating out with glamorous blondes each night distracted her from asking him the obvious question about where it was that he lived. She remained silent.

He twisted slightly in his seat as he checked for traffic coming through the awkwardly-sited roundabout just off the Bridge. 'Tell me where to go once we reach Broughton St. Those one-way streets in Kirribilli can be a bit tricky.'

Nicola gave directions to her apartment block. Tom stopped his car in the 'No Standing' zone and turned to face her, resting his left arm on the back of her seat.

She smiled at him tentatively and said, 'Thanks Tom. For being so kind. For coming to my rescue, as ever. You've given me the quiet time to recover my equilibrium. I'd invite you in for a drink, but I'll be busy with Thea for the next hour.'

'Thea?'

'My two-and-a-half-year-old daughter. I may not have mentioned her.'

'That's right. You have not.'

Nicola was suddenly nervous of his coolness of tone. But she didn't elaborate. She'd always made a point of keeping her private life hidden from her colleagues at work. Women faced enough discrimination in the workforce without adding the complications of child care issues to the mix. Would he take her less seriously as a professional now that he knew she was raising a young child?

There was a brief silence. Then he asked, 'Does she have a father too?'

Nicola paused for a bit, chewing on her lip before she replied, 'Well … kind of. Must go. Thanks again, Tom. I appreciate the ride. You're considerate. See you tomorrow.'

Nicola jumped out of the car and was gone.

'Kind of!' What did she mean by 'kind of'? Did she mean her ex? Did she mean that bloke who'd been on the phone, that fellow George? Was George her ex? Or was George the new father figure? He felt strangely compelled to know.

Over the last half hour Nicola had seemed to warm to him, to be grateful for his help, but her body language gave nothing away. Sitting with her in his car, in the same 'No Standing' place he'd utilised less than two weeks ago, he'd hoped she would show some signs of leaning his way. Even a fraction. Physically, or emotionally. If only she knew the strength of her pull on him, a pull he couldn't quite understand. Of course, as any man would be, he was itching to get his hands on her. But it was much more than that. Unlike any woman before her, she was getting under his skin.

She didn't seem to be in any hurry to invite him in, that's for sure. What was going on here? God, the woman was tantalising but infuriating. Full of secrets. Why did she think it wasn't important to have mentioned before that she was a mother, with a daughter? Surely she could have trusted him with that basic piece of information. You never knew where you stood as a man with this woman. She kept him off balance, same as Catherine had, but in a different way. Less fatal attraction, more puzzling made-for-each-other moments.

CHAPTER THIRTEEN

Nicola collapsed onto her settee with a stiff drink after putting Thea to bed. How was she going to explain her complicated story to a man like Tom? It was the main reason she was trying to steer clear of him, and other men. Even her tentative 'kind of' had been a mistake.

It was none of his business, when all was said and done. But she was a slave to the truth and unable to lie when confronted with Tom's direct question. Thea did have a father, of course. But who was it?

Grappling with this issue was the worst of her private demons. Everyone else might discuss the most intimate of the private details of their life at the drop of a hat. On their mobiles on the train, in voices loud enough for all their fellow passengers to overhear. On talk-back radio. In magazine interviews. But she wasn't like that. She'd always been a private person. Her mother was one of the few people who knew how special Thea was to her.

She wasn't ready to open herself up again. More time was needed. Maybe she needed counselling. Maybe a good listener would break down her reserve—the right kind of listener. Testing the waters, sussing out what kind of man Tom was, didn't seem like a good idea in hindsight. He'd not reacted well to the news she even had a daughter. What would he think if he knew the whole story?

George Woodard's surprise call had brought it all back. Her first marriage to David. How it ended more than three years ago. Its legacy. Thanks to the medical profession, she was already one month pregnant when David walked out on her, before they knew the outcome of a gift donated by a stranger. Artificial insemination using donor sperm had given her Thea, an AID baby.

Nicola was confident that the stranger would have been carefully vetted and was probably a medical student. A student, anyway. They often donated sperm for the money. Her daughter would likely inherit academic genes. One day Thea might be legally allowed to find out who her genetic father was and she hoped Thea would enlighten her at that point.

In the meantime, Nicola was left with continuing uncertainty about so many issues. How could she answer questions from doctors like 'Is there any family history of allergies?' She couldn't say. Where did half of Thea come from? It kept her awake, some nights, wondering about that stranger.

Other parents loved to talk about how their little Johnny was the image of his father. It would be wonderful, a pipedream, to laugh with Thea's unknown father about his genetic stamp on her. She envied other parents these simple daily pleasures of raising a child.

Nicola hadn't given a passing thought to these issues before she embarked on the course in life leading to Thea's arrival. Back then, of course, she'd expected to be sharing whatever concerns arose—sharing them with David. It was meant to be the two of them. It was meant to be teamwork. Going it alone was immeasurably harder.

All things considered, things had gone well enough, until today's phone call from George Woodard, the counsellor working alongside the doctors at the fertility clinic. It was the unexpectedness of that phone call, and its receipt at work, which had tilted her off balance.

Nicola was expecting her file at that clinic to remain closed for many years to come. All she was required to do was keep the staff informed of her contact details. As an overseas resident originally, she'd given them her mother's home address and home phone number, and had later informed the clinic's receptionist of her new home number at Kirribilli. How the clinic became aware of her mobile number was a bit of a mystery. They must have rung Nicola's home number this afternoon and Stephanie must have passed it on. She must speak to Stephanie about that. Stephanie was too trusting. The caller could have been anyone—even that mysterious person who sent the roses.

Now George had rung her at work on an extremely personal matter, something she didn't wish to broadcast at work. And he'd asked her to come in to the clinic to discuss her case. Why? Was there a problem with the donor? Had Thea inherited a genetic time bomb? Nicola swigged a giant gulp of her drink, anxiously fearing tomorrow afternoon.

'Hi there Nicola. Good to see you again.' George Woodard greeted her in the reception area.

'And you. Time has simply flown since I saw you last, George, and a lot has happened.' Nicola tried to smile, but her muscles had locked. Her eyes darted across his face looking for signs of the answer to the question she feared to ask, 'What's all this about?'

George patted her on the shoulder. 'Let's go down to my office.' He shepherded her along the corridor.

When they were both seated, George continued: 'It's three years last November since you were here. I believe you have a little daughter now.'

'How do you know that?' Nicola's sharp voice indicated her suspicion.

'Quite routinely, I assure you. When my receptionist rang your home number she spoke to your nanny person. A two-way conversation ensued, with your nanny speaking on the phone while simultaneously giving directions to a small child in the background.'

Nicola relaxed her guard. No-one had been spying on her and Thea. Except for that mystery roses person. It bothered her that an unknown admirer knew where she lived but her heart still fluttered whenever she dreamed that it might have been Tom.

George made small talk. 'How's she getting along?'

Nicola realised he was trying to smooth the path towards the point of this meeting. She smiled. 'You've got me onto my favourite topic.' She fished a photo out of her wallet and thrust it at him. 'There, don't you agree that she's absolutely gorgeous?'

'She certainly is. How old is she now?'

'She'll be three next birthday, in August.'

'Ah. August. We were correct.' George gave a self-satisfied smile.

'About what?'

'Our records show that you withdrew as a patient of the clinic after two appointments, but you've now confirmed that exactly nine months after the second appointment your daughter was born. Her name's Thea, isn't it? That's the name my receptionist heard.'

'That's right, Thea.'

George nodded but made no comment.

Nicola surveyed the pensive face across the desk. There sat a man obviously waiting for her to elaborate. 'It's a long story.' She sighed.

He sat forward, eyes alert, and said, 'And a story this clinic would like to understand.'

'First things first. Can you tell me why, now, you asked me to come in to the clinic today? Am I in trouble for some peculiar reason? Has Thea inherited health problems I should know about?' Her words rushed out as her stomach churned with anxiety.

He relaxed back in his chair with a calming smile. 'Not at all, Nicola. Let me reassure you on both counts. It's another matter entirely' He shuffled some papers on his desk. 'We've been steadily going through our file records covering the last five years, analysing the outcomes of the work of our clinic. Our belated discovery of your case history has made us question all of our internal systems.'

Her nerve endings ceased twanging. She could handle business matters. 'Sounds like something right up my alley. Management controls are my forte at work.'

He raised an eyebrow at her. 'Smart cookie, eh? You understand where we're coming from, then.' She ignored his patronising comment and nodded impatiently for him to continue. 'Part of our review process involves re-assessing the way in which we judge the suitability of couples for treatment. We pride ourselves on providing the right counselling and advice before the invasive physical work begins.'

'And you've decided that I'm an example of how your screening mechanisms failed?'

'No, in your case, there was no doubt about your suitability. What we need to establish is why you cancelled so soon after treatment commenced, before you knew of its outcome. That's unique in our experience.'

'Not something you can chat about over the phone, on an out-of-the-blue call.' She reined in her sarcasm. He was beginning to irritate her. This was all about his interests, not hers.

He had the good grace to look down, unable to meet her eyes. He cleared his throat and continued, 'The reason isn't recorded on the file. We're trying to guard against it happening again.'

'Risk management, eh?' Disdain coloured her voice.

'Yes. Clinics like ours are an expensive investment in medical resources and we need to make sure that we maximise their benefits. We're starting to attract a lot of criticism for the numbers of marriages which fail after IVF and other fertility treatments.'

'And you want to know what happened to mine.' *After all this time. Incredible.*

'We deem ourselves bound to look after everyone's interests, including those of any children which might be born as a result of our work.' His slick answer sounded infuriatingly sanctimonious.

'I gather you want me to tell my story.' *Why should I?*

'Please, if you would. I'm here to listen. Take all the time you need.'

The word *need* triggered something in her brain. She stared at her shoes, weighing up the benefits and costs of accepting his invitation. She reminded herself that George was a professional counsellor. Even if he'd got off to a bad start with her today, she'd dealt with him okay in the past. *Who else can I safely tell? It might be cathartic. I've kept it all bottled up to date.*

Nicola took the plunge. 'Where to start?'

'At the beginning is usually best.'

'Right.' Nervously she licked her bottom lip. 'When I first came to the clinic I'd been married to David for five years.' She wriggled in her chair, trying to find a more comfortable position. 'We married young, straight out of uni.'

'Meaning you both lacked worldly experience?'

'I guess that's right. We were teenage sweethearts. Neither of us dated anyone else. At first we were happy, but I became increasingly depressed over failing to fall pregnant.'

'Understandable. Many women do.'

'Medical tests eventually confirmed the reason. David was sterile. He took the news badly.'

'Such news is no bolster for the male ego.'

'You're so right. I was pretty devastated too. For us both.' Her eyes prickled with tears at her memories. Her bounce upwards from the springboard towards all her hopes and dreams had bombed and she'd nosedived to the depths of the swimming pool below.

George passed her a tissue but she blinked the tears away and gritted her teeth. 'When I realised he couldn't cope with the news, I began to investigate our options. Adoption. Artificial insemination. I hated the idea of it.

So undignified. So horrible to imagine that stuff being squirted into you. So artificial. It didn't mesh with my romantic ideals.'

'I agree it's one of the toughest decisions any woman could make.'

'Absolutely.' She sniffed back a few remnant tears. 'My worst fears were realised when I came to this clinic and the dreaded experience became my reality.'

'That's where our file records begin, with your first appointment.' George glanced at his paperwork, then pressed her for more. 'Did David go along with it willingly? We have his letter of authority here on file.'

'Not at first. Eventually. He signed the permission forms but his heart wasn't in it, I could tell. His signature was given so that I could be a mother, basically.'

'Did it make you think twice, if you felt his heart wasn't in it?

'No, I saw his signature as a mark in his favour. I suppose some men wouldn't have agreed.'

'That's true. And he did come to Sydney with you.'

'Yes, we travelled to our home town of Sydney together, on leave, and the first ... er, treatment was performed.'

'Which didn't work, because you returned by yourself the next month.'

'Correct. Overcoming our infertility problem became an expensive undertaking. All those airfares on top of everything else.'

'Quite. It takes an exceedingly determined woman to see this process through.'

'That was me, determined. I grew up as an only child of a widow and I craved what I'd missed out on, a family life with several children.'

'Craved?'

'I needed to feel good about something. Creative.' Nicola shrugged. 'Dad died when I was small. That left my mother struggling to pay the bills.' Nicola nodded. 'I was sensitive about that at school. The other kids had so much. I didn't invite them to my modest home. I spent a lot of time at home alone while she was at work, wishing I had a brother or a sister for company.'

'Like so many of us, you needed to repair the damage of your childhood? Reset your course in life?'

'I guess that's it. But David all along had other ideas.'

'He left you?'

'That's right, almost as soon as I returned to PNG, straight after the second insemination. I couldn't wait in Sydney for the follow-up appointments as I needed to get back for a meeting with a visiting World Bank delegation. David opted to get out while the going was good.'

'What do you mean?'

'In my more charitable moments I like to think that David probably didn't deliberately leave me holding the baby, so to speak. Neither of us knew whether I was pregnant or not. I was pretty stressed. The prognosis didn't look good. David probably plucked up his courage to leave me while I was in Sydney on my own, no doubt aided and abetted by Susie, both of them hoping that the treatment hadn't worked again.'

'Susie?'

'The other woman. I knew nothing about her. David married her straight after our divorce came through, when Thea was a baby.'

'Ah, another of our couples is divorced. I'm sorry to hear that.' He made another note.

'It might have happened anyway. In hindsight, I can see that we married too young. We grew apart once we entered the real world beyond school and university.' She gave a small toss of her head. If she was honest, her new direction in life offered far more rewards than life in the David era.

A tentative smile crossed George's face. 'You've pointed me to the weakness in our system. We should have insisted on both parties attending each and every appointment. We made allowances for the distance you were travelling. We may have picked up David's ambivalence if we'd seen him again after the first session.'

'Possibly. I'm so glad you didn't.' Her heart swelled with gratitude. 'I wouldn't have my gorgeous little girl. She's my whole reason for living. You need somebody to love.'

'A fundamental truth. Couldn't agree more.' George nodded vigorously then stopped suddenly as a pensive look clouded his face. 'But if you'd been free, not shackled by having to care for a baby, you might have met someone new and you might have found a second chance for a more normal family set-up.'

'*Or*, I might have been so bitter and twisted about David that no man would have been interested in me anyhow. That's how it's panned out. I *am* angry about David. I *have* been on my own. At least I'm fulfilled in one area of my life, as a mother. Having someone to love has energised me.'

'Good. I'll make a note of this meeting and the fact that you, at least, are satisfied with the outcome even though you're raising the child as a single parent. Of course, we still need to review the files for the donor.'

'You know, George, that's almost the worst part about this process, as you lie there on the surgery table under bright lights, your body recoiling instinctively as you are artificially inseminated. You wonder where this sperm originated, what your baby might turn out to be because you have no idea about the father.'

George nodded sympathetically. 'I don't have his details to hand but he wasn't one of our regulars, as I recall. Some men are. They take pride in how many children they have fathered.'

Nicola gasped. 'Will Thea end up meeting and wanting to marry an unknown half-brother?' She frowned in concern.

George reassured her. 'I'm sure all is well. By donating sperm, men today still expect anonymity. But moves are afoot to change this. We expect that laws will eventually pass giving children the right to know the identity of their father, once the child reaches legal adulthood. We're trying to think ahead and avoid complicating the situation when children like your little Thea turn eighteen.'

'Complications?'

'We like to guard against trouble, should she want to make contact with her biological father. We wouldn't want the donor to shut the door in her face.'

'Now you know why I didn't sleep well last night, thinking about all those donor issues. I hope he has a kind heart and is intelligent as well as having the good health record that, three years ago, you assured me he possessed.'

'I agree. I hope so too.' He scribbled some notes on his paperwork. 'Well, Nicola, it has been a most interesting session. We'll be addressing our internal systems to make them more rigorous.' He stood, led her to the door and shook her hand as she left. 'Thank you for coming at such short notice. Goodbye, and good luck.'

CHAPTER FIFTEEN

February's humidity had given way to Sydney's spectacular autumn weather. Nicola was sipping on her morning tea and staring out the window at the bluest of clear blue skies when the phone rang. It was Tom.

'I have an idea, Nicola. Instead of meeting in my office this afternoon, let's meet a bit earlier and have our meeting over lunch. Outside somewhere, in the fresh air.'

Her heart did a little hop, skip and jump. 'That sounds like a wonderful suggestion. Sometimes I go stir crazy, trapped inside this building. It looks glorious outside today.'

'Sure does. Do you mind walking a bit?'

'Not at all. Do you have a place in mind?'

'I most certainly do. I thought we could walk down to the Quay—ten minutes each way. There's a café on the terrace of the Museum of Contemporary Art. Have you been there?'

'Coffees only. Not for lunch.'

'Great. I'll book an outside table before everyone else in town has the same idea as me. I'll meet you in the downstairs foyer at twenty past twelve.'

Nicola spent the morning wishing the time away. At last, as the waiter showed them to their table, she pinched herself. *This is really happening. To me. Lunch with Tom.*

The waiter quickly returned carrying their drinks order. Tom, facing the soaring white sails of the Opera House, took a swig of his light beer. Nicola, sipping on her mineral water with her back to the harbour view, squirmed a little whenever she caught him eyeing her off instead of the spectacular architecture behind her.

To distract him, Nicola shifted her seat sideways, looked around her and said, 'You know, Tom, I appreciate your choice of venue. I like places with historic significance on a grand scale.'

Tom quirked a lazy eyebrow at her. 'What do you mean by that?'

She laughed at him. 'Careful with your questions, I might bore you with my answers.'

'Carry on, I'm listening.' He cupped his ear in exaggerated emphasis, more in fun than as a taking-the-mickey gesture.

She smiled in response. *This is too good to be true. A high finance man who listens!* 'We're sitting almost on the exact spot where modern Australia began.'

He spluttered on his beer. 'What? Not the turn of conversation I expected. Right here?'

'Yes. The European settlement of Australia began right here. This is where they first stepped ashore in Sydney Cove in January 1788.'

'Oh yeah, you mean the First Fleet. Of course. This was the spot, was it?' Tom put his beer on the table so that he could scrabble for his sunnies and she watched him surveying the scene in silent contemplation for a few moments. 'I should have known. Just never put two and two together. I've seen the memorial up in Argyle St.'

'Me too.' She grimaced. 'Its location is too cramped. The aesthetics don't please me either.'

'Agreed.' Before his sunglasses settled on his nose and hid the direction of his gaze, she noticed him staring past her at the busy ferries churning in and out of Circular Quay.

He mused, 'You know, Nicola, the leader of that voyage, Captain Arthur Phillip, is one of my heroes. I'm a sailor too. What an impressive bloke.'

'The right man for the job,' said Nicola, thrilled that Tom even knew about Phillip. 'He led one of the most amazing voyages in the whole of human history.'

Tom flicked a fly away from his beer. 'Pretty brave of him to take it on, I reckon. That trip across the unknown Southern Ocean to an even more unknown destination, responsible for all those people, must have filled him with trepidation.'

He hadn't begun squirming in his seat out of boredom. What a guy. This was business talk with a twist. She kept it going. 'Absolutely. In eleven little ships, laden with crew, convicts, marines and stores.'

'Ships not much longer than today's maxi-yachts.' If his posture was any guide, Tom's sunglass-shielded eyes seemed directed her way. His attention wasn't flagging. A flicker of hope that they might be on the same wave length coursed through her.

She risked a bit more. 'Except for James Cook's accounts, he was stepping off the edge of the known world.'

'They didn't have our mod cons. I'd think twice before taking it on, even today, and I'm an experienced deep-water sailor.' His admiring tone reminded her of one of those sports commentators covering the annual Sydney-Hobart Yacht Race.

Surprise, surprise, Tom was actually engaging with her nerdy world. Or rather, her mother's world. Her mother was a librarian. Nicola had been raised on books and ideas and stories about history. Everything about Tom's body language indicated his similar interest in Nicola's world.

Taking heart, she continued: 'He proved to be even more amazing once he got here. His leadership was crucial to overcoming the alien climate, infertile soils, unfamiliar vegetation and dangerous wildlife which for several centuries had deterred European settlement on the West Australian coast.'

He pushed his sunglasses down his nose, peered at her over the top of the lenses and winked. 'Save me, please. You're reminding me of my primary school lessons about those Dutch East India Company traders who were blown too far to the east after rounding the Cape.'

His words carried no tone of reprimand and his wink was so playful. She grinned in response. 'I'm impressed, Tom. You actually listened at school.'

'Sometimes. I liked the bits about adventure and exploration.' He laughed.

She chuckled. 'You mean you're a Type A personality from way back?'

'Maybe. Look at the job I chose to do!' He gave her a coy grin. 'What about you?'

'Me? I was always a studious type. Can't you tell?'

'Yep, so far. Prove it some more, teach.'

Nicola enjoyed his teasing ways. 'You're on. I will.' She smiled sweetly at him but raised her chin slightly to indicate her serious intentions. 'Europeans did know about the western side of the continent, but Cook didn't realise he had discovered the eastern shores of the same land mass.'

She stopped and glanced across the table, checking to make sure she still had Tom's full attention. History bored the pants off most people. Would he step into the gap in conversation and change the subject? When he continued to sit calmly, looking with interest towards her, it added immeasurably to her sense of mental attraction to him. Encouraged, she continued, 'That meant that Phillip had no real idea of the enormity of his ultimate place in history, as the founder of modern Australia.'

Tom was quiet for a moment. 'I'm quite fascinated by

leadership,' he countered eventually. 'Without Phillip's able leadership in the early years the whole expedition would have failed.'

Nicola nodded her agreement. She was delighted to discover this side of Tom. Fancy meeting a man who knew anything at all about Australian history. Especially a man heading a major bank's financial trading room. Men in his line of work generally talked markets, rates, dollars, percentages, ups, downs, in staccato incomplete sentences. How far could she push this conversation? She pressed on. 'And there's more, as they say. Once they got here, they all nearly starved to death.'

'There's never been any prime agricultural land around these rocky shores. They even called this place The Rocks, where we're sitting.' Tom twisted in his seat, his glance encompassing The Rocks rather than the Opera House.

'Not knowing how to work these thin old soils forced the new settlers to experiment, to improvise.'

Tom shook his head sadly and said, 'Two centuries on we know they should have taken more notice of the Aboriginal ways.'

'Ah, our First Peoples. If only.' She sighed. 'Phillip was enlightened for his day and did his best for them. He shouldn't have to cop the blame for what's happened to them since 1788.'

'He otherwise left a strong mark on our culture', said Tom. 'Phillip knew food supplies were running out. He insisted on everyone having equal rations, even as available food was progressively reduced.'

'I'm impressed Tom, you know this story well.'

'As I said earlier, he was my kind of guy. His approach radically overturned the prevailing ethos of the class-conscious society they'd left behind, and started something new here. Egalitarianism.'

'Right! Here's to Arthur Phillip.' Nicola clinked her glass against Tom's and took a generous sip of her sparkling mineral water. 'All this talk is making me thirsty.'

'It's making *me* hungry. What are we going to eat? Let's get that waiter back and order something. I'm starving.'

They ordered their food and sat in companionable silence for few moments, watching the tourists milling about taking photos and the lunch time crowds strolling along the harbourside walk below them.

Nicola waved her hand in their general direction. 'Look at them. A good percentage of those people would've been transported here, had they lived back then.'

'Eh?'

'You're wondering where I'm going with this?' A wry grin creased her face. 'The thought occurred that I bet a good number of those people have been fined for something or other in their lives.'

'Join the crowd. I've had a parking fine or two.' He gave her a quizzical look.

'Don't you think it's ironic that the crimes of most convicts who settled Australia would scarcely rate a judicial fine in today's world?'

He chuckled. 'Australian history is full of irony.'

'Most of the founding settlers weren't bad people, just poor people.'

'You're so right. I copped plenty of good-natured flack about being an Australian when I lived in London, but the Poms seem to forget that that's where our convicts came from in the first place. From *their* society. England, Scotland, Ireland and beyond.'

She loved that Tom was proving to have a good sense of humour, which she rewarded with a smiley-face. 'In the end, we've had the last laugh.'

He raised his empty beer glass at her in silent salute. 'The consignment of poverty-stricken convicts to the far side of the world was a unique and quite remarkable way to found a new nation, but it delivered an unexpected outcome. Men mired in the misery of large, crowded, dirty, foul-smelling cities soon proved capable of seizing their golden opportunity to make a better future for themselves here.'

'You're waxing lyrical there, Tom.'

A sheepish look crept over his face. 'Sorry. Now I'm being schoolmaster-ish. I thought about it a lot when I was in England. It was part of working out my personal identity. Many of our early settlers worked hard to create a better life. They helped each other. They developed ingenious solutions to the problems of their new environment. They laughed that they may not cry. Their struggles and their dry, witty brand of humour forged many of the unique qualities of today's Australians.'

'Do you know whether *you* have any convict forebears?'

'Nope, I don't know. If I did, I'd be proud of them, especially if they came early, during Phillip's time, when people needed to be brave and work hard. Colonial society in its earliest years here didn't carry free-loaders. Phillip ran a boot camp. Tough love. But it made the place.'

Nicola looked around and did a bit of time-travelling. 'It's hard to believe that in 1788, when he arrived here in Sydney Cove, human shelters in the whole vast continent of Australia amounted only to caves, simple bark humpies and small huts made from grass or stone.'

Tom brought her back to the present. 'And now look at what's here.' He pointed, and Nicola swivelled in her chair to absorb his view of the Opera House and the Bridge.

In turn, she pointed towards *her* view of the soaring skyscrapers of a major financial centre, squashed by topography into a small central business district. 'I agree, a lot has happened in just over two centuries.'

'I realised while I was away that, between us all, we've created a highly successful nation.'

Nicola laughed a little. 'And the owners of Sydney's prime residential real estate are willing to pay millions of dollars for a view of the same waterways which the city's founders enjoyed for nothing.' Oops. Tom was likely one of these millionaire owners. She closed her big mouth.

He replied drily, 'I believe the First Fleeters paid a

different price. They suffered the anxiety of geographic isolation, lack of contact with home, the hunger pangs of near starvation and fear of the local Aborigines.' He paused before adding 'Who were equally fearful of them.'

'Tom, you surprise me, you really do. Do you read books about Australian history?'

'Being a sailor, one who often sails over there on the main harbour, this part of our national story appeals to me. So, yes, I've read a few relevant history books. For the small band who arrived with the First Fleet in January 1788, it was almost two and a half years before any contact was made with the outside world. I call that a *true* survival story.'

'Not like today's reality TV shows, eh?' Nicola couldn't bear to watch them. 'Whenever I feel lonely and isolated I remember those poor convicts and their unwilling marine guards. The marines too were separated, either unwillingly or out of duty, from their families and shipped off with the First Fleet to the other side of the world. Loneliness is a relative concept.' She sighed heavily.

Tom jumped right into the opening she'd inadvertently left for him. 'Nicola, now that we've proved ourselves as serious-minded weirdos, you've got a friend in me.' He raised his hands to mimic air quotation marks around the title of that popular song. 'Whenever you feel lonely, all you have to do is think of me,' he teased.

She looked down at the table and fiddled with her menu. Damn. In my lonely moments I do think of him but just as I was getting comfortable with him, he crossed the line too early for me.

She raised her head and found him watching her curiously. To her relief he snapped into business mode. 'Okay. Just kidding. Let's get on with the reason for this lunch. It *was* meant to be a meeting about work.' He sat up straight in his chair, like an officer at passport control. 'Don't know how we got off onto the First Fleet and all that jazz, but it was interesting. I can't think of any other woman who'd even think of all the things you're so knowledgeable about, Nicola. You're truly a surprise package.'

She gazed at him, assessing how to take those words. Was this a compliment, or was he writing her off as a complete nerd, happy and willing to be teased but nothing more in the flirtatious world of male-female relationships?

Her reply was forestalled by the waiter bringing their food, and the moment passed.

Once their lunch plates were cleared away, they turned to business matters and covered a wide range of their management control topics.

Nicola was intoxicated by the man, the venue and the conversation but she was a slave to her watch. Ingrained habits die hard. 'It's getting on for two o'clock. I'm not used to long lunch hours like this. Time to get back to work, Tom.'

'Do we have to? I could stay here all afternoon. We are working and I'm enjoying this meeting, out in the fresh air.'

'You have more scope for breaking the rules than I do.'

'Meaning what?'

'You meet with clients and lawyers away from work, your office hours are more flexible.'

'This table proved just as good a space as an office desk for sketching out some flow diagrams on the back of a paper serviette, in far more congenial surroundings than usual.'

She shoved the paper with its boxes, lines and arrows into her handbag. 'Agreed. I'll think about your ideas. Thanks.'

'You know, this is the first time in five weeks we've ever engaged in a proper conversation. It's good to know that you don't have a completely *one-track* mind.'

His emphasis was deliberately and cheekily provocative. She recalled his filly remark on the day they met. Her mouth curved into the beginnings of a wry smile. With the First Fleet topic well behind them, she was back *on track* with him as a work colleague.

'About work, I mean.' He grinned.

Nicola couldn't help laughing. He was the one with the one-track mind but at least he hadn't repeated his earlier 'friend' line. He'd derail her from her chosen track if she didn't watch out. How could she not succumb, in a small way, to his devastating physical presence and his attentive interest in her, and her interests?

Right at that moment, when both were smiling broadly at each other, John Wrigley walked along the promenade below them, on his way back to the office. Wrigley looked up towards the balcony when he heard Nicola laugh.

Tom tilted his head in Wrigley's direction. 'I'm sure you're aware of this but watch out for him, Nicola. He's trouble. A malicious gleam crossed his face when he noticed us. He'll start a rumour about us. We don't want to give him any opportunity to exaggerate what he thinks he saw. Let's go.'

'I certainly don't want him to undermine my credibility.' She frowned.

'Exactly. He'll imply to the other men at work that you achieve your success by offering sexual favours to the boss.'

'Would he think that? Is that your reputation?'

'In some circles, yes. You'd be surprised how easy it is to be misunderstood.' Tom feigned a hang-dog expression.

It cut no ice with Nicola. She retorted, 'Well, I might have thought that once too. You give off that aura. But I have to say that you've always been a perfect gentleman around me. Have I misunderstood you?' She reflected for a moment. 'Or should I ask, perhaps, what's wrong with me?' She felt sure they were safely back in teasing mode.

'Nicola, you know perfectly well that this isn't the time and place to answer either of your questions. For now, work calls. Wrigley has to be set straight.'

Instead of signalling for the waiter to bring the bill, Tom stood up, pulled back Nicola's chair for her, then followed her to the front desk where he extracted his wallet from inside his coat pocket and slapped down his platinum Amex card.

She quietly observed this casual display of his wealth. A millionaire, clearly. Maybe he had sent those roses a few weeks ago! Her heart did a little happy dance.

'We'll follow Wrigley back to the office. If we walk quickly we should be able to catch up to him before he gets to the lifts. I'll make sure he realises this was a business discussion, in lieu of the normal 2.30 slot.'

'It was, wasn't it?' Her innocent-sounding question carried a false ring.

Nicola didn't expect an answer and Tom didn't provide one. Intuition told her that today they'd crossed a boundary. Today's lunch signified the beginning of something entirely private and personal.

They hurried up Pitt Street. When they reached the ground floor of their building, crowded with people returning from their lunch break, John Wrigley smirked at them across the foyer.

'So you two are an item now, eh Tom? Didn't take long.' All eyes were now upon them. Nicola kept quiet, stood erect and stared him down.

'Never heard of a business lunch, John?' Tom's tone was scathing.

Wrigley scoffed. 'Looked more like the set-up for the casting couch to me.' A few of the onlookers snickered.

'You mean you see a man and a woman sitting at a table together at lunch time, you automatically put one and one together and make three. I always knew your maths were suss, Wrigley, but you've just made it clear that your world view is limited too.'

Publicly humiliated, the man opted not to challenge his boss any further, but his lips curled into a sneer and his eyes narrowed with salacious intent as he looked towards Nicola. She knew that trouble lay ahead. Wrigley would bide his time to make life more difficult for her.

CHAPTER SIXTEEN

Maddie was on the phone. 'Pete's away for the weekend, Nicola. Thought I'd come and keep you company tonight. I want to catch up on all the gossip about that hunk you mentioned last time I was over. Any action happening there?'

Nicola laughed at her friend's willingness to blunder into an area where angels feared to tread—Nicola's private life. Maddie's direct approach was rather refreshing.

'Since you asked, the answer is no. But it will be good to see you anyway. I get a bit tired of watching telly on my lonesome on a Saturday night.'

Oh, darl, no telly tonight. A good gossip over a few drinks is what I had in mind.'

Dinner was over. Thea was in bed. Nicola and Maddie were in a mellow mood. They plopped themselves in the sitting area, setting a bottle of wine, a wine cooler and two glasses on the coffee table in front of them.

Nicola jumped up, returned to the kitchen and came back with a large packet of dry cheesy nibbles. 'My quick fix for soaking up alcohol,' she said as she tore it open. 'Not very elegant but effective, if this turns into a long night.' She offered the packet to her friend.

'Not yet. Later. The night is young.' Maddie wriggled herself into a comfortable position. 'You know, last time I was here, you talked about David a bit. But never mentioned why you two broke up.'

'I told you before, I was trying to avoid the blame game.' Nicola hoped that her stand-offish tone would discourage the third-degree.

Maddie sailed on. 'I know it's none of my business, but I'm willing to bet you've been keeping a lot of that stuff bottled up. It's always seemed odd to me that David doesn't feature in Thea's life.'

'You've caught me at a vulnerable moment, you know.' Nicola's voice trembled with the memory of her recent meeting with George.

'You mean you've been hiding stuff? I knew it.'

'Not exactly hiding, just not telling all.' Nicola grimaced slightly.

'Right. In that case, how about telling all to me. You know I'm your friend and you know you'll feel a whole lot better. It couldn't be that bad, after all. You're a private person, that's all, you find it hard to unburden yourself. How come David never comes to visit Thea?'

Nicola almost dropped her glass. No-one had ever asked her that specific question before because she kept to herself so much on weekends. To hell with it. Maddie was her friend. 'Because he's not her father.' A whoosh of relief swept over Nicola as that particular fact escaped her mouth.

Maddie's smile was triumphant. 'Ah hah, now why does that not surprise me? I've been thinking along those lines for a while. Did you have an extra-marital affair that went bad?'

Nicola sighed. Her friend was breaking down her barriers. 'No, nothing like that.'

'There's only one other way you could have got that gorgeous girl. Out of a test tube.'

'You're on the right track now.'

'Really? I'm all ears. I've heard it's stressful … traumatic … going through that whole process. What was the problem?'

'David was sterile. I can easily have babies. I fell pregnant on the second try. And the first try turned out, in hindsight, to have been at the wrong time of the month. I would probably have got pregnant first go, under normal circumstances.'

'So Thea is an IVF baby?'

'That's how people generally refer to it, but technically, in her case, she's an AID baby.'

'AID? What's that?'

'IVF babies usually start life in a proverbial test tube, using the husband's sperm and the wife's egg. AID means I was artificially inseminated with a donor's sperm.'

Maddie's eyes were like saucers. 'OMG, you're kidding me.'

'Nope.' She checked her friend's startled expression. 'You know what I mean, don't you? The cattle industry's based on the process. The thoroughbred horse business too.'

Maddie spluttered on her wine. 'Of course, I understand completely. A rough gig for you. Everyone knows that the real thing is much more fun.' Maddie gave her a cheeky grin.

'I agree.' Nicola's forlorn voice did not match Maddie's upbeat tone. The real thing was in her past.

'Tell me more. All of this happened while you were living up there in PNG, I take it.'

'It did.'

'How did David take it, when he knew he was sterile? You were away from all the usual sources of information and support, living there. I bet it was pretty tough going.'

'I think he took it badly. He was quiet and subdued for months afterwards.'

'How about *you*?' Maddie's sympathy and concern oozed across the room.

'I was devastated. There was I, a young healthy woman, perfectly capable of having a baby, desperate for a baby, and doomed to barrenness.'

'They say women who want a baby will do anything

to get it. I'm beginning to understand that drive myself. I'm still waiting for Pete to pop the question.' Maddie directed an ironic grin towards Nicola. 'Go on.'

'At the same time, I felt for David. The news hit his self-image hard, and I knew he was consumed with guilt on my behalf. At first, anyhow.'

'Did you talk about it?'

'Not really. Not enough. You probably don't know yet what it's like, when you're stuck in your comfortable old routine.' Nicola smiled at her friend.

'Nope, it's all new and exciting with me and Pete.' Maddie couldn't keep the sparkle out of her voice.

Nicola drawled, 'We'd been together for years. Since school.' She paused to let that fact sink in. 'He travelled for his work as a professional engineer, I didn't. At home on weekends we read the papers, visited the beach and the local market and often shared a meal or a picnic with friends.'

'If I may venture an opinion, that sounds pleasant enough. Plenty of couples do that.' Maddie added hurriedly, 'Just saying.'

'Point taken, but we didn't talk about 'us' and our feelings. Our conversation at home was limited to the usual everyday topics of people who live together—the weather, the local news.'

'More like buddies than lovers?'

Nicola nodded and sighed. 'After we found out, his trips away became more frequent and more prolonged. A few days at a time stretched into the whole week. Sometimes he stayed away on the weekend as well. The weekends when he was home developed into chill-out zones for him.'

'So what *did* you talk about?'

'Not much. He wouldn't talk about the elephant standing in the corner.'

'What, even when you were sitting at the table together, eating dinner?' Maddie's eyes widened in disbelief.

'Not us. I'd cook, we'd eat in silence, save for some background music. Then I cleaned up and washed up.'

Maddie rolled her eyes. 'And what did David do while you did all the work?'

'As I recall, his favourite after-dinner destination was his bed. He started going to bed early, earlier than we'd ever done before, saying he felt a bit knackered.'

Maddie wrinkled her nose. 'What did *you* do to pass the night away?'

'I usually picked up a book and read for a few hours before I headed off to bed.'

'Did he show more interest in you then?'

'No, he was usually sound asleep. We still shared the marital bed, but by then a strip of no-man's-land ran down the middle.' Nicola slumped in her chair. The memory was painful.

Maddie shook her head in disbelief. 'Did you think that was strange, for a young couple?'

'Of course. I gave myself a good talking to. I knew I needed to make more of an effort with David. I thought his shock discovery must explain his lack of sexual interest in me.'

Maddie took a swig on her wine as she stared across the room at Nicola. 'I can see it must have been a real dent to his ego.'

Nicola nodded. 'Poor man, a low sperm count makes no difference to the physical act, but a huge difference mentally. I think it changed his view of himself quite a bit. I tried to make him understand that there was no difference for me. But I was emotionally gutted too. The news certainly built up something of a wall between us.'

'Did you try to change things? Trot out new sexy underwear?'

Nicola wriggled in embarrassed discomfort. 'Nothing worked. David showed absolutely zero interest in me.'

Maddie gasped. 'That must have eroded your confidence as a woman.'

'It did, and it has ever since, despite knowing that infertility problems caused many problems in marriages.'

'But I suppose you tried to deal with it alone, as you usually do.' Maddie's warm words surrounded her with the warmth of a mother's hug.

'You understand me better than I realised.' Nicola gave her friend a rueful smile. 'Yes. I thought about adoption and then moved on to considering AID. I researched the topic and found the name of a good clinic in Sydney. This is my home town, don't forget.'

'I'm curious. How did you broach the idea with David?'

'As tactfully as I could. One expert suggested that men sensitive about their infertility sometimes needed a quiet space to read, digest and process unwelcome information. I followed his recommendation and left some brochures on David's bedside table. A week or so later I casually asked if he'd read them.'

'Had he?'

Nicola shrugged. 'It seemed so, but he was non-committal. Said he'd think about it. A few days later I asked him to attend the clinic in Sydney with me during our upcoming scheduled leave. I told him that I hoped that things between us would improve once we'd been to the clinic together.'

'And did they?'

'Marginally. David did sign the letter of authority giving permission for treatment by artificial insemination. Reluctantly. And when we were in Sydney he did come with me for the first appointment. That was in October, nearly three and a half years ago now.'

Maddie stared at her friend. 'So even after that he still showed zero interest in you.'

Nicola took a gulp of her wine. 'That's right. And that first time it didn't work. I flew back to Sydney in November, by myself, for the second insemination at the right time of the month, but David took for granted all my efforts.'

Maddie's jaw dropped. 'Jeez, you must have been devastated that he let you down so badly. That he didn't support you.'

'I was. Anyhow, the reason for his lack of interest soon became apparent. The doldrums had broken into the steady downpour of the wet season, in early December, when David dropped his bombshell.'

'My God, what happened?' Maddie eyes could not be open wider.

CHAPTER SEVENTEEN

'This story takes more than five minutes to tell. Are you sure you want to know?'

'Of course. I'm in no hurry to leave and there's plenty of wine left in that bottle. It's time you unburdened yourself.'

Nicola gave her friend a grateful look. 'Well, all his onsite work in other places was 'on hold' because of the weather, so he'd not been away that week. Based at office headquarters, he seemed to be suffering some kind of cabin fever. I'd been home from work for about five minutes when David came through the door and stated abruptly that there was something he needed to discuss.'

Nicola thought back to that moment. She sighed heavily. 'Well of course I'd known for a while now that something was seriously wrong with David. I wasn't surprised that at long last he deemed a discussion to be in order. But his behaviour that day was totally unexpected.'

Maddie gasped. 'You mean he went troppo or something?'

Nicola shook her head. 'No, nothing like that. Normally, at least he said hello first. And he always avoided initiating any conversations of substance. That was usually my task.'

'Men! Tell me, just why do we bother with them?'

'Exactly. Let's drink to that.' Nicola pulled the bottle of Pinot Gris out of the wine cooler and topped up their glasses. 'Here's to that infuriating species—men!' She leaned across to clink glasses with Maddie and gulped down a mouthful of fortifying liquid. 'Am I boring you?'

'Not at all. I'm riveted. I'm getting to know the real Nicola at last.' Maddie smiled encouragingly at her friend.

'In that case, where was I? Ah yes, he was rather tense about whatever it was that he planned to say. Wouldn't look me in the eye. That kind of thing.' For a few seconds Nicola stared down thoughtfully at the glass in her hand.

'Don't keep me in suspense. What did he say?'

'David told me to sit down and make myself comfortable. That he'd get us both a drink. I knew then he was preparing me for something big.'

'Sure, the 'sit down' bit certainly signifies that bad news is on the way.'

'It's funny how the little things stick in your mind when something major happens. I remember that David disappeared into the kitchen. I heard the kettle being filled and switched on. The clatter of a cup and saucer. The teapot being emptied and rinsed. The kettle neared the boil and was turned off briefly while David swilled hot water through the teapot. He knew I liked the pot to be warmed. The whistle on the kettle indicated its return to the boil.'

'C'mon, is this detailed emphasis on the tea-making ceremony relevant to your story?'

'It is. I heard the quick clank of a beer can top being removed. David then appeared with the drinks tray, placed it on the small table between us, and sat down. I looked at him, somewhat puzzled, but my curiosity was soon satisfied.'

Maddie lent forward in her chair, eager to satisfy hers. 'Whatever did he say?'

'David clenched his beer can as if for reassurance and told me that this was about us. Then he said he didn't quite know where to begin.'

'Sounds ominous.'

'Eventually he said something like Oh, what the hell. I went along with the AI idea to please you, because I knew you wanted a baby. What woman doesn't? We agreed on that point.'

Maddie nodded her head. 'Me too, I'd love a baby one day. Soon, I hope, if Pete shares my goal. We haven't quite got to that stage in our relationship.'

Nicola smiled sadly. 'If what you've said about the call of nature is true, you will.'

'Thanks, but don't get side-tracked. This is your story time, not mine. Keep going.'

'Yes ma'am.' Nicola paused for recollection. 'David

looked at me rather uncomfortably. Then he started talking. He told me that he'd never cared about having children, one way or the other, but lately he'd begun to understand the importance of children, and he didn't want to miss out.'

'At least that was positive.'

'Yeah, but then he said that after reading the literature about the process, he realised that the treatment at the fertility clinic may not work. He confessed that he'd never been keen on the notion of artificial insemination and that his visit to the clinic in October had truly opened his eyes, confronting him with the reality of the process.'

Maddie's sharp intake of breath echoed in the room. 'He wanted to back out, you mean?'

'Yes. He'd decided that humans aren't like cattle, or horses. He could never raise a baby produced so clinically. Or a baby who was half mine, but was produced from some other man's donated sperm.'

'Nice time for him to drop that in your lap.' Maddie scowled.

'Right. I wondered where all of this was leading and soon found out. David said that he'd applied his engineering brain to the problem, the logical brain that I kept reminding him about, and he'd found the solution.'

'And what was that?'

Nicola briefly closed her eyes, shutting out her memories. Then she said, 'I can see him now, shifting uncomfortably in his chair and refusing to look at me. Eventually he told me that in the course of his travels that year he was introduced by work colleagues to a secretary in one of the regional offices of his department. Her name was Susie Smith.'

Maddie's eyes narrowed. 'I can tell what's coming.' She covered her ears in mock disbelief.

'Smart woman. You got it.' Nicola raised her glass to acknowledge her friend's perception. 'I was too stupid back then. Naively I asked him how was Susie Smith a part of the solution for us. David replied *Er, not exactly for us. Definitely not.* I said *Well then, what has Susie Smith got to do with our problem?* I can tell you, Maddie, I was totally mystified.'

Maddie said, 'But older and wiser now, eh! How did he answer?'

'He looked at me and bit his lip, nervously, before telling me that Susie was a single mother, with two children who needed a father, and that during his trips away he'd been seeing a lot of Susie and her children. The penny began to drop for me. I said *So David, what you're trying to tell me is that you've found someone else.* He admitted this was exactly what he was trying to tell me.'

Maddie exclaimed, 'What a rat! Someone who'd already borne two babies.'

'That's right.'

'Someone else's babies.'

'Yes, but he didn't care about that. They were lovely kids, he said, but it wasn't like he needed to pretend they were his, or anything. That was one of his big problems about AI.'

'The pretending, you mean?'

'Yes. And the 'pot luck' aspect. He already knew what Susie's children were like, and who their father was. They were a known quantity, genetically-speaking. Her kids were quite young, but they remembered their father.'

'What's his story?'

'He'd divorced Susie and disappeared and wasn't the most popular guy in Susie's household. David was. Mr Popular, I mean. He was there in the flesh, and he was nice, the perfect father figure. And his lack of sperm meant Susie was free of contraception worries for the rest of time. Two kids were enough and she didn't want any more.'

'And he planned to sprint along a fast track to an instant family, just like that.'

'Exactly. Well Maddie, it's obvious I took a few shocked minutes to absorb his words. I stared at David as if he'd suddenly crashed to earth from another planet.'

Maddie snorted. 'I'm not surprised. He had. What happened next?'

'Well, then David told me exactly what he thought of me. That we'd been together since we were kids, virtually, and we'd drifted apart. He was bored with me. My work bored him. My interest in my garden bored him. My friends bored him. He didn't like the music I played. He couldn't tell me how glad he'd be not to have to make any more cups of tea, involving all that fuss. Susie didn't drink tea, thank God. Susie liked a beer, like he did. Life was supremely better and brighter when he wasn't with me.'

'You! Boring? The man was mad. I bet your hot shot at work doesn't agree. What's his name again?'

'If you mean Tom Forrester, let's not start on him right now. We work together, that's all.' Nicola kept quiet about her lunch with Tom during the week. How she'd loved his company and longed for a repeat performance. A note of wistfulness filled the room.

Maddie gave Nicola a searching look. 'Right then, back to your story.'

'All the pieces fell into place for me, Maddie. But I was incredibly angry with David. I asked him why, in all of those long years we'd been together, he'd never mentioned any of these sources of such earth-shattering discontent, or any other ways in which I displeased him, but now, out of the blue, he was leaving.'

'I bet he had no answer to that. Men, their brains sure are below their belt line, not above.' Maddie looked suitably disgusted.

'You're right, on both counts. All he said was he was sorry to upset me, but he'd decided over the last month to move in with Susie on a permanent basis. In fact, he planned to leave almost immediately, so he could spend Christmas with her and the kids.'

'I see. Simple as that. And what were you supposed to do for Christmas?'

'Exactly! And all the Christmases to come. I pictured myself all alone. He said that my friends would rally round and I'd be alright, although he did have the good grace to look uncomfortable about it.'

'My heart bleeds for him'. Maddie's sarcasm was palpable.

'It was a real shock to me, Maddie, that David could be so matter-of-fact and calculating. I'd always suspected that I was a habit with David, more like a pair of comfortable old shoes than a source of passionate commitment, and here was the proof of his attitude towards me. We'd drifted into an early marriage from which he was easily able to walk away.'

'Too easily.'

'But there was something hugely more important at stake here.'

'You mean the AI treatment?'

'Exactly. David said airily that I'd have to cancel the appointments. He didn't want to find himself shackled to the long-term commitment of raising a baby with me. I was still young and, unlike him, I could have children. His wonderful Susie thought there was still a chance for me to find someone else. Someone more my type. Do you know what he had the hide to say to me, Maddie?'

'No, quick, tell me. I can't believe this guy.'

'David pronounced that he and Susie thought I should return to Sydney as soon as possible and start a new life. He opined that I wouldn't meet anyone else in PNG because all the expat men were married.'

Maddie snorted in disgust. 'That didn't stop him and Susie, did it?'

'But he said that was different.'

'Of course he did. There's always a double standard

where men are concerned. How did you stand being married to a guy like this for so long?'

'I ask myself the same question. It's one of the reasons I steer clear of them now. I think my trusting nature will get me into trouble again.'

'Don't write off Mr Tom Forrester just yet. He might be altogether different from David.'

'He'd want to be. Anyhow, David and Susie clearly believed that they'd got my life all safely mapped out, to relieve their consciences. David even said that they tried to think of me but, in the end, they naturally came first. My thoughts and feelings came a poor second. He and Susie were happy. That's all that mattered to him. The kids were great, Susie was great, and the sex was great.'

Maddie nodded sagely. 'Ah, the sex. The seven-year itch syndrome. Don't blame yourself, Nicola, he was enjoying the novelty of a different partner.'

'Easy to say, but my sense of rejection was pretty overwhelming. And I was devastated at David's capacity to turn his back on me so blithely, and to think only of his needs, even leaving me to do the dirty work and cancel the appointments at the fertility clinic. He was heading off to greener pastures, ignoring all the awkward stuff.'

'Of course. I bet you cried when you had to cancel out.'

'Well, I would have, but …,' Nicola smiled.

'Of course. You were already pregnant. Now I get it.'

'I'd better finish the story. After my initial shocked

paralysis, my anger rose to the surface. David wasn't a man. He was a mouse. Good riddance, I told myself.'

'I'm not surprised.'

'But it wasn't good riddance to the baby I'd been longing for. Before I flew at him in a rage, because he was taking away my baby, I needed him to be out of my sight.'

'I hope you kicked him out in no uncertain terms.'

'Well, no, but I probably should have. This was PNG, after all. A lot different to here. Not many places to go at that hour of the night. The bed of the oh-so-desirable Susie was miles away, wasn't it, a plane journey away.'

'So what did you do?'

'Immediately, while I could still control my despair and could salvage some pride in my rejected self, I told him he'd better go out somewhere for the rest of the evening, drive around, whatever, and he could sleep in the spare room when he returned. Tomorrow, he must move out.'

'And you went to bed crying.'

Nicola recalled that moment. Her uncontrollable shaking. Her astonishment. Her disbelief. Her rage.

'Eventually. First, I tried to calm myself down. I went into the kitchen and poured myself another cup of tea. I was tempted to pour the boiling water over David instead. How dare he do this to me? It wasn't fair.'

'Unfair and unkind. Did he leave the house, as you asked?'

'He did. I didn't know where he was going, and didn't

care. All I knew was he was taking away my chance to have my own baby.'

'Oh, hon, it must have been horrible for you.' Maddie clucked in sympathy. 'What did *you* do, after he left?'

'In a daze, I got out the photo albums of our life together. I spent a long time looking at our wedding album. Two fresh faced youngsters, barely out of their teens. Babies, that's what we'd been.'

'How sad.'

'By now it was quite late. I piled a few leftovers in the fridge onto a plate. I stood at the kitchen sink, shovelling some food into my mouth on autopilot, staring unseeingly past the pawpaw tree leaning drunkenly at the back steps into the darkened garden. It was important to eat, wasn't it? Keep up my strength.'

'That's a funny thing to remember, a pawpaw tree.'

'I guess so, but that's what always reminds me of PNG. Then I went back to the living room, sat at the table again and looked at the next album, and the next. All that innocent fun. Before we knew any of the hard facts of life. Before we grew up. Why hadn't I seen this break coming? Maybe because I'd lost interest in him too, was my painful conclusion.'

'Always brutally honest with yourself, aren't you!'

'Maybe. Anyhow, when I heard David's car returning, I hastily retreated to the bedroom, closing the door. Our bedroom door. David came in to the house quietly.'

'Where had he been?'

'I found out later that he went to a friend's, and made

some lame excuse for his visit. He said nothing about his planned new life.'

'Typical. I bet he left you to do all the dirty work and tell your friends.'

'Yep. He couldn't deal with their disapproval.'

'It must have been a heart-breaking night.'

'It was gut-wrenching, having a suddenly estranged husband sleeping in the next room. Not sleeping with me after all those years. To live through the first night of the end of a marriage.'

'Did you get any sleep?'

'Not much. There were tears, of course. I needed lots of tissues. But quiet tears. No need to let David know I was crying. I tossed and turned all night. What was I going to do now? My world was upended. And all because my husband had a low sperm count. Practically non-existent. And not motile. It all seemed so unfair at the time.'

'It was unfair. Especially on you.'

'True. But as the night dragged on, an inner voice kept telling me that David was right, we'd drifted apart. We simply went through the motions of a marriage. We'd become comfortable flat mates, sharing a living space and offering each other basic good manners but leading separate lives internally, in our heads. We no longer shared intimacy. In our adult years, as we left our student years behind us, our paths had diverged.'

'That's not surprising, since you were babies when you met.'

'My pride was hurt, that David preferred someone

else to me, but a worrying little voice intruded insistently and told me that I was ready to embrace change.'

'Once the shock wore off, you mean.'

'Correct. At first all I could think about was betrayal and the end of my hopes for a baby.'

'You didn't realise then that you were already pregnant. That the second AI treatment had worked.'

'That's right. For a while I thought my late period was due to stress. By the time I was nauseous in the mornings and twigged to its cause, I'd resigned, packed up my belongings and removed myself to Sydney. I'd even signed a contract accepting the position with the Grosvenor Bank.'

'I bet they weren't too pleased to find that their new recruit was pregnant.'

'True, but they accepted that I'd recently separated from my husband and had taken the job in good faith. And they quickly found out, once I started, that they were getting value for money from me.'

'It can't have been easy as a single mother and a career woman.'

'I've managed, like thousands of other working women, despite sleepless nights and endless physical and emotional exhaustion.' Nicola sat up straighter and a confident, defiant grin flashed across her face. 'Thank God my workforce skills were in demand. My income amply covered accommodation and child care costs.'

Maggie exhaled loudly. 'Wow, what a story. Not your average gossip session. But I'm glad you told me. You've coped with a lot. And pretty much all on your own. You're an inspiration. I'm glad your ex doesn't visit here at all. If he did I'd give him a piece of my mind, I can tell you.' Maddie grabbed the wine bottle and sloshed its remaining contents into their glasses. 'Here's to you, the biggest bottler I've ever met.' She raised her glass with gusto. 'You put on such a good show in public. What the world sees as your public face bears little relation to everything hidden underneath that reserved and self-controlled shell of yours.'

'Is it that bad?'

'No, darl, of course not.'

Nicola heaved a sigh of relief. 'Thanks, Maddie. I must say it's been good to tell the whole story to such a good listener as yourself. I told some of it to the counsellor at the fertility clinic the other day.'

Maddie did a double-take. 'What? You went back there? Is there a problem? Has the donor passed on a genetic problem?'

'No, but of course I worry all the time about where she came from. It worries me more as time goes by, probably because I don't have anyone to talk to about it.'

'Fair enough. Understandable. Did the clinic reassure you about that aspect?'

Nicola shook her head. 'The staff can't provide any details. The topic was covered in broad terms and they didn't flag any problems. I guess I'll have to take comfort from that. In essence they were spring-cleaning their records.'

'That's a relief, then.'

'Maybe for them,' Nicola conceded. 'For me, it brought that whole distressing period of my life back into focus. I've been trying to put the David and Susie era and its associated rejection and stress out of my mind. Except for one aspect still making me angry.'

Maddie leaned forward eagerly. 'You mean there's more?'

Nicola shrugged. 'Sad's probably a better word than angry. Had things gone according to plan, I could have had a second child, donated by the same anonymous man. Things have *not* gone right. It means Thea will grow up without a sibling. As a child I always longed for the companionship of a brother or a sister.'

'Let *me* be your pretend sister.' Maddie's hands of friendship reached across to clasp Nicola's.

She squeezed back. 'Believe me, I couldn't wish for a nicer one.' She gave a half-hearted grin of apology. 'Especially when sisters can say *please go home now*. Reliving the tale has quite exhausted me.'

'No wonder, hon, and it *is* getting late. I'll say goodbye and let you get some rest. But you might find that talking about it, now that the passage of time has given you some perspective, will begin to set your mind at rest. Leave you more open for better things. Better men than David.' She gave her friend a farewell hug, and then an irrepressible grin. 'Maybe Tom Forrester.'

Maddie collected her belongings and headed for the door. Nicola waved to her as the lift doors closed and retreated inside her flat. Phew. She collapsed in an exhausted heap on her bed. What a way to end a Saturday night, churned up and emotionally drained. Telling both George and Maddie had certainly brought it all back. But Maddie was right, it was good to face your demons. Verbalised, they were never quite as bad as they seemed.

If George was right and the laws were likely to change, sixteen years wasn't *that* long to wait before she'd know the identity of Thea's father, before she'd know the genetic destiny of her daughter. Maybe during those years she'd regain her confidence that someone would love her again, one day. Other than Thea, of course. What would she do without Thea? But without her bidding, the image of a certain tall, handsome man at the office danced at the edge of her brain.

CHAPTER EIGHTEEN

On this Saturday morning in early autumn the air was crisp, the sky blue, the day bright and shiny and sunlight sparkled on the harbour, turning each little wave crest into a glittering diamond. The day called out for walkers to get out and about.

As Nicola headed the stroller leftwards to descend Broughton St's steep slope, she surveyed the city skyscrapers on the opposite shoreline, seemingly a stone's throw away at this narrowest point of the harbour. She glanced down at Thea's little head and chubby knees and mentally contrasted the two extremes of her lifestyle. They could scarcely be more opposite—on weekdays she confronted the hard-edged financial world and its challenging dealers, on weekends she was the archetypal Mum as she man-handled a four-wheeler. A jaunty spring entered her step as she realised how much she enjoyed her unique brand of dealing and wheeling. Her face creased into a smile. This was going to be a happy day.

They turned right at the water's edge and followed the road leading under the Harbour Bridge towards the Olympic Pool and Luna Park. Thea loved to see the clown entrance to the park, not yet open for the day. She jiggled up and down in her seat, tilted her head up as if to count the clown's row of grinning teeth and threw her arms out wide with excitement. A passer-by, enjoying the sight of a captivated child, exchanged an amused glance with Nicola.

They ambled along the boardwalk and onto the concrete footpath. Metal riggings clanked as the boats rocked at their moorings in Lavender Bay. Joggers puffed past them on their daily run. Nicola soaked up the simple joys of being alive.

They reached the steep flight of steps leading up to King George St in McMahons Point. 'Up, up' chirped Thea.

'Sweetheart, I can't carry you and your set of wheels up all those steps.'

'Want a hand, lady?' An obliging young man jogged up behind her.

'Oh, fantastic. Thank you.' He picked up the stroller and its human cargo and hoisted it up the stairs. Her muscles were no match for his. At the top he held the stroller steady on the sloping path until she wheezed to a halt beside him and took over control of the handlebars.

'Thanks a million. You've warded off a few howls of protest.' She smiled her gratitude.

'No worries. C'ya,' and off he ran.

Nicola surveyed the steep incline which was King George St, ascending straight up the hill to the ridge line above Lavender Bay. It promised to challenge her efforts to keep fit. She'd let Thea decide. 'We've walked a long way today, haven't we darling. Will we keep going? Will we walk up this big hill? See what's at the top?'

'Big 'il, Mummy.' Thea lunged forward against her seatbelt, signalling her keenness to start moving.

'Okay, let's go.' Half way up Nicola stopped for a rest. 'It's steep, isn't it poppet? When we get to the top, let's get ourselves a drink. Poor Mummy. She's tired. You're getting too heavy to push around.' She stood still for a few seconds to allow her heart to slow.

Thea twisted in her seat to check out her mother and Nicola said, 'Soon you'll be big enough to walk all this way by yourself.' Thea giggled.

Breathless from her exertions of pushing the toddler up that steep slope, Nicola looked for an outdoor café in Blues Point Rd where she could easily park the stroller and not create a traffic hazard for passing pedestrians.

She extracted Thea from her chariot and perched her on the chair beside her. Thea liked to be a grown up like her Mum. Nicola ordered a latté and water for herself and a babycino for Thea. Rummaging in the stroller's hold-all compartment she found Thea's water bottle and Thea flipped the lid to suck noisily from the inbuilt straw.

Nicola took a more ladylike sip from her water glass as she glanced around at the other patrons. 'It's busy here today, Thea. Lots of people out and about.'

Her chattiness died as she spied Tom sauntering out of the newsagency two doors up, carrying the Saturday Herald under his arm and juggling his sunglasses onto the bridge of his nose. A warm flood of elation swamped her from head to toe.

He turned in her direction and walked down the footpath towards them. He almost dropped the paper when he saw her, pausing for a second before coming over. 'Nicola! I didn't expect to see you here.'

'Nor I you.' A few brain cells clicked into gear. 'Is this where you live? Where your apartment is? McMahons Point?'

'Sure is,' he drawled. 'See, it was no trouble to drive you home a few weeks back. It's not far from where you live.'

'True. We walk most Saturday mornings, but normally don't make it this far. It's usually either too hot, or too cold, or too wet, or we don't have enough time. Today's so perfect that we kept on going, right round Lavender Bay. Someone even helped me up those stairs at the bottom of King George St.'

Tom glanced at Nicola's pint-sized tablemate. 'This must be your daughter.'

'It certainly is. This is Thea. Say hello to Mr Forrester, Thea.'

'H'wo.' Thea smiled at him coquettishly, angling her

head in that endearing way that small children somehow manage to achieve maximum coyness.

Nicola pulled Thea's chair towards her, to make room for a third chair at the table and looked up at him. 'Please sit down and join us in a coffee, if you're not in a hurry.'

'Not in any kind of hurry. Especially now.'

Tom dragged across a chair borrowed from another table, sat down and winked at Thea, who stared at him with fascination. He signalled to the waitress to bring another coffee.

He winked at Thea again, waited patiently for her to respond with another coy smile and then played a silent version of peekaboo with her, using a section of his newspaper. The child began tilting her head to see round the paper, giggling, instantly a devoted fan.

'Hmm, she's taken an instant fancy to you.' Nicola watched his performance in amazement. This new side of Tom, so different from his work persona, tugged on her heart strings too. 'Tom, were you a pre-school teacher in a prior life?' Asking if he had children of his own sounded too much like a leading question.

'Nope. No real experience with kids. Only what I see others doing with their kids when I'm out and about.'

She added his child-friendly nature to her expanding list of personal qualities she admired in Tom.

He abandoned peekaboo and tucked the paper behind him, out of the way. 'I know you have to kind of keep your distance at first. They're wary of being touched or picked up by strangers. She's no different from most kids.

Plus, she takes after her Mum, I think.' Tom gave her a wry grin.

'Eh? What do you mean?'

'Don't think I haven't noticed how you keep your distance from us all at work.'

'Oh!' Nicola reached out for her coffee, avoiding his direct gaze.

'You're clearly the type who likes to hold back, observe, form a considered judgment based on careful observation.'

She looked at him and gulped. 'I'm sorry if you think I've been unfriendly, Tom. I thought we were getting along just fine when we had lunch the other day.'

'I was beginning to wonder if I'd grown two heads or something.' His eyes twinkled with mischief.

Two could play his teasing game. 'You pride yourself on being an expert at reading people? I won't concede any ground in my case, but you picked Thea pretty well.'

'Thanks. I reckoned that a few party tricks might appeal to her. She's got that inquisitive, fun-loving look about her. Thank God they worked. If I'd scared her, you might have spent the next five minutes pacifying her.'

'You've won her over completely. It's hard to believe you don't have any kids of your own, stashed away at home.'

'Not even a wife. Divorced.'

Her mood kicked upwards. He'd neatly cleared those particular decks and set her mind at ease. But she wondered why Tom sat strangely silent, studying the pair of them across the table, especially her daughter. She switched her gaze from him to Thea and immediately sucked in an urgent intake of air. Seeing Tom and Thea side-by-side, it was impossible to miss the eerie likeness. Especially their eyes. A pang of sadness jolted through her. Her pipedream of laughing with Thea's unknown father about his genetic stamp on her would never come true.

He looked up eventually and joked, 'If I didn't know better, I'd say she was mine.'

Nicola gasped. Tingles of exhilaration raced through her body. Of course. Had he ever been a sperm donor? It would perfectly explain that uncanny match of eye colour. She took a deep, calming breath. Even if theoretically possible, an almost unbelievable coincidence like this didn't seem likely. Sperm donors were men who needed extra money. Why would he, of all people, ever get involved in the whole process of ejaculating into a container in a medical clinic, while eyeing off the girly magazines left there to inspire the required 'performance'?

It would be the answer to all her prayers, to know who the donor was, especially if it was Tom. How could any mother wish for a better father for her child? But it was impossible, surely. And tricky. If she said anything, now, about Thea being an AID baby, Tom might take instant offence at her implication that he would sell his sperm for money. Her tingles of pleasure turned to pain, as if she carried a heavy burden.

Surely, if he'd ever been a donor, he'd know it was feasible for him to have children he knew nothing about.

But his expression gave no sign of pondering the possibility. He continued to smile at the joking remark he'd just tossed her way. Anyhow, he'd been living in London for years. She didn't know his movements for certain, but the timing didn't fit. She wrapped both clammy hands around her latté glass, distractedly seeking a source of comfort.

Should she say anything about Thea's AID origins? It had proved hard to trust her friend Maddie with the story, and she hardly knew Tom.

These thoughts flashed through her mind in a microsecond. Aloud, she countered in a shaky voice: 'There is certainly a remarkable likeness in the eye department.' Her rational self regained charge over her wishful thinking. 'But we both know she's not yours.' Her voice rang with conviction. 'The facts speak for themselves. I don't remember knowing you back then.' She gave a cheeky toss of her head. That felt better. She could handle Tom in teasing mode.

'You could have fooled me!'

They both laughed. The moment passed … but she watched as Tom alternately focused his attention on a child who would pass as his, anywhere, and on the mother who'd borne her. Nicola wondered what he was thinking each time she caught his gaze on her.

They finished their coffees in thoughtful silence and she called for the bill.

'Let me get these.' Tom left a crisp new note inside the wallet and as they rose to leave the café he asked, 'What are you doing now?'

'We're walking back to where we came from,' Nicola mumbled into Thea's lap as she strapped her back into the stroller.

'Then I've got an idea. Why don't you join me for lunch?'

Her head jerked up in surprise. 'What, here?'

'No, at my place.'

'But what about Thea?'

'She's invited too. I'm sure I can find something she'll eat.'

The idea thrilled her but mothers had to be practical. 'How will we get there? You won't have any baby seats in your car.'

'My place is just down the road, down the hill, on the point. We can walk.'

She pulled a face. 'It'll be a long walk home, all the way back up Blues Point Road.' That sounded ungracious, unduly negative. 'What I mean is, it's not as steep as King George St but it's a long hill, especially when you're pushing a baby carriage.' She hoped he'd understand.

'No problems. Later I'll call a water taxi to pick you up at the McMahons Pt wharf and deliver you both back to the Jeffrey Street wharf at Kirribilli. Come on, why don't you?'

I'd better not seem too keen. He'll think I'm a desperado. 'Aren't you busy with work? I never think of you as having any time off.'

'It so happens that I'm completely free this entire

weekend.' His upbeat, carefree voice resonated with energy and let Nicola's habitual restraint off its leash.

'Well, er … why not? Thea loves going to explore new places. But are you sure you won't mind a few sticky finger marks?'

'She doesn't look as if she'll wreak carnage. Let's go.'

CHAPTER NINETEEN

Nicola stood on the balcony. 'Tom, it's magnificent. This must be one of the best views in Sydney. Luna Park. The Bridge. The Opera House. The city skyline. The harbour itself.'

'I thought so when I bought the place. It *is* kind of special. I love to sit here on the balcony and watch the yachts racing, and the ferries buzzing about, and the weird and wonderful watercraft crammed with tourists all snapping away, and the cruise liners coming in from overseas. Pretty good vantage point for the fireworks displays as well.'

'Couldn't be better.'

'Despite all the activity, it's still quite restful to sit here absorbing the panorama and letting it all wash over you.'

'I'll have to be careful with Thea. It's a mighty long drop to the ground.' Nicola peered over the balcony edge in trepidation.

'Don't worry, the glass panels are high enough to deter adults from falling. Unless she climbs up on something, she should be quite safe. We can watch her while we're here. When we go inside we'll lock the balcony door to keep her from wandering out here on her own.'

'Again you sound as if you know a thing or two about managing children.'

'Yeah, a couple of my friends have brought their kids here since I came back to Sydney. They've alerted me to the safety problem. Might not have thought of it myself.'

'You've never had any children yourself?'

'No, my ex-wife didn't want kids.'

'Did *you*?' It was suddenly important to know.

'As a matter of fact I did. Still do.' He stared out at the harbour, as if miles away in his thoughts. 'But you have to find the right woman. One who wants kids, and wants them with you.' He looked back at her and gave a nonchalant shrug.

'You should have no trouble lining up the candidates there.' *I for one might be tempted, having seen you in a new light today.* 'I saw you deep in conversation with a glamorous blonde in Martin Place a few weeks ago. What about her?' She tried to keep her tone light and playful, but his answer was seriously important to her.

'Who, Catherine? No way. That was my ex-wife.' Nicola silently let out the breath she'd been unaware of holding. 'She ran off with that well-known property tycoon Paul Baxter precisely because she most definitely did *not* want kids. Our divorce went through about eighteen months ago. She's married to him now. Don't get me wrong but he's welcome to her.'

'You've surprised me there. Can't believe any girl in her right mind would do that to you, of all people.' Nicola gulped. She was giving the game away here. This off-duty Tom was proving to be irresistibly attractive.

Tom's exultant look proved that she *had* said too much. He wagged a playful finger at her. 'Well, Miss Nicola, speaking as one responsible workaholic to another, I have to tell you that some people like to fill their days with fun and frolic, and Catherine is one of those. As a younger man I was attracted to that degree of extraversion, but we soon found that we didn't suit. We were too different, and we wanted different things out of life.'

She smiled at him. 'It doesn't sound as if you're too bitter and twisted about it.'

'Well, I am in some ways. I suppose I did love her once, for her gaiety. I must have, because I married her, but when I look back I think she set out to get me, and used every possible feminine wile to achieve her ends. She even told me once that I was a trophy husband.'

'Because of the job you do, the money you make, not to mention the way you look?' She could risk joshing him.

He displayed enough good grace to look embarrassed. 'Yeah, something like that. Catherine was a social climber, not used to it. She latched on to me at one of those parties as soon as she found out my, um … attributes, as you put it.'

Nicola laughed. 'And did she go with you to London? Maybe she harboured visions of meeting the Queen at one of those summer garden parties at Buck House.' Nicola couldn't immediately think of anything higher in English social status than the Royal family.

'God, no. By then she'd found Paul, another 'life of the party' type like her. I went to London on my own and she organised the divorce while I was away.'

'How enterprising of her.'

'Yes, it saved me a lot of trouble.' He grinned. 'Now, that's enough about Catherine. Let's get onto more important matters like what we're going to have for lunch.' He shepherded them inside and locked the balcony door. 'I have some fresh salmon in the fridge. I went to the fish markets early this morning. Does Thea like salmon?'

'She's a human garbage bin. She'll eat a small portion. Let's try the Three Bears approach—you can have one and a half serves, I'll have one, and she can have half a serve.'

'Sounds good to me. Right, then I'll turn on this grill plate. It's magic, this griller. No splatter, great exhaust fan.' He busied himself with preparing the salmon. 'Some salad components are in the crisper, and I hope there's some bread in the freezer. Plus some ice cream. If all else fails, I think kids like bread and ice cream.'

'Very true. They do.'

'I'll thaw out the bread. You can assemble the salad.

No, come to think of it, you watch Thea and keep her happy, and I'll do the salad. It won't take long.'

'That sounds domesticated.'

'I pride myself on learning how to look after myself, living alone in London these past few years.'

'I'm surprised you were ever at home alone.'

He gave her a cheeky look. 'Well I was. Quite a lot.' He opened a cupboard and extracted two wine glasses. 'Would you like a glass of wine to go with lunch? Perhaps some Pinot Gris? Or even a red? Salmon has a strong flavour.' From the fridge he pulled out several bottles of wine. 'I'm currently going through a Rosé phase myself, it's a summery choice. I'm making the most of being back home. Of having a real summer. Even if autumn has arrived.' He grinned.

Nicola desperately needed a relaxation booster. This man at close quarters was again profoundly disturbing her senses, as he had in the lift a month back, then in his car, and at lunch the other day. She clamped down on her skittish state of nervousness and tried to act normally. 'That's an excellent suggestion. A glass of wine I mean. I'll have the Pinot Gris.'

'Coming up. Tell you what, I'll show you where the cutlery and table mats are located. Can you and Thea set the table? It will help to keep her occupied.'

Nicola laughed. 'I'll trust her with placing the table mats.' She looked about her as she laid out the cutlery, keeping an eye on Thea while she surveyed Tom's domain, a bachelor pad with a difference.

The refurbished apartment would have been clinical in the hands of anyone else. The internal walls and the floors were stripped back to the clean lines of a box. But they gleamed with high quality finishes. And some special art work.

'Tom, whose work is this? It's marvellous.'

'Would you believe that my mother is an artist? This is some of her work. She has a great talent for conveying the human figure, and she particularly loves the back views of people. That one there shows her three grandkids and some of their mates leaning over a balcony wall.' He pointed to a painting near the table. 'The composition is perfect, as the kids range in age making them, height-wise, all steps and stairs, and kids have such gangly postures. The colours are great too, don't you think?'

'Agreed, she's an exceptionally talented lady. Does she live in Sydney?'

'She used to. Mum moved to Melbourne to be near my sister when I headed off to London. She'd have been alone here otherwise, because my father died about five years ago. My sister's married to an architect there and they have three kids.'

Nicola gazed longer at the painting, then stood in front of several others in the same style. Clearly his mother's. 'Not what I'd expect your mother to be though, an artist.'

'You mean with the job I do?'

'Yes. Why aren't you writing, or doing something else in the creative arts field?'

'Genes will out. My Dad was an engineer. Good with numbers.'

'But I see you also have an artistic eye, the way you've set up this apartment. Or did your mother have a hand in it?'

'I have to confess that it's all my work. Correction—ideas. I used skilled tradesmen to do the refurbishment. Even had I been here, I don't spend enough time at home to do it myself. I bought the apartment before I went to London, and rented it out.'

'Like this? Lucky tenants!'

'No, as it was when I bought it. I knew in advance that I'd be returning home in January, so I asked my architect brother-in-law to oversee my planned renovations in advance of my return.'

'But he lives in Melbourne, you said.'

'He's always in town on business and knows a thing or two about council planning departments and tradesmen. Even so, I was surrounded by a complete mess when I first got back. The work hasn't been finished long. All I've needed to do, personally, is arrange the furniture placement, hang the paintings and organise the contents of the cupboards. Stuff like that.'

The walls facing the harbour comprised a series of clear glass floor to ceiling panels, which slid along to create an open-air room in fine weather conditions. The dining table was positioned to create an alfresco eating space when the panels were open.

'Let's eat here and make the most of a beautiful

autumn day. We can keep a close eye on Thea while we eat. There'll be no unobserved sneaking across the balcony if we sit her between us on this side of the table, looking outwards. I'll find a few cushions so she's high enough to reach the table.'

'It's a perfect place to eat, the way you've placed the table.'

'Thanks. We're looking eastwards. I bought this particular apartment for that reason. It suits me because the rising sun wakes me in the morning, and you of all people know I need to get up early.'

'And I live so close to you as the crow flies, on the eastern side of the Bridge.' Her hand indicated the direction. 'What a coincidence.'

'Not really, when you think about it. I'm sure I live here for the same reason as you—proximity to the office, combined with a scenic and interesting environment.'

Nicola nodded in agreement. 'This apartment must have a good aspect for the afternoons also.'

'It does, it's great. It's those on the western side of the building which cop the heat and glare of summer's setting sun. I still get all the benefit of that sun, without the heat, as it lights up the Bridge and the Opera House and the Darling Harbour area with a special glow.'

'I see you're a man who thinks of everything. You have a discerning eye.'

Tom flashed a look of appreciation her way. 'I'm certainly using it to good effect right now.'

Despite her plan to keep all men at a distance, a little

thrill sparked up her heart-rate. It sure worked wonders for your morale, being the focus of attention of a debonair man. But it was dangerous territory this, being chatted up. She adroitly changed the subject.

'I think we should eat, before Thea gets too tired and starts whingeing. Then we'll have to go, as she usually has a long nap after lunch on weekends. Full-time child care is tiring for littlies.'

Tom's eyes danced with humour but he meekly said, 'Right. Coming up.'

As they waited on the wharf for the water taxi to arrive, they watched the Manly ferry picking up speed as it passed the Opera House after leaving the Quay. The throbbing sound of its engines carried across the water and gave Tom an appealing idea. 'I've had such fun with you both today, would you like to do it all again tomorrow? Feel like a trip to Manly on the ferry? I'd like to make the most of this fantastic weather and my free weekend.'

He could hardly believe that he heard himself saying it aloud. How could he have possibly known what a day like today could mean to him? He'd always loved every minute of the time he spent with Nicola at work, and he'd discovered that time spent with her away from work was even better. How was it possible to feel so right with someone, so sympatico, after such a short space of time?

Nicola's reference to the Three Bears at lunchtime had struck a major chord with him. It resonated, made him happy. The simple joys of being a family had blown him away. Already he was beginning to understand how it was that other guys became so willingly embroiled in single parent families.

His offhand tone of voice was designed to keep the pressure off Nicola. His invitation to spend the day together was casually extended. No need to make it too obvious that he'd give anything to spend more time with her—and Thea, as a welcome addition. Nicola's daughter was enchanting, so like her mother to look at. Even the same dark, curly hair. But there was something vaguely familiar about her. Too familiar, strangely disturbing, uncannily resembling his baby photos. And as for those eyes of hers, the minute he'd engaged with them in the café this morning, he'd felt someone walking on his grave.

Nicola returned his invitation with a straight bat. 'Tom, that would be wonderful. Thea would love it.'

'What about Thea's mother?'

'Well, yes, I have to admit, I'd love it too.'

Nicola rushed to meet Tom at the Jeffrey Street wharf. She looked forward to every minute of today.

His tall figure dominated the entrance to the wharf as he peered in her direction, seemingly on the lookout for her. She hurried down the steep slope, with the safety strap wrapped around her wrist as a precaution against losing control of the stroller. The prospect of her precious cargo rolling away from her down the hill and tipping into the harbour was too terrible to take the risk.

She panted up to him. 'Are we too late, Tom? Have we missed the ferry?'

A broad smile was his answer. 'Relax, Nicola. The ferry's still on its way.'

He was wearing shorts, of the type sailors wear, a loose sports shirt, deck shoes, sunnies and a cap. A camera was slung around his neck. 'You look so different away from the office, Tom. Yesterday too.'

'Same goes for you. Where's that prim tailored suit of yours gone to?' He eyed off every detail of her sunhat, designer sunglasses, long-line long-sleeved blouse top, capri-style pants and flats.

'Suits and babies don't combine too well, I'm afraid.'

'You look great whatever you wear, Nicola. You have an innate sense of style.'

'Thanks.' She smiled at him. 'I need to cover up a bit, as I burn easily. Hence the long sleeves, and so on.'

'We don't need to linger in the direct sun. I'm sure Thea has to be protected too.'

'That's true, but she's been liberally coated with sunscreen. I've got more in my bag.' Nicola pointed to the massive carry-all bag toted round by all mothers of young children.

He squatted on his haunches to greet Thea. 'Hello little one. Are you ready for a ride on the ferry?'

'Mmm, fairy.' Thea beamed at him, her new best friend since yesterday.

'Don't mind her', Nicola laughed, 'fairies and ferries are all the same to her.'

They stood on the wharf, watching the ferry with its creaming wake chugging in to collect them. The turmoil of the threshing water as the ferry reversed its engine thrust and approached its mooring characterised her inner turmoil. Excitement to be spending the day with Tom, anticipation of the moments when he made her feel good to be alive, fear of losing the battle in her resolve not to trust men again.

The metal gangplank clanged onto the wharf. Tom picked up the stroller and its miniscule passenger and followed Nicola across to the ferry deck. An outside seat provided plenty of parking room for her set of wheels. They sat quietly as the ferry's throbbing engines propelled the small craft, crossing the magnificent harbour virtually beneath the landmark Harbour Bridge and past the inimitable Opera House. It was a short ride to Circular Quay, where they'd catch the famous ferry to Manly.

A dash between the wharves at Circular Quay saw them scramble aboard their second ferry as the gates were about to bang shut. Upstairs seats offered a better view and Tom hoisted the stroller and its little passenger up the wide staircase on this larger vessel.

The old motto of the Manly ferry run, in popular demand by poster collectors—'Seven Miles from Sydney and a Thousand Miles from Care'—suited Nicola's mood today. A day out. Carefree. With Tom. The pulse of the engines reverberated under their feet, setting the rhythm for the day ahead.

Tom interrupted her daydream. 'I'm a bit of a camera junkie. It feels as if I'm on holiday today and I like to take happy holiday snaps. Do you mind if you special ladies feature in some of them?'

She smiled happily and shook her head. 'As long as I get copies. I don't have many of us together.' She thought about that for a moment and said, 'You'd better take some while Thea's still fresh, clean and tidy. Later she might be tired and grumpy, or asleep.'

'Right.' Tom opened his camera and clicked away. Nicola alone. Thea alone. Nicola and Thea together. She noticed he took care with the angles as he framed each composition.

'Like your mother, eh Tom, making art with your camera instead of a paint brush? Don't forget to send me copies.'

He smiled. 'Of course. I'll take some more later, when we get to the beach.'

As the ferry churned its way across the harbour, she noticed Tom paying close attention to the 18 footers. Grabbing his camera again and zooming the lens, he took a few photos of them too. 'I told you the other day that I'm a sailor. See those skiffs flying along over there, Nicola. They're practising for the race this afternoon. Normally I sail in one of those 18 footers in the Sunday afternoon races.'

'You do? I'm impressed. They're totally spectacular. Sydney Harbour's famous for its 18 footers. They're so fast!'

'Yep. They rip along. Even on a fairly calm day like today. The wind will get up later and make the race more fun.' He stood suddenly to get a better angle for a shot and called over his shoulder, 'The 18 footers are just about the fastest monohulls in the world. They virtually plane along the surface of the water.'

As he resumed his seat she said, 'They're hard to handle, I hear.'

'They carry a lot of sail for their size, generating a high power to weight ratio. Those guys hanging out on the trapeze try to counterbalance it. You need to be strong to sail those babies.' Nicola could now understand Tom's spectacular physique.

She was fascinated as the crew members scrambled around, as fast as monkeys. 'You need to be an action man too, addicted to speed and excitement, by the looks of it.'

'Anticipation of danger is the key to success. You need a keen awareness of everything happening around you, and extremely fast reflexes, to stay out of trouble.'

'Not for amateur sailors.'

'Nope. It's easy to have a major accident, even when you're experienced.'

'I see why you do the job you do—you Type A personality you. You love the adrenalin rush.'

'Love it. Love the challenge. And where the 18 footers are concerned, the fresh air and physicality of it simply adds to the buzz.'

'So why aren't you sailing today then? The Manly Ferry is pretty tame by comparison.'

'Because I had a better offer.' His voice carried a cheeky twinkle. 'Seriously, I came back from London too late to join any of the regular crews. I'll get involved at the start of next sailing season, but for now I simply fill in when needed. No-one needed me today. All the established crew members made sure they were around for today. It's club championship day.'

Nicola pointed at his brown legs. 'So that explains the tan and …'. She checked herself from commenting on his muscles.

'It does. I've been a sailor pretty well all my life. We wear full body suits on the 18 footers, but hanging around boats and marinas does lead to a fair bit of exposure to sunshine.'

'Did you sail in England too?'

'I did. I shared a weekender with some other chaps at Hamble. We escaped from London most weekends of the sailing season, and competed in the race series there.'

'Where's Hamble?'

'Near Southampton, on the English Channel. Not far from Portsmouth, where that First Fleet of yours was assembled.' He grinned at her.

'Stop teasing. I know I was a bit over the top with my history lesson that day we had lunch.'

'Today I'm the teach.' Another amused grin. He'd been to charm school, this man. 'Hamble's a small, ancient village with a pretty good sailing club. It's been a centre of maritime activity for centuries. Me and the boys used to love sailing there.'

Me and the boys. An image flashed into her mind, picturing them as chick magnets in the evenings after the races. An unexpected stab of jealousy silenced her response. She gave a nod of acknowledgment.

The ferry pulsed past the zoo and the defence force

area at Middle Head. It began to roll heavily in the incoming ocean swell as they crossed between South and North Head. Beyond stretched the Tasman Sea and the vast expanse of the Pacific Ocean. The horizon rose and fell and water sprayed over the balustrade of the lower deck.

Tom was still in sailor mode: 'Big swell for such a calm, clear day. Some strong winds blew out there in the Tasman a few days ago.'

Nicola braced herself too late, and was thrown against Tom, who was holding the stroller as a precaution. He steadied her with his free arm. She could think of nothing better than staying right where she was, in bodily contact with him. It triggered a flash of longing, a wish to explore the skin-to-skin sensations of this particular man's flesh, before the pendulum inside her brain swung back to full self-control mode. She shifted position to regain her personal space and covered her confusion with the opportunity for subterfuge provided by Thea's presence.

'This is fun, isn't it darling, we're having a fun ride. It's like the Big Dipper at Luna Park.'

'Dippa, dippa,' came Thea's gleeful response.

'If you both like the roll of the ocean waves, I'll make sailors of you yet,' chimed in Tom. Despite her surge of joyful anticipation of future outings with him Nicola let that observation pass without comment. He had to be making small talk.

The ferry slowed as it made its way across the calmer waters of Manly Cove and reversed its engines in a swirl of roiling water as it reached the wharf. With the gang-plank in position, the jaunty passengers swarmed off the crowded vessel. Most headed for The Corso, a short promenade which led straight to the surfing beaches.

As they walked down The Corso, Nicola tried not to bump Thea and the stroller into anyone's ankles. Tom came to her rescue. 'Let me carry her. In this crowd, she'll see more at our eye level than she will riding along down there, surrounded by bare legs and a view of far too many broad backsides.'

'Wonderful. Thanks. Thea has a bad habit of kicking out at any stray ankles within her reach. My bulky bag can take her place in the stroller.'

Tom picked Thea up and clasped her against his chest. One of her beatific smiles dazzled him. 'Nicola, have you sent this kid to charm school?'

It was weird that half an hour ago she'd had exactly the same thought about him. 'No, she's obviously taken a shine to you. Children are like puppy dogs. They use their senses to decide whether they like you, in which case they wag their tail, figuratively speaking of course. And you know how dogs cringe and slink away with their tail between their legs if they fear you, and snarl and bite at you if they dislike you. Kids are much the same.'

Other children were being carried on their father's shoulders. Thea reached up to pat Tom's shoulders, saying 'Me, me.'

'You want to extract every ounce of fun from your

exciting day, missy? You want to be Queen of the Castle?' He hoisted her up.

'Look Mummy, look, kween.' She looked down in triumph at her mother.

'I see you. You're having fun, aren't you?'

'So am I,' said Tom. 'I'm having a wonderful day.'

They reached South Steyne Beach and surveyed the scene. This famous stretch of coastline stretched for a few kilometres northwards under three different names but in reality was one continuous surfing beach, flanked by Norfolk Island pine trees.

'Fancy having fish and chips for lunch, beside the beach?' Nicola asked.

'Is the Pope a Catholic?' He grinned at her and she had her answer.

'Thea loves chips. I think all kids must love them.'

'Big kids too. I don't say no.'

'It's a special treat for her. I don't cook them at home.' Nicola gave herself a silent kick for sounding too defensive. Tom wasn't the dietary police.

Others shared the same lunch idea. The queue was long, but it was worth the wait. They found a place to sit, unwrapped their parcel, spread out their modest feast and squeezed some lemon juice over it.

The usual flock of predatory seagulls came diving and squawking around their table, preying on the thousands of visitors who threw their scraps to these fearless scavengers. Frightened at the invasion, Thea began to cry, so they partially covered their food as a deterrent to the birds.

Happy now, Thea scrambled between her two adult protectors, alternately sitting on Nicola's lap, clasping a chip in each hand, and then Tom's lap, finally settling comfortably on his. Nicola watched with growing amazement at Tom's skills with her precious baby. Their mutual acceptance required no fussing, no special attention. As she watched them, it struck her anew that any stranger observing them would take them for father and daughter, they looked so alike.

Lunch over, Nicola rolled up the scraps in the paper and looked around for the nearest bin. Tom put a restraining hand on her arm as he reached for his camera again and spoke to the young couple sitting across the table from them. 'Would you mind taking a few shots of the three of us?'

'Not at all mate.'

Tom adjusted the settings and handed over the camera. 'Thanks. Just point and click.'

The obliging young photographer squinted through the view finder, finger at the ready on the button. 'Hold your daughter up a bit higher, so she's in the shot better.'

Tom reached across and put his arm round Nicola's shoulder, pulling her towards him and Thea to create a better, closer grouping.

'Ready? Say cheese!'

Click. A family shot. A perfect shot. Nicola tried hard not to think about her broken dream of days like this, with a husband, and children so readily identifiable as belonging to them. Their daughter, that young man had assumed.

She resisted the pull of snuggling into Tom. He'd think she was too needy for affection. A physical distraction was sorely needed. By her at least. She wriggled along the bench, away from him. 'We can't come to the beach and not get sand between our toes. Thea will love it. How about it?' She tilted her head at the staircase leading down onto the beach. He gave her the thumbs up in reply.

Nicola chucked their rubbish in the nearby bin and took Thea by the hand. Tom grabbed the stroller and folded it for carrying so that sand didn't jam its wheels. He slung Nicola's bag over one shoulder. With their shoes kicked off, their bare toes squeaked on the dry sand. Thea had fun sifting the loose grains through her fingers, and more fun scampering on the firm wet sand at the water-line, trying to outrun the incoming waves as they swirled up the beach. She lost her footing several times in the rush of water and collapsed in a squeal of giggles and wet curls.

'I did remember to bring a towel and spare clothes for Thea but I should have brought a bucket and spade, to make sand castles. I didn't think,' said Nicola.

'Next time,' promised Tom.

Nicola was exuberant. He planned on a next time.

CHAPTER TWENTY-ONE

Sandy feet were still gritty in their shoes. Drips of melted ice cream had been scrubbed off Thea's face, hands and change of clothing. They were on their way home, seated side by side on the ferry heading back towards the Quay. Thea had nodded off in her stroller.

Tom sat close to her on the hard bench seat. He'd kick-started her emotional bonds to him so successfully that Nicola could easily have rested her head on his broad shoulder and dozed off herself. She must resist the temptation. He was merely filling in his free weekend with them. She and Thea were an entertaining novelty to him, not a fixture in his life.

Tom leaned over, checked Thea's state of wakefulness and breathed a sigh of relief. 'Now that she's asleep, we can talk. We've spent the whole day together, happily I think, it's been great fun, but it's not easy to have a conversation with a two-year-old around.'

'Almost impossible. Does it worry you?'

'No, not at all, but I've been keen to discover what *you* do in *your* spare time.'

'Spare time! What's that?'

'Mmm. Point taken. Maybe you don't have any spare time right now, but some must have been available in the past. Do you play sport? Have a hobby? Have a secret passion?'

Her secret passion could easily become him. She was keen to hide this from him. 'I'm not like you Tom, with your sailing. But I do keep fit, or try to. I love to walk.'

'Like yesterday.'

She nodded. 'Many wonderful walks surround the harbour foreshore. Lots of hills and dales provide a bit of a workout.'

'With the added advantage you can do this with Thea.'

'Some of the pathways are a bit unfriendly for a stroller, but someone usually comes to my aid when I'm confronting an actual flight of stairs. One or two stairs don't cause problems.'

'What do you enjoy most about the walks? The exercise? The company? The scenery?' He waved a hand to encompass the sights of the harbour inlets they were gliding past.

'All of the above, plus getting away from the traffic noise. I love the sounds on the harbour. And the birds are fantastic—the flash of a rosella's red and blue plumage, the song of a magpie, the busy-ness of a hundred birds chattering away in the treetops.'

'I agree. Sydney's so lucky to have this thin strip of national park surrounding its crown jewel.' He pointed at the bushland as they rounded Bradley's Head. 'When do you go for these walks? On the weekends, I guess, like you did yesterday.'

'Yes, we try to get out most Saturday and Sunday mornings for a couple of hours.'

'An awful lot of wheeling. That child chariot of yours must be almost worn out.'

'You can buy spare wheels but she'll be able to walk everywhere by herself before that happens, fingers crossed.'

'Okay. What else?'

'What do you mean, what else?'

'I'm trying to discover your passions. Other than me, of course.' His irony was palpable.

She gave him a bashful glance and ignored the jibe. 'In my youth I loved to dance.'

'Oh, ho, old lady, a Twinkle Toes, eh? I'll bear that in mind, for future reference.' He hummed a few bars of a waltz and they both laughed. 'Anything else?'

'This is like the Spanish Inquisition. I'd have to say it was music. I can't play, but I love listening to music. In PNG I was restricted to CDs, but after I returned to Sydney, before Thea was born, I haunted the Opera House. For the time being I'm back to CDs.'

'Do you listen while you work at night? I assume you take some of your work home.'

'Yes, I do take a lot of my work home, but no, I tend to do one or the other where music's concerned. I'm an active listener to music. I like it to infuse my body with its power. When I listen, I sit and listen, rather than use it as background music.'

'Then we have that in common, Nicola.'

'You mean you're a music lover too?'

'That I am. Especially opera.'

'Really? An action man with a yen for high culture?'

'Must be my mother's influence. My sister and I were raised on Verdi, Bizet and Mozart. Look ahead, we're nearly at the Opera House. In a few months, when the season opens again, you'll have to get a babysitter organised and come with me to a performance by the Australian Opera.'

'Oh Tom, I'd love that. It beats everything else hands down as a form of theatrical performance.' Nicola wished she'd made her response more personal. He'd been hinting at a real date and Tom had looked a bit crestfallen that the attraction was the opera and not him. Today had been the best of days. She was beginning to feel as if she'd known this man all her life. Even if she was out of practice with the dating game, she must make it clear that she did respond to passion.

'Opera is so exciting, so thrilling, so melodramatic, so over the top. Life's dramas are compressed into a cataclysmic few hours in a theatre.'

'Yep. It's magic alright.'

'The human voice is such an amazing instrument. When a soprano or a tenor hits the high notes, or voices are combined in perfect harmony, it sends shivers down my spine.'

'Heard some of the world's best voices in London.'

'The closest I've got to the best is Pavarotti, on a CD.'

'I'm told he's pretty wooden as an actor, but who cares, once he opens his mouth?'

'Sometimes, when I'm driving out to see my mother, I play that greatest hits recording of his, with the volume turned up, and let it overwhelm me. Thea seems to enjoy it too. She listens.'

Their ferry passed the Opera House on Bennelong Point, cut back its engines and cruised into Sydney Cove, busy with vessels coming and going from the wharves. Tom seemed in no hurry to collect up their belongings and make preparations to leave. He continued to chat. 'Ah! I was wondering about your family.'

'It's smaller than yours. I'm an only child. My father died when I was young and my mother always worked to support us. She's a librarian. She's been working out in the Hawkesbury area for a few years now, so what with the distance, her schedule, and mine, I don't see a great deal of her.'

'That's too bad.'

'We're close though. We try to catch up for an hour or two most weekends. Often we meet half way between, for a picnic or something like that. Mum loves to spend a bit of time with Thea.'

'But not this weekend.'

'No, she's on holiday in England and Europe, with a friend, timing her tour before the peak season begins. The fares and accommodation charges are lower, and most of the attractions she wants to see will be open.'

'Have you been there yourself?'

'Yes, er ...,' she trailed off.

'When you were married,' prompted Tom.

'Yes, with David.'

'Does he maintain any contact with Thea?'

It was odd that Tom had tensed up. 'No, he lives in PNG,' she replied.

Tom suddenly released his breath with a whoosh. Even odder.

'And besides ...'. Her nerve failed her. She couldn't bring herself to say *he's not Thea's father*.

'I see.' Tom's slow smile puzzled her and she wondered why he didn't ask her to explain 'besides'. Instead he said, 'Feel free to talk about being married before. I know it probably brings back some painful memories, but you can't pretend a large chunk of your life never happened.'

'That's true. But the whole subject opens up a discussion I don't want to have right now. We're about to disembark. It would take too long to explain properly and I don't want to spoil our lovely day.'

'OK. We'll talk about it some other time, when you're ready.'

They'd swapped ferries at the Quay and were back at the Jeffrey Street Wharf. Tom glanced at the stroller. 'Thea's *still* sleeping.' His surprise resonated in his voice.

'She often sleeps for a couple of hours and today all that fresh air, sun, surf and sand will have made her extra tired.'

'I'll give you a hand up the hill with that stroller. Then I'll catch a cab home from your place.'

'Oh thanks, Tom. It *is* a pretty steep climb and she's getting bigger and heavier with every week that passes.'

In no time they reached Nicola's front door. 'Come in Tom. Welcome to my home.'

Tom closed the door behind them and looked around the room. Nicola was a bit nervous about his response. 'As you can see, not in your league. No sweeping harbour views. There's a glimpse of water between those two buildings in front of mine. But I do get some sunshine. That's important.'

She knew the trendies would consider her flat old-fashioned but she liked it. The furnishings were a bit shabby-chic but her placement of paintings and objects created a unique living space. She wasn't a slavish adherent to the current dictates of interior designers. Her colours were subtle, the tones blended in. Maddie described this room as restful and 'homey'. Even her settee had that sit-on-me comfortable look, with arm rests and a back high enough to lean your head against.

Tom let out a sigh of contentment but Nicola was still a bit jumpy. It was important to her that he liked her space and he hadn't said a word since coming through her front door. She rushed on to fill the void: 'It's been a long day. Do you need to use the bathroom before you leave? It's through there. First door on the right.'

Tom returned a few minutes later, smiling. 'Never seen a bathroom like that before. It's full of Melanesian artefacts, alongside a collection of bath toys. It lived up to the surprise of this living room. You've certainly created a lovely, interesting place to call home.'

To Nicola's anxious ears, he didn't sound at all critical but filled with wonderment and even vaguely amused at her eclectic taste.

'Do you like it? To me, those artefacts looked better grouped all together. They're from PNG. I'd have to move them if the bathroom was in regular family use. The steam would ruin them.'

'Especially if I was in there.' He waggled his eyebrows at her, definitely flirty. 'I take long showers.' Damn the man, was he trying to get her steamed up over him?

'I take quick showers.' Nicola retorted. That should short-circuit the direction of his thoughts. 'Thea has her bath in there each day, but children's bath water tends to be on the tepid side. Not steaming hot.'

He gave her a cheeky look and grinned.

She rushed on. 'That assemblage of artefacts wouldn't suit this living area, and there's nowhere else to put them in this small apartment.' Her pragmatism should kill off his shower fantasies.

His cheeky look faded. 'You have an eye for place-ment, that's for sure. You've created a dramatic contrast to this room, using objects meaningful to you.' She loved that he sounded kind, not condescending. 'You spent a long time in PNG?'

'Five years. My artefacts bring back many memories.'

'Five years! You must have been a baby when you went there.'

'Pretty young, yes. It was a big adventure, that's for sure.'

'So how did you make the switch from jungle girl to city slicker so easily?'

'Well, no-one would ever describe me as a jungle girl. Even so, it wasn't easy at first. The hardest part about coming back to civilisation was being confronted by excessive consumer choice.'

'Wouldn't bother most of us.'

'It did me. I had to make so many decisions, even during a simple trip to the supermarket. Which brand of tea? What flavour biscuits? The range of milk left me reeling as to what to buy. In PNG we were offered full cream milk air-freighted in from Australia, and that was it.'

He raised his eyebrows in surprise. 'I've never been exposed to that kind of life experience. Some valuable lessons there. It must be a reason why you're good at your job. You know how the other half lives. You can appreciate the full range of risks.' He gave his chest a brief pat. 'Those of us who mix almost exclusively in the financial capitals of the world can easily lose our perspective.'

'Thanks for that.' His self-aware comment followed by his diffident half-shrug had pleased her. 'I can see why you've done so well too. The fact that you'd even say that shows that you're a thinker.' She smiled at him.

There was an awkward pause. She shifted her weight nervously from one foot to the other. What would happen next? It was years since she'd had a man in her house. Had he interpreted her smile as a come-on? Would he try to make a move on her? Her stomach nerves tightened in pleasurable anticipation.

'Speaking of thinking, I think it's time for me to head off home.' He spoke briskly. 'Sunday night and all that. No doubt you've got heaps to do to prepare for the week ahead.' Not waiting for her response, he opened his phone and summoned a cab.

Moving towards her door, he said, 'It's been a fabulous

weekend. Over the last few days you've taught me something exceptionally special—that the magic is in the everyday.'

'Have I Tom?' Warmth flowed through her body, despite the let-down of his business-like mode of departure. Being a parent, she knew already that what he said was true. Seeing the world through a child's eyes turned many everyday moments into magic. It thrilled her that he was receptive to the same instincts.

'You have.' He gave her a confidence-boosting smile of appreciation. 'But I'll have to put the magic on hold temporarily.' He tilted his head to the side as he watched her and said, 'I have to go to New York and Washington on Tuesday, for about a week, to attend some meetings.'

'I remember you mentioning them when we lunched at the Quay that day.' She swallowed hard as she tried to hide her disappointment. She'd miss him.

The taxi tooted its horn out in the street. 'So long, Nicola. Can't do this in the office, but I can here.' Placing both hands gently on her shoulders, he kissed her lightly on the forehead. He paused for a moment, brushed her lips lightly with his, a mere feather's touch, quickly opened the door and was gone.

CHAPTER TWENTY-THREE

After a weekend unlike any other in his experience, Tom was suffering from a case of Mondayitis. On Monday mornings he was usually raring to go. Today his office held no allure. *Your daughter.* Yesterday's assumption by that stranger echoed in his brain.

Yesterday morning, waiting for Nicola and Thea to join him at the wharf, he'd not been sure she would come. Babies got sick without warning. Catherine had taught him that women changed their minds at the last minute, got cold feet and backed out of arrangements at short notice. Would Nicola have second thoughts and trot out an excuse on Monday for not turning up? Hell, by concentrating too hard on playing it cool on Saturday, he'd forgotten to obtain her mobile number so he couldn't contact her yesterday to confirm. Her home number was unlisted, like his, and the office phone network was useless after hours. His heart had lifted when he saw her appear at the top of the hill, pushing that stroller.

His world had changed since meeting Nicola. His reservations about becoming entangled in a step-father situation had started to erode as soon as he met Thea. The kid was delightful. Spending time with them wasn't what he'd expected at all. Sunday was even better than Saturday. Burning with curiosity he'd asked the sixty-four-thousand-dollar question and received its totally unexpected answer. Thank God. An 'ex' living overseas was unlikely to turn up at Nicola's front door.

This morning he grudgingly admitted that many of his original prejudices were sadly misplaced. His interest in Nicola was becoming more and more serious. A luscious, intelligent female who was totally determined not to flirt with him in any way was proving irresistible. All day yesterday the words 'a fine romance, with no kisses' had been on replay in his head. At the last minute he'd succumbed to her temptation, carefully, not wanting to push his luck. His goodbye kiss had triggered a small kick of triumph in his guts that she'd dreamily closed her eyes and not pushed him off. He hoped she was warming to him.

He was falling for this intriguing woman but he sensed she was holding back on him and that it had something to do with her first marriage and her daughter.

Impatiently, he picked up the phone and made a call. 'Hey, Birko, remember when Nicola Pearson started here at the Federal Bank six or seven weeks ago and you gave me a bit of background about her?'

'Yeah mate, vaguely recall the conversation.'

'You said something about Sarah telling you Nicola had a child. Have you ever met this kid?'

'Can't say I have. Sarah has, when Nicola was on maternity leave. She went round to Nicola's quite a bit during the daytime, to see if she was surviving, because she seemed to have no support most of the time. No family to speak of. Her mother lived out west, somewhere, and worked full-time as I recall.'

'Does Sarah still see Nicola?'

'She hasn't kept up regular contact, because Nicola went back to work full-time and our number three arrived and Sarah has been too busy.'

Tom squashed a tinge of disappointment. Sarah was his last chance for obtaining the lowdown on Nicola's past. 'Did Sarah ever say anything about the baby?'

'Can't remember. The usual I suppose. All that 'isn't she gorgeous' stuff. You know the way women gush over babies.'

'Not really. It's a big gap in my life experience.' Tom's reply was terse.

'I've told you before, Tom, most women aren't like Catherine.'

'Thank God. Did Sarah ever say anything about why Nicola was on her own?'

'Interested, are we? Nah, all I know is there was a marriage breakup.' A phone rang in the background and

Birko said 'Hold on.' He broke off for a second, barked 'I'm on the other line' to someone at his end and then came back to Tom. 'But now that you remind me, I do recall Sarah being quite excited after a visit to Nicola's. When I got home one evening she couldn't wait to tell me.'

'What was that?'

'Well, she'd been at Nicola's that day, and Nicola let slip that she didn't know who the baby's father was.'

Birko's choice of words floored Tom like a kick in the guts. He sucked in a deep breath then let out a quiet sigh of satisfaction. His sneaking suspicion that Nicola was somewhat scared to let go with him might be true.

'Did Sarah elaborate? What on earth did she mean by that?'

'Dunno. I ask you, how would any woman not know? Unless she was a promiscuous sort. Sarah was quite surprised herself.'

Tom didn't want to go there. Nicola didn't strike him as promiscuous. 'How did Sarah come by this information?'

'All Sarah said was she admired the baby's unusual eyes and asked Nicola if the baby inherited them from her father. Nicola promptly burst into tears. Then she wailed that she didn't know, because the father could have been anyone. Then she clammed up. Hormones. You wait, Tom. This 'getting a baby' business is a bit of a roller-coaster ride. It goes on for a while even after the baby is born.'

'As I said, I wouldn't know from first-hand experience. Young babies seem to be off my radar screen at present.' That sounded churlish, even to his ears. Neutral gear would likely achieve better results from this tricky conversation. 'What else did Sarah say?'

'She said that she didn't think Nicola was the type to sleep around, but maybe she lived another lifestyle in PNG.'

'Like what?' Tom made an effort to keep calm, resisting the urge to snap at Birko.

'Maybe they were all bored out of their brains up there and engaged in wife-swapping parties ... or something ...'. Birko trailed off.

'Really! Does she seem the sort?' Birko was close to lighting Tom's fuse.

'Not to me, no, not when I worked with her,' Birko hastily responded. 'Always business-like and ethical. No feminine wiles on display. But maybe Sarah's interest in Nicola fizzled out, if she suspected more than me. Dunno.'

Tom was ready to bop his friend. Nicola wasn't the type to sleep around, he'd swear to it. 'Nicola's ex-husband seems to play no role in her life—or Thea's. Did you two ever think it might have been an IVF-related baby using a donor's sperm?'

'Hell, no. But of course. We should have thought of that at the time. We've never had that kind of problem, ours is completely the opposite. I just have to look at Sarah and she gets pregnant.' Birko was silent for a moment, as if processing this new idea. 'We didn't think. We jumped to conclusions and assumed that Nicola's unconventional background was the explanation. Maybe Sarah's woman's intuition let her down. I must tell her.'

'Yeah, I'd like to know whether the IVF scene fits with Sarah's perceptions of Nicola.'

Birko's voice took on a curious tone. 'It sounds as if you have more than a passing interest in our mutual colleague.'

'You could say that.'

Birko let out a low whistle. 'It'd suit you down to the ground, wouldn't it mate! A child with none of those complications you were so afraid of, that you mentioned last time we spoke about Nicola. No access weekends and all that disruption. No clever manipulation by children of their biological fathers versus their step-fathers.'

'True, but I think you're jumping the gun. First, get the girl.' Tom gave a wry laugh.

'You don't sound too confident. Not like you. Normally you barely have to snap your fingers and they come running.'

'This one is different. She's the 'once bitten, twice shy' kind.'

Birko's *hmm* came down the line. 'Well, er … maybe we could do something to help.'

'Like what?'

'Oh, an idea has popped into my head. You'll find out soon enough.' Birko chuckled and clicked off the call.

Tom spent the rest of the day in a disoriented frame of

mind. At home that evening he hunted around for his old photo albums. He'd been thinking all day about that stranger's comment at Manly. *Your daughter.* That young man noticed the likeness too. Before leaving for his overseas business trip, he urgently wanted to compare his baby photos with those he'd taken yesterday. His instructions, way back when, had been made crystal clear to all parties.

CHAPTER TWENTY-FOUR

Tom cursed the interruption to his preparations for his trip and grabbed the ringing telephone. Birko on the line. He relaxed. They exchanged the usual opening greetings before Birko drawled, 'Have followed up on your call, mate.'

Tom tensed as he waited for Birko's news.

'Last night I asked Sarah about Nicola. Thought I'd let you know that Sarah does think, on reflection, that Nicola's baby might have something to do with infertility treatment.'

'Why's that?' Tom just managed to stop bursting out with 'yes, yes, yes'.

'Sarah's heard a few programmes about IVF on the radio since she lost regular contact with Nicola. In one of those broadcasts she recognised the name of the interviewee as a doctor Nicola had mentioned. But she can't recall his name now.'

'Thanks Birko. Interesting.' An understatement. If only Birko knew! 'That all makes sense to me. Did she say anything else?' *I've missed my vocation as a detective, not giving anything away.*

'Yep, she said that Nicola sometimes made cryptic comments like *I wish I knew,* as if she was upset, whenever Sarah talked about stuff like our kids' allergies and where they came from.'

'She sounded upset about it?' Feedback from a friend of Nicola's was important to Tom, helping him to process his theories about those photos he'd examined so closely last night.

'So Sarah said. But she never elaborated. Women usually blab on about their private lives without needing any encouragement.' Birko's long-suffering-husband tone quickly changed to a brighter note. 'Now, while I'm on the subject of women, we're having a party for Sarah's birthday on Saturday week. Can you make it?'

'Yeah, that sounds great.' His social life needed a boost. 'Is it a special birthday?'

'Nope, a plain old vanilla-flavoured one. It's an excuse for a get-together. We've all been so busy it's hard to keep up with our friends.'

'This wouldn't have anything to do with the idea that popped into your head when we spoke yesterday, would it?' Suspicion replaced Tom's pleasure at the prospect of seeing his friends again.

'Maybe, mate, maybe. I had to check first with Sarah. She's my social secretary. Do you want to bring someone?'

He paused. 'For example, Nicola?' A sly snicker wafted down the line.

'No.' Tom snapped his answer.

'No need to bite my head off.' Birko sounded a bit taken aback at Tom's curt reply.

'Sorry, mate.'

'Then I'll tell Sarah you'll be coming on your own. She'll be surprised.'

'Well, old son, you know how it is. Sometimes you need the softly, softly approach.' Tom sure hoped it would work with Nicola.

Birko chuckled. 'No-one else in the offing? Love life in the doldrums then?'

'Let's just say I'm playing it cool at present.'

'OK mate, I get the message. Mr 'Play it close to the chest' has Ms Nicola Pearson in his sights but is biding his time.'

'Could be. Let's wait and see.'

'You definitely don't want to ask her to come to the party with you?'

'No. She'd probably make up some excuse. She's still nervous about anything that even hints at a proper date. With me on my own, I mean.'

'You mean you've tried and been knocked back?'

'Nope. But I did meet up with her by accident last weekend. Turns out she lives near me. She's fine when she's hiding behind her daughter.' Tom chose not to confess to his friend the full extent of the weekend time he'd spent with Nicola and her daughter. He'd already given Birko and Sarah plenty to talk about where he and Nicola were concerned and his growing feelings for her felt private, special, in need of protection from the well-meaning commentary of friends.

'The child you're so interested in.'

'Yep … a lovely kid.' Tom smiled at his memories of last weekend. 'Listen Birko, Sarah and Nicola have been friends in the past. I don't mind at all if you and Sarah invite her.'

Birko laughed. 'OK, so that's how it is. You don't want to frighten the horses. Will do. See you soon then. Can't make our lunch appointment this coming Friday, by the way, the big boss is in town, so I'll see you at the party.'

'Right. I'll be away myself. Should've called you. Have to go to a few meetings in New York and Washington. I'm flying out later today. But I'll be back in time for your party.' Tom wouldn't miss it for the world. Nicola might be there.

'Hope you'll be able to stay awake on the night. There's a big time difference between the east coast of the States and Sydney. All that jet lag won't boost your party mood.'

'Don't worry, mate. I'll be firing on all fours that night. And thanks.'

Tom hung up the phone and crossed his fingers and toes that Nicola would come to the party. She'd have a fair idea that he and Birko must be friends. If she made a special effort to organise a babysitter and come by herself, it would give him a better clue to her possible interest in him. Nicola was a dedicated mother and, from her conversation on the weekend, it didn't seem as if she ever went out in the evenings. If she turned up at Birko's, it would be a positive sign.

If she came, it would be his big chance, finally, to break down her guard without a child inadvertently playing gooseberry. He couldn't wait. No prompting was needed where he was concerned, he'd fallen for her in a big way and he'd take her to bed in a heartbeat, but he respected that she was that rare someone who couldn't be rushed into a physical relationship. What excited him was his pretty fair idea that, once committed, she'd give it her all, like everything else she did. His body responded to that idea in ways that were totally frustrating.

CHAPTER TWENTY-FIVE

Nicola and pyjama-clad Thea rushed for the ringing phone, giggling. It was a game they played. Who could get there first? Nicola snatched it, and scooped up her running child in the other arm. 'Hello, Nicola Pearson speaking.'

'I know this comes out of the blue.'

Nicola recognised the voice instantly. 'Sarah!'

Nicola cuddled her squirming child, soothing Thea's disappointment by whispering 'It's an old friend of Mummy's, darling, you can talk to her in a minute.' No matter who was on the phone, Thea had to speak.

Sarah laughed. 'Yep, it's me. Phew, I'm glad you beat Thea to the phone.' Relief sounded in her voice. 'I've a few calls to make to households such as yours. It's never easy when a small child picks up the phone and you have a one-sided conversation with them, trying to persuade them to get Mummy.'

'I know, I know. It can take forever.' Nicola wondered why Sarah had chosen this moment to call her, after so long without contact.

'That's if they don't hang up on you—or walk away leaving the phone off the hook.' Sarah kept the chatter going.

'The joys of parenthood. But it's fun.' Nicola was not going to make it easy for her supposed friend to bridge the gap of recent times.

'I'm glad you can see it that way. Last time we spoke your life wasn't much fun.'

Fun! It all came rushing back to Nicola. The trauma of going back to work when Thea was a few months old. The wrench every morning, having to leave her precious baby at that crèche. Her nights of interrupted sleep from Thea's teething troubles. Thea still woke up cold in the night after kicking off her covers, or wailed in distress when she couldn't find Blanky in the dark. Nicola counted herself lucky to get a good night's sleep before heading off to work each day. Yeah, not much fun at all, having no supportive husband by her side like Sarah. Lonely too. Nicola opted to remain silent and let Sarah digest the meaning of the words she'd just spoken.

The seconds ticked by. 'I'm sorry I haven't been in touch.' Sarah sounded sincere.

Nicola forgave her. *Friends are hard to come by when you're a full-time working mother of a two-year-old.* 'It's good to hear from you again, Sarah. It *has* been a while. How are you and how are the kids?'

'Oh, you know, battling on. The kids keep us on the go all the time. Number 3 changed me from a normal, sociable human being to a frazzled mother who never has time for anything but running around after children. Not that I mind, it will pass. My precious baby's two now and that's it. Definitely. No more.'

'I haven't seen him for a year, then, at your party last year. I suppose he's at the Terrible Two stage, saying no to everything.'

'That he is.' Sarah laughed. 'Thea's almost past that stage, I'm sure. She must be getting towards three, such a gorgeous age for little girls. Those big baby eyes, the coy head on the side as they look at you, the lisping way they talk, the giggles. Irresistible!'

Nicola started at that word. She'd never contemplated the extent of Thea's appeal to others. Was Thea the big attraction for Tom, a gorgeous little novelty in his life, a plaything, a source of fun times without all the responsibility? Her mind flashed back over the times they'd spent together, with and without Thea's presence. It was possible. Beyond work matters and helping her once as a friend, when she was distressed, he'd never pushed for spending time alone with her—but as soon as he met Thea he seemed keen to spend every waking moment with them. In those moments she'd seen an attractive new side of Tom, a family man.

Deep down, her gut instinct whispered that his attitude to Thea, and herself, ran at a deeper level than as playthings. Heartened by these thoughts, she replied,

'You're right Sarah. Even though I do say so myself, she *is* pretty irresistible.'

'I'm ashamed that I haven't seen you and Thea for so long.' Sarah's *mea culpa* resumed. 'Haven't even called. I should have rung to see how you both are, especially when you left Grosvenor, to see how you're liking the new job. Birko was gutted at losing you. But he knew you had to do it. You can't pass up these career opportunities.'

Nicola's olive branch was at the ready. 'No need for apologies, Sarah, I could have called you too. But during the day we're both miles apart and busy, with no opportunity or time to meet for a quick coffee, and at night we're too tired to pick up the threads of an old friendship. Anyhow, night's your time with Birko and it's my time with Thea and finishing off my take-home workload.'

'True, true, but this phone call reminds me that we last spoke at this time last year. Which gets me to the reason for my call. We're having another party. Again, it's for my birthday. On Saturday week. Can you make it?'

'A party invitation!' A little thrill lit up the pleasure centre of Nicola's brain. 'How exciting. As I recall, it's not even a special birthday.'

'That's true, but Birko and I haven't seen our friends for ages. We thought we'd make an effort to be sociable for a change. No presents. Your presence is all we want.'

'I understand. Of course I do. I'm no social butterfly either. Would love to come. I haven't seen you all for so long.' That was true but her thoughts had turned immediately to Tom and the possibility of seeing him at the party.

'Wait on, first I'll have to see if my childminder Stephanie is free to babysit. Saturday night is party night for students too. Remember? We were like that once.' They both laughed. 'Can I get back to you?'

'Sure. Do you want to bring someone?' Sarah's casual conversational style shifted tack, became more pointed.

'Me? No, there's no-one on the scene.' *I sound like a desperado.*

'Then you'd better wear your glad rags in case one of our friends takes your fancy!' Now Sarah was sounding suspiciously like a matchmaker.

'Like who? Everyone seems to be married these days.' Tom wasn't. Would he be there?

'Now that would be telling. Wait and see.' Sarah would make a good quiz show host, spinning out the gap between a contestant's answer and the judge's verdict.

'Stop teasing me, Sarah. Should I dress up or dress down?'

'I thought we could doll ourselves up a bit. I get tired of my jeans and runners, don't you?' Sarah sighed.

'Well, in a manner of speaking. In my case, I get tired of my suits and heels.' Nicola groaned.

'I'm sure I would too, if I needed to be at work in the city every day. Yes, let's be glam for a change and wear our party dresses. Maybe not the full glitter regalia, but something pretty.'

'Sounds good. It'll be a lovely change of routine for me.' A brief girlie moment engulfed Nicola. 'Might have to go on a shopping spree next weekend. My party wardrobe's rather limited.'

'Perfect. Get yourself in the mood. Before I go, where's that gorgeous little girl of yours? She's gone all quiet.'

'She's lying on the couch beside me, listening and sucking on a corner of her Blanky.'

'She must be well and truly talking by now and I want to say hello.'

'I'll put her on the line. Don't worry, it'll be quick. I won't walk off and leave the phone in her charge. It's her bedtime. We were just about to read stories.'

Nicola held the phone to Thea's ear. 'Say hello to Mummy's friend Aunty Sarah.'

'Lo.' Silence followed. Chatterbox Thea was struck dumb, but widened her eyes, nodded vigorously and smiled a lot as Sarah talked to her. A disembodied voice coming down the line was still a novelty.

Nicola took pity on her busy friend. 'Now say bye-bye to Aunty Sarah, she has a lot of calls to make today, so she has to rush.'

Thea dutifully piped up with 'Bi bi Arn-tee Sair.'

Nicola gentled the receiver away from a reluctant Thea. 'Good girl.'

'See you on Saturday week, Sarah, thanks', Nicola called out towards the descending hand piece. 'Now, darling, we'll hang up the phone, like this.'

The receiver back on its rest, Nicola hugged Thea to her. Another little thrill of excitement lifted her spirits. A party. At Sarah and Birko's. Tom was bound to be a friend of theirs. Would he be there? She knew he'd gone overseas today. Would he be back in time? Did she want him to be there? There was a little blip with her heart. Yes, came the immediate response. Quick, she must ring Stephanie and hope to God she'd be free. Panic struck. Where was the best place to shop for a party dress?

CHAPTER TWENTY-SIX

Nicola piled the breakfast dishes into the dishwasher and gave the kitchen bench a final wipe. Thea was strapped into her stroller by the front door, squirming to escape. It was time to leave for work. Same old morning routine, but April had arrived and life was so different now. Full of fresh possibilities. Tom was in her life.

How the last week had dragged. How keenly she'd noticed Tom's absence. The oh-so-special weekend of barely two weeks ago had highlighted the big gap in her life. Tom filled that yawning chasm perfectly. At the office a phantom Tom inhabited the corridors where for almost two months she'd thrilled each time she bumped into him. With him away, the trading room no longer held its appeal. No longer did her heart skip a beat with a secret joy when she braved that particular lion's den. The contrary was true. Tom's empty office dampened her spirits a little, its vibrant life force missing.

Her slightly melancholic office mood over the past week had always lifted as she returned home to Stephanie and Thea each evening. She'd grabbed a few moments of 'me time' this week, dawdling along from the station, soaking up the ambience created by the rays of the setting sun as it turned the harbour into a golden mirror. One wonderful weekend had turned these streets into dreamland, the private world she and Tom shared away from the office.

Nicola had spent the week reliving every moment of that weekend and, like a kid at Christmas, counting the number of sleeps until he returned from New York.

He'd taken her by surprise. Just when her life was all mapped out, her future as a career girl and single mum digested and accepted, he'd turned up to destabilise her plans. Chemistry was working the magic predicted by Maddie and she was beginning to contemplate letting down her long-maintained and rigidly-held emotional guard.

This morning, as she slammed the front door behind her and pressed the button for the lift, Nicola asked herself 'Why have I wasted so much time being a tortoise, retreating into my tough protective shell?'

She pushed the stroller into the lift, still lost in her thoughts, for once not paying full attention to Thea's burblings. No-one could deny that Tom had the X-factor. His brief brush on her lips at her front door had easily demolished her mental ban on getting close to anyone again. If Tom had lingered he'd have found her warm and wet in all the right places, her lips and arms craving to meet his. But there was more to it than a powerful sexual attraction. Tom seemed to be a responsible man, with integrity. He was living proof that good men did exist.

As she bumped Thea down the front step of her building and onto the pavement, she muttered to herself 'Maddie's right, I must stop hiding away from life. I must free myself of the shackles of the hurt inflicted by David. I must flutter free, like a bright butterfly. I must savour what life has to offer.' She grinned as she imagined Maddie's lecturing words and looked forward to her next tête-à-tête with her friend, when she would say to Maddie, 'I shouldn't have been such a scaredy-cat. I can see that now.'

The handles vibrated against Nicola's palm and tightly-curled fingers as the stroller traversed a patch of concrete pavement made uneven by the roots of the street trees. Nicola looked down at Thea, redirecting her thoughts. *It won't be good for you to grow up as an only child, the sole focus of my attention. I'm probably a slightly bitter mother. That won't teach you the important lessons in life, little one. Tom may or may not be the final answer, but he's the perfect starting point for me.*

She deposited Thea at the day care centre and made for Milsons Point station. Standing on the crowded commuter train as it rumbled across the Bridge to Wynyard, Nicola ruminated further. *My own childhood should have taught me something. Mum loved me, but she didn't remarry and make a new life and demonstrate how to love a man and make a happy family. I'm running on automatic, repeating the patterns of my past. I've been a fool. I'm an April fool.*

CHAPTER TWENTY-SEVEN

Within hours she was a different kind of fool.

It had all happened in the lift as she was heading out to grab a morning coffee. That little capsule did more than save time and energy on the internal stairwells, it transported people up and down in life. Up, up with Tom, in the lift after Valentine's Day. Down, down in the lift with John Wrigley today, April Fool's Day.

The life doors were already closing when an arm shot through the gap, tripped the sensor light and sent the doors into reverse. Wrigley barged in, ruining her safe little world. A cruel sneer flitted across his face when he saw her there alone. 'Heard the latest, Nicola?'

Typical. No manners. Normal people started with a *Hi!* or a *G'day*. She shook her head. Nothing that this man could say was of the slightest interest to her.

'Tom's up to his old tricks in New York.' Wrigley leered at her.

After a week without him, any mention of Tom was like rain to a parched garden. Was he setting the market on fire with a daring trading position? Was he running in the New York marathon? No, it was the wrong time of year. Nicola had no idea what John Wrigley knew of Tom's past. But any news of Tom *did* interest her. Come in sucker: 'Old tricks?'

'Yeah', drawled John, 'he's always had an eye for the chicks.'

Anxiety nibbled at Nicola's chest.

'And vice-versa.' Wrigley's smirk said it all. That snide rendition of *vice-versa* implied that Wrigley took her for the latest female to be smitten by Tom and also that he wanted to hurt her. She recalled the day down by the Quay, when Wrigley had seen them lunching, and laughing. She realised he couldn't retaliate against Tom for certain comments by the lift, afterwards, but she was a soft, easy target for a man with a grudge.

Nicola tried to act nonchalant with a toss of her head. 'Really? Good for Tom.'

John determinedly flung mud at her face. 'Crazy, really. He must know the dangers. There's always someone on the scene, snapping pictures. Especially in New York.'

Nicola clenched her teeth and her forehead tensed up. What pictures? What scene? Wrigley soon enlightened her. 'There's a photo of him in the gutter press, taken this week at a swanky restaurant, cosying up with a pretty dishy-looking bird, name of Lucy. Blonde. All over him. Both laughing. So my New York buddies tell me. I've just been on the line to them. Market's active today.'

John Wrigley had always delighted in baiting her but with this revelation he might just as well have punched her in the stomach. Nicola took a deep breath and fought to control her reaction. Hiding her shock as best she could, she parried with 'You keep tabs on Tom, do you?'

'No way, but it's today's talking point in our trading room.'

'Gossiping about Tom?' She managed a dispassionate tone, as if they were talking about the weather.

'We were too lowly for you, you made that clear. We were all laying bets on you and Tom. Looks like you didn't measure up after all.' He edged sideways, crowding her into a corner of the lift. 'He's moved on.' Wrigley's triumphant gloat spoke volumes to Nicola. If he couldn't have her, he could enjoy his role as spoiler.

She sidled along the wall towards the front of the lift, ready to make her escape when they reached the ground, and found the strength to retaliate in kind. 'You *are* a nasty little man, John. Despicable, actually. I should have you up on a charge of sexual harassment, except for not wanting to waste my time on you.' She had no intention of giving a creepy worm like him any opportunity to be linked with the words 'sex appeal' in any legal case, even if the words did not apply to him.

Undaunted, Wrigley retorted, 'If Forrester's looking elsewhere, he's found out you're the Ice Queen, has he?'

'Are you looking for trouble? Be careful, John Wrigley.' She summoned up her best schoolmarm's voice.

Nicola tossed her head in the air as the lift doors opened at the ground floor level. Maintaining her sang-froid, she stepped out ahead of Wrigley and marched away without a backward glance. She held her spine rigidly erect, but her legs wobbled like jelly. Overt confrontations didn't suit her temperament but she was proud she'd found a few comebacks against that slimy creature. She badly needed that coffee. Its warmth would soothe her jitters.

Her calm façade didn't crumble until she returned to her office, takeaway cup in hand, slammed the door shut behind her and slumped into her chair. She'd been floating on cloud nine for the past ten days or so. Today her fluffy white cloud crashed up against a giant, black thunderstorm. Tom and Lucy? A tear of disappointment slid out and she dabbed it away. This was what guys were like. They had a one-track mind. How could she have thought otherwise? She'd been kidding herself that something solid and worthwhile was in the offing. She was an idiot, no doubt about it.

Tom wasn't the man she thought he was.

The lump in her throat swelled and she gave up the attempt to drink her coffee. Tom had shattered her dreams of love and family. She gritted her teeth, sat up straight and squared her shoulders, hastily resurrecting her personal stone ramparts.

CHAPTER TWENTY-EIGHT

On the flight from New York to LA, Tom battled with his jet lag. The fourteen-hour time zone difference always caused him to struggle to keep his eyes open in the dead time after lunch, and kept him wide awake when he should be sleeping. Like now.

His mind drifted back a few days. It had been so good seeing his cousin Lucy again, being enveloped by that genuine warmth and affection of hers. Her embraces came from the heart, with no holding back. It had been a great relaxing night.

But for the hundredth time on that sleepless flight his thoughts returned to Nicola. Meeting up with Lucy had reminded him that you couldn't find two women at more opposite ends of the spectrum. After years of living in her adopted city, Lucy had morphed into a typically breezy and extraverted New Yorker, dolled-up to the nines and ever-ready for showy kisses on both cheeks.

It had turned out for the best that he'd made no effort to contact Nicola on this trip. These few days had given him some breathing space. Behind her gloss Lucy was insightful and had always been a friend. Once she twigged that Tom was unusually reticent over dinner, she'd winkled out his secret love and stepped in as a self-appointed but well-meaning counsellor. She'd reminded him that absence from life-changing situations, distancing yourself, helps you to see things more clearly, to focus on priorities, what's important.

His aroused body ached for release from sexual tension. Nicola was so frustrating, such an enigma. He'd been totally disappointed that she pulled back from that kiss at her front door. To be fair, she didn't exactly pull *or* push back, she simply didn't lean forward into it. But she *did* close her eyes, dreamily too. More warmth flooded through his body as he thought back to that moment.

Her aloofness towards him didn't fit with the warmth of her attitude to Thea, or her willingness to enjoy bodily contact with Thea at every opportunity. Why was she so reserved with him? Was it just him? What was she hiding, that she was so uptight? Surely there was more to it than the secret he suspected surrounding Thea. He'd make it his business to get to the bottom of this, just as soon as he got back to Sydney.

CHAPTER TWENTY-NINE

Nicola peered in the bathroom mirror, putting the finishing touches to her makeup. Her hands shook a little. She must do something to quell her nerves. *Breathe slowly, deeply. It's just a party.*

She stood before the full-length mirror and fell in love, all over again, with her carefully-chosen outfit. The red, satiny long-sleeved sheath with a low back line was slightly stretchy and hugged her slim figure in all the right places. A hint of cleavage and exposure of her long, well-shaped legs all projected a far sexier image than her professional colleagues were used to seeing. She'd even surprised herself.

The red high heels perfectly matched the dress. Tippy-toed triangles on the front portion were held on her feet by an almost transparent but slightly shimmering mesh curving across the remainder of her toe area and a double strand of dainty ankle-straps. A metallic bag picked up the shimmer in the shoes. On the outside Nicola was elegance personified.

Inside, she was a nervous wreck. She feared she'd lost her skills for making small talk away from the office. Social chit-chat with strangers didn't come easily to her. Business functions were one thing. Everyone knew the rules of social etiquette. In that sense the business world was a controlled environment. But parties were different. Random. Anything could happen once people consumed a few drinks. Nicola could expect a few home truths directed her way about her single status. And some of the married men would try to chat her up. They always did.

None of this would matter if she knew for sure that Tom would be there. She'd have someone she knew to talk to, other than the hosts, and they'd proved they could converse easily.

This was ridiculous. She was letting down the side— Team Woman. Where was her pride? How could she even think like this, look forward to seeing him again, when she knew about Tom and that Lucy woman, over there in New York? If Tom was the two-timing kind, she needed to find out tonight, while she still had the will power to resist.

He'd come back to work yesterday. Their meeting schedules hadn't coincided and neither rang the other. Nothing unusual about that. They were not embroiled in the throes of a hot office romance. She'd passed him in the corridor, he with a spring in his step, as if he didn't have a care in the world. Men! Mack, the equities trader, was with him. They'd exchanged a few words, but nothing personal. Nicola had been cool towards Tom, aloof almost, but uncertain about him, her stone ramparts a bit more crumbly than they should be.

With Mack present yesterday, not a word had crossed Tom's lips about the party so Nicola wasn't at all sure he'd be there tonight. But his words in the corridor were accompanied by a speculative gleam in his perceptive eyes. They'd signalled a promise of some kind, but did he think of her merely as another conquest, like Lucy?

No matter. Tom had catapulted her into a new vision of the world, and herself. The past week had taught her that this particular leopard, Nicola, could change her spots and open herself up to new experiences. It was years since she'd let her hair down at a party. It was years since she'd kissed anyone. Apart from that fleeting kiss from Tom at her front door, David was the last man to kiss her properly, and his kisses at the end could only be described as half-hearted. Her body craved more than a kiss, it craved intimate physical contact with another human being, skin-on-skin whole body connection, but since David her mind had always said 'no, not this man'.

Tonight it was different, Lucy or no Lucy. Niggling insistently at the back of her mind was the thought that there could be an honourable explanation for that compromising New York photo. She should give Tom the benefit of the doubt.

That's what her rational mind was saying. Innocent until proven guilty.

Her subconscious mind was saying 'yes, yes, yes' to Tom. That's where it started with her—her mind. She'd never identified with women who chose men as random sexual partners purely for physical exercise, release of tension and personal gratification. She needed to feel an intellectual bond, share a sense of humour, admire a person's qualities, share value systems before her mind would relax enough to accept a man into her physical space. Such a meeting of minds was happening with Tom.

She thought back to the day they'd met. Those remarkable blue eyes. His dark, almost black hair cropped close to his skull. His straight nose and strong jawline of classic film star quality. His height, his trim torso. His deep baritone voice. All in all, his very sexy example of maleness had triggered her long-repressed female instincts.

He was proving incredibly seductive, as if he was calling to her, 'Come to me. We need each other.' She even sensed that he was the kind of man who'd understand about Thea. If he knew, that is.

She walked out to the living room with butterflies beating against the walls of her stomach. Her shoulders were painful with tension. Her mind was skittish. Tonight would change her life. Either Tom would be there, and something would happen, or he wouldn't be there, and she'd know she meant nothing to him. She'd know she was nothing more than an idle flirtation, another New York-style Lucy, filling up an empty time slot in Sydney.

Their precious hours together hadn't conveyed that impression, but heck, having married her one and only boyfriend she was no judge of men, was she!

Stephanie looked up from the TV screen and gave a small yelp. 'Oh my God, Nikki, you look great. Really great. Fantastic.'

Stephanie occasionally followed the lead of Thea's child care supervisor by calling her Nikki. Nicola didn't let it bother her tonight and responded with a smile of gratitude.

'I can't believe my eyes, Nikki, that dress is sensational. That shade of fire engine red is perfect for you. It suits your dark hair and fair skin.'

'Thank you, Stephanie. It's nice to receive a compliment.' If she was a cat, she'd be purring.

'And those shoes. They're to die for.'

Nicola pirouetted in her new shoes out of sheer joie-de-vivre, which suddenly burst forth from some deeply-repressed place.

Stephanie's eyes narrowed as she examined Nicola again, as a fashion stylist would. 'OK, so I may be a jeans-clad student on a budget, but I just love dresses. Don't you? Why don't you wear them more often?'

Nicola rolled her eyes skywards, exasperated. 'Good grief. Because I work full time. Because work means suits. Because dresses mean play, and I never have time to play.' She relented and smiled. 'Except with Thea, of course. And the mandatory attire for playing with kids is jeans. As *you* know full well—look at you. You're in the uniform.'

Stephanie tossed her head. 'I'm warning you, the way you look tonight you'd better get ready to fend off the blokes. They'll have a different kind of play in mind.'

Nicola thrilled at the prospect of a playful Tom. 'You're on a full-scale campaign to bolster my ego, aren't you! Thanks.' She grabbed her bag and car keys. 'I'd better get going. You've got my mobile number. Give me a call if you need me. I won't be far away. The party's at Mosman.' She took a peek into Thea's bedroom and turned back to Stephanie. 'I'm confident she'll be fine. She's been asleep for half an hour and these days she rarely wakes at night. Thanks a million for giving up your Saturday night.'

'I've already told you, I've got an assignment due, so you're doing me a favour. I'll be keeping my nose to the grindstone while simultaneously earning extra pay from you. Win-win. Even better, I know my way around your kitchen. There'll be something there to tempt me when I need a break from brain strain.'

'I'll try not to be late home.'

'No worries. When I get tired I'll grab a pillow and a blanket and sleep on the couch here. It makes no difference to me if I go home in the morning. No need to worry about getting back by twelve, or anything. You never go out. Enjoy yourself.'

'Thanks. I'll try to obey.' Nicola smiled her appreciation at Stephanie.

'By the way, your hair looks gorgeous too. How did you achieve that shape?'

'With a lot of Prison Lotion.'

'Huh?' Stephanie blinked in surprise.

'Just kidding. I can never remember the brand name but nothing else keeps my hair under control, imprisoned, so that's my pet name for the product.' As she walked towards the door she directed a grateful smile towards Stephanie. 'You're doing wonders for my confidence. Thanks again.'

'Don't forget. Let your hair down.'

'Yes sir.' She stood at attention in the doorway and saluted cheekily. 'I'll try to reform. I'll try being a femme fatale for the night.'

'You won't have to try too hard. You already are.'

Nicola shrugged. 'Not that I've noticed. Anyhow, I think most of Sarah and Birko's friends are married couples. Except for one friend of theirs—at least I think he's a friend. He's single.'

'Thank heavens there'll be one. Hope he's not gay.'

'Definitely not gay.' Recalling his kiss at her front door sent an ecstatic shiver up her spine.

'Oh ho! So you know this guy?' Stephanie bounced in her seat with enthusiasm.

'Yes, I do. Actually, I work with him.' And how she secretly loved every moment she spent with him.

'Oh! Wow-ee. Maybe there's a bit of matchmaking going on.' Stephanie's gleeful voice filled the room.

'I hope not. I don't even know if he'll be there.' But how she wanted to see him, New York or no New York.

'I see you dressed for him, in case.' Stephanie teased.

'Well ….,' Nicola paused, then laughed. 'Maybe I did.'

'Hallelujah. There's hope for you yet. Get going. Have a good time.'

Driving to the party a few suburbs away, Nicola reflected upon the difference between David and Tom. Definitely the X-factor. Yes, that was it. Sparks flew when she was around Tom, he gave off that aura. David was a damp squib by comparison. Until she dropped into Tom's world, she'd never seen a real-life example of someone with sizzle, except for movie stars on the big screen, a world of air-brushed make-believe if ever there was one.

She'd definitely dressed to light Tom's fire. Lady in red. Would he be there?

Nicola had trouble finding a parking spot in the densely populated environs of Birko's house. The suburb of Mosman was city-central for the bankers and lawyers of Sydney. Well-heeled. Genteel. Up-market. But not her cup of tea as a place to live. Despite her suspicion that she was regarded as a control freak by her colleagues at work, she preferred the more bohemian atmosphere of Kirribilli. It was more quirky, more disordered. Maybe she liked that aspect of her neighbourhood because it provided the antidote to her day job.

The night was crisp and clear. Nicola clasped her pashmina a little more tightly to protect her bare back from the cool night air. Autumn was well underway. The pashmina would be essential if this party turned out to be an outdoor event.

Apprehensively, she rang the doorbell, taking a moment to slip the pashmina off her shoulders so that it draped gracefully from her arms. No need to spoil whatever dramatic impact the dress might make on Tom. If he wasn't there would her keyed-up anticipation crash down to flat-as-a-pancake disappointment?

Tom answered the door. His face lit up.

Elation overwhelmed her as her heart skipped at least two beats.

Tom murmured, 'My evening just got a whole lot better.'

Nicola gave him one of the special, unconditionally happy smiles normally reserved for her daughter. But her old habits with him kicked in automatically ... she should stay cool ... for as long as possible, anyway. Besides, Lucy was yet to be explained. She responded tartly 'And hello to you too, Tom.'

'Sorry, Nicola. Didn't mean to blurt out one of those predictable lines. I can't help that you blew me away. You look good enough to ... er ... eat.' His smile had the touch of the big bad wolf spotting little red hiding hood for the first time. Damn, why did she choose red for her dress? *Don't forget Lucy.*

'Come in, come in.' Tom slipped into mine-host role. 'Birko's trying to settle one of the kids who keeps coming out for a drink of water, Billy I think, and Sarah's busy with a last-minute crisis in the kitchen. Something about birthday candles which have gone missing. I've been delegated the job of chief door opener. Come in and meet the others.'

Tom put his arm lightly against her back to shepherd her from the front door. Nicola could hear music and the buzz of conversation in the rear courtyard area. His touch on her skin thrilled her and sent a little shiver down her spine, a shiver he must have detected. Nicola baulked slightly. All she wanted right now was to stay close to him, like this, in the entrance hall. No need to bother with all those people inside. She glanced sideways at him. As if sensing her hesitation he returned her look. His fingers splayed and pressed a little more firmly against her bare back. 'Later, Nicola, later,' he whispered.

'You two look as if you already know each other quite well.' The comment from the other end of the hall dripped with sarcasm.

Oh no. Nicola had seen this woman in action before. It was Jodie, from Grosvenor Bank, entering the hallway from the rear part of the house. Jodie, always on the prowl for a sexual encounter, and tonight showing a great deal of cleavage, almost all of it if truth be told. Looking as if she too had dressed to catch Tom's eye, she directed a malevolent glare at Nicola.

'As a matter of fact Jodie, we do know each other. We've worked together almost every day for the last two months. Haven't we, Tom?'

'We've been a team, alright. How come you two know each other?'

'When I worked with Birko at Grosvenor Bank,' Nicola replied. 'Jodie worked in the back office.'

'I almost didn't recognise you, Nicola. Not in a suit tonight, I see. You certainly look as if you're out to impress someone tonight.' Jodie's sneer was palpable.

'She sure has impressed me,' responded Tom. 'I'm on my way to get her a drink. I see you already have one, so if you'll excuse us, I'll leave you here to mind the doorbell in case someone turns up while I'm busy. Birko will be back in a minute, so can you wait here until then?'

Jodie scowled ungraciously. 'He'd better be quick then. Don't want to miss all the fun.'

'Thanks Jodie. This way, Nicola.' Tom steered her out to the courtyard, where a small bar was set up and a waiter circulated with a tray of drinks.

'What will you have? I can recommend the champagne. That's my choice tonight. Veuve Cliquot. Luckily Birko's champagne tastes match his champagne income.' He laughed.

'That sounds festive. Yes please. I'll restrict myself to one glass though.' She selected a tall flute from the waiter's tray. 'Champagne goes straight to my head. I'm the world's expert on making one glass last for hours.' She lifted her glass at Tom in a silent toast. 'If I have my glass now, the effects will wear off before I have to get in the car and drive home. Don't want the booze bus to spoil my evening.' *Stop rabbiting on, girl.*

Tom directed a quizzical gaze her way.

Nicola reflected for a minute on what she'd said. 'Did I sound too much like a party pooper?'

Tom looked steadily at her and said quietly 'Maybe you won't be driving yourself home this evening.'

Nicola looked back at him. His eyes met hers. A promise glinted there. Something was definitely going to happen tonight. A flush of warmth drenched her all over. Her spine tingled in eager anticipation.

Hastily she said, 'Let's move onto the balcony, where it's not so crowded.' She could cool off out there, in the fresh air.

They stood as close as birthday party etiquette tolerated and sipped their drinks, surveying the show of fairy lights adorning the garden. Nicola wondered if Tom felt keyed-up like her. She took a big gulp and floated on a cloud of champagne bubbles to another time and place where Tom dominated the scene playing in her mind.

'Penny for your thoughts, Nicola.' He tapped her glass with his. 'Where were you?'

'Doing a bit of time travelling, that's all.' She smiled apologetically.

'Forwards, or backwards?' His keen glance and the

glint of awareness in his eyes suggested that he knew the answer was forwards, with him.

'Now that'd be telling.' She played the coquette, just as Thea had done when she met Tom.

'What would be telling, Tom?' Jodie sidled up beside him, waving her empty glass. 'Aren't you going to top up my glass for me?'

'The waiter's over there, Jodie. We were having a private conversation, about something at work.'

'Didn't look like work to me. But if you say so, Tom.' Jodie flounced off.

'Poor Jodie. I gather that you're well-practised at giving her the brush-off.'

'You could say that. She was hanging around before I went to London. When *I* go time-travelling, *she* is definitely not in my future. There was one like her in my past. Once was enough.' Tom smiled at her. 'But you know about that already. My ex-wife Catherine. You've seen her. The stunning blonde, that day in Martin Place.'

'Stunning is the word. Like your blonde friend in New York last week.' Nicola spoke matter-of-factly, expressionless in her voice and manner, but she watched him closely to read his body-language.

'What?' He looked genuinely startled at the turn in conversation. 'Oh! You mean Lucy? The blokes in the office gave me heaps about her when I got back yesterday.' How could he be so nonchalant about something so important?

'John Wrigley gave me heaps about her too, while you were away.' She pulled a wry face.

'Did he? Now why was that?' His voice carried a teasing note but his steady, assessing gaze hinted that he wondered if she was the jealous, harping, nagging type. He continued, 'Mack noticed that you were pretty offhand with me yesterday. In fact, he said 'What's up with her today?' I wondered too. Just put it down to that wall of yours. Sometimes there's an entrance gate. Sometimes your wall is ten feet high with barbed wire on top.'

'Am I really that bad?'

Tom smiled at her but chose not to answer that question, leaving Nicola to ponder that piece of useful feedback. He took a sip of his drink. 'I take it you've heard about the photo of me with Lucy?'

'Yes.' Why wouldn't he put her out of her misery?

He grinned. 'Lucy's my cousin. She lives in New York. She's one of those types who call everyone 'darling' and smother you with hugs and kisses when you meet.'

Nicola's tight grip on her champagne flute relaxed as her tension visibly drained away.

Tom grinned again. 'Lucy's husband took that photo when we were out to dinner. My mother and sister down in Melbourne wanted to see a shot of us together. He's a journo and I was once active in the New York social scene, so it got into the papers. The cryptic caption was an in-joke for the family.'

'Your staff here don't know about the family connection?' She needed more reassurance from him about the two competing worlds he inhabited.

'Nope, they prefer to pick up on random bits of my life and I don't bother to correct them. It's none of their damn business. Wrigley in particular is a troublemaker. You know that. He's also a lousy trader and close to losing his job.' He frowned. 'Very close.' He frowned again. 'Why did you trust anything he said?'

'I didn't entirely believe him. I wanted to give you the benefit of the doubt. But picturing you with Lucy did come as a bit of a sucker punch, after the weekend we shared. I thought we'd made a real connection. I didn't trust my judgment of you. Felt defensive.'

'You raised that internal drawbridge of yours?'

She loved that he seemed to understand her. 'I feel *much* better now.' She raised her glass at him in a show of happy self-confidence.

Tom smiled his relief at her. 'Feel that you can trust me after all?'

Nicola nodded. For a moment she reflected on the importance of trusting each other's word, until she remembered that she was effectively hiding something pretty major from him. All the issues of trustworthiness came alive again for her. But this was neither the time nor the place to unburden herself.

As he seemed in the mood to unburden himself, she directed their conversation back to his admission earlier in the evening concerning the stunning blonde in his past.

'While we're talking about the women in your life …,' she murmured.

'Are we?' he teased.

'Briefly, yes. Tell me again why you think you and Catherine couldn't make a go of it. You talked about her a bit when we had that impromptu lunch at your flat.' Might as well slap all her sources of insecurity out on the table. 'Why weren't you happy with her?'

'Going straight for the jugular tonight, I see! First Lucy. Now Catherine.' His eyes held a spark of amusement.

Nicola was contrite. 'Sorry, don't mean to pry. I'm just curious. Trying to figure out what makes you guys tick.'

'Guys generally, or this guy in particular?' He pointed at his chest, with an ironic question mark in his eyes and an upward quirk at the corner of his mouth. My, he was good at this bantering game.

'I think you know the answer to that.' In effect, she was conceding her interest in him.

'I think I do.' She was certain that his eyes could look inside her head, like a CT scan.

He surprised her with a quick click of his champagne flute against hers, as if he was toasting her. 'Well to oblige a fair damsel, I'll expose myself and bare my soul.' He grinned. She responded in kind. Bare bodies better described their current train of thoughts.

Suddenly he switched to serious mode. 'To be honest, apart from all the obvious reasons I mentioned to you at my place the other day, there was no calm in my soul, no quiet inner satisfaction, no contentment, as if all was right with the world.'

'So you're seeking that most elusive of human beings, a soul-mate?' A whoosh of elation rushed through her. He was definitely the kind of man she'd longed for.

'In a word, yes, now I am, because I've realised it's important. You can feel more lonely married to the wrong person than being single. But I think that's more than enough about me. My past is no secret. You're saying almost nothing about yours. I've begun to think that you must be keeping a few important secrets about your past, Nicola Pearson.'

Nicola gulped. She was saved from answering by the arrival of more friends. The moment passed. Social chit chat took over.

***

'Have you had enough to eat, Nicola?' Tom breathed the words into her ear.

Standing behind her in the crowded living area, he was close enough to wrap his arms around her. She longed for his touch.

'Oh yes, plenty,' she blurted out. 'The food was delicious.' What else could she add to disguise the direction of her thoughts? 'The birthday bit went well too. Sarah blew out all her candles in one breath. I was impressed. Those three kids obviously maintain her fitness at peak level.'

'She's always on the run, I'd say.' He answered her prayer and put his arm around her again, as he had at Birko's front door. 'Now that the official celebrations are over, the rest of the night is ours. Come back out onto the balcony with me.' His voice lowered to a whisper and his eyes conveyed more meaning than did his simple invitation.

She nodded her silent but willing agreement. They moved outside. The other guests remained inside, lingering over the dessert offerings and the coffee.

The moon swathed the waters beyond Balmoral Beach in a silver shimmer. Nicola wasn't immune to tonight's magic. A quiet crackling of her senses began, like a match igniting some dried-out twigs, as Tom steered her into a more private nook on the balcony. The flame developed into a slow burn, like a bushfire creeping through the forest-floor debris of a valley, waiting for a breath of wind to puff it up into the tree canopy, fanning a full-blown conflagration as the blaze raced up the slope.

The seductive power of Tom's low voice fuelled the fire of her fevered anticipation. 'Ever since our few moments in the hallway, earlier, I've been dying to get you alone again.'

He moved a little closer and gazed down at her intently. 'Did you know Sarah organised this party especially for us? I overheard her talking to Birko before you arrived. She asked him what was the good of friends who didn't act as the fairy godmother when there was some kind of Mexican stand-off between a man and a woman ideally suited to each other?'

'She meant us?'

'Yes. Do you know why I didn't invite you to come with me tonight?'

His eyes captured hers. She was mesmerised. Eventually she confessed, 'I did wonder.'

'I wanted to see if you'd come by yourself. If you'd choose to come yourself, hoping to see me here. If you'd show interest in me, as a man.'

'I did. I do.' It was a whisper, as he drew even closer and took both her hands in his.

'I'm starting to see that, thanks to Lucy.'

'Please, Tom, don't remind me. I'm not the jealous type. Just out of practice with this dating game.'

'I knew that all along. That's why there's something I desperately need to say to you. Remember Valentine's Day?'

'I remember it vividly. A beautiful surprise came my way.' Her right thumb began stroking his left hand, making slow gentle circles.

His face came closer to hers. 'I have a confession. Mr Anonymous. It was me. I sent you the roses.'

'You! Oh Tom, over the last six weeks, how I've wished it was you.'

Pent up emotion overcame her. Nicola melted against Tom and his strong arms opened to wrap around her and pull her close against his aroused body. As she tilted her face upwards, their lips met fully for the first time. She was molten, fused to him. It was a miracle—exactly how Maddie predicted it would be. A volcano erupted and engulfed her in a flow of molten lava. Nature was telling her everything.

How many minutes went by? She couldn't tell. Through the waves of blissful sensations swamping her body, Nicola was still sufficiently aware of proprieties to register, vaguely, the murmur of voices approaching. Passionate kisses and exploratory hands were for private delight, not for public display. Forcing herself to disengage, she struggled to resume some semblance of normality. 'You're a miracle worker, Tom Forrester.' It was the barest of whispers.

'In what way, Nicola Pearson?' His baritone voice was low and husky, but a pair of smouldering eyes challenged her to acknowledge the reality of a sizzling physical attraction.

'You know full well. In every way I can think of. Especially this way.' A sledge hammer had demolished her wall of reserve. She was back to being a teenager, flooded by uncontrollable hormones. She reached up and fluttered her hand over his lips.

'Would you like more?'

'You know I would.'

'Well then, my glorious moonlight lady, we can't stay here. I'm burning for you. Come home with me. Right now.'

CHAPTER THIRTY-ONE

Monday morning. Tom tried to focus on work after the best thirty-six hours of his life, spent with Nicola, in bed with her at every opportunity, whenever Thea was asleep.

Tom picked up his copy of the Fin Review. He drew in a sharp intake of breath. Staring at him from the front page was Paul Baxter, Catherine's husband. Done for fraud over a major property transaction. Facing charges. Likely to go to gaol if convicted. Tom had always known this spiv had it coming.

He knew he should feel sorry for Catherine. There'd been a time when he'd cared enough about her to get married. Bad idea, in hindsight. For her too. She'd found out the hard way that the grass wasn't greener.

Catherine's come-uppance was upon her. But, on reflection, his life was great, fantastic. It wouldn't hurt to be charitable.

Tom picked up the phone. Rang her number. Got voicemail. Left a message. Catherine rang back later that day.

'Have you rung to gloat, Tom?'

'Actually, I rang to see how you are. I thought all this would've hit you hard. Keep your chin up. The media storm will eventually pass.'

'You know, sometimes I think I did a silly thing, leaving you.'

'I don't. You know we weren't suited.'

'Well, that's telling me.' She paused, then continued. 'On the matter of suitability, I think there's something you should know. I wasn't going to tell you, but since you're proving yourself to be, um … er, a friend in need, shall we say, I should 'fess up, and clear my conscience.'

'That sounds particularly ominous, Catherine.' In his experience, Catherine and her conscience didn't meet too often.

'It's about that, um … IVF clinic.' Her voice trailed away.

'You want to explain that trick you played on me? Bit late now.' Tom's scorn replaced his concern.

'No need to be mean, Tom.'

'Just speaking the truth. Your conscience didn't stop you playing along with the concept of IVF, to keep me happy, while you went on the prowl for another fella. One like you, who didn't want kids the way I did.'

'I didn't know how to tell you. I knew your ideas of me as a woman would change.'

'Right. Let me get this straight, then. You mean that for all that time, all those months, you pretended … *pretended* … you'd discovered that you couldn't have babies. Fortuitously for you, we never got past stage one of the investigations. They tested me first. If they'd had time to move on to you, you would've been unmasked. You were still on the pill.'

'I was panicking at the end. That Paul wouldn't take me on before you found out.'

'That became obvious.' Tom knew that irony was wasted on Catherine, but the 'fessing up was a new angle on her character. 'So what exactly is it that you haven't told me?'

She sounded defensive. 'It all happened a few weeks after you went to London.'

'What happened?'

'A letter was forwarded to me, from the fertility clinic.'

'What did it say?'

'It was about your … er … frozen sperm sample. The one set aside from your tests.'

'What about it?'

'Asking what we wanted to do with it. What you wanted to do with it? Should it continue to be stored, for future use by us, or could it be used by another couple, or should it be destroyed?'

'That issue was one of the loose ends I almost forgot to tie up before going to London. In my efforts to put your behaviour out of my mind I blanked that out too.'

'Tom, um …,' she began in a faltering voice.

He interrupted her. 'I don't know why they contacted you. As it happened, I did remember at the last minute, while I was packing my bags. I rang that clinic, leaving clear instructions for the sample to be destroyed. The whole experience of family formation left rather a sour taste in my mouth. I was definitely a bitter man.'

Catherine's tone of voice shifted to defiance. 'Well, maybe the message wasn't passed on, or maybe the letter was sent because of your call.'

'What do you mean by that?'

'The letter requested your written instructions, for the file. The letter didn't refer to any phone call from you. It looked like the receptionist might have sent out one of those standardised things. It contained a tick-the-box set of options.'

'And you opted for the 'destroy' option, I trust. We had no further use for it and you possessed no right to decide that I should become the unwitting father of someone else's child.'

'Well, er, no, I didn't.' She sounded edgy.

He recognised that evasive tone. 'Catherine. What exactly did you tell them?'

'I … um …,' she tailed off nervously.

He growled, 'Which box did you tick, Catherine?'

'I gave permission for it to be used by another couple. Thought a couple might be glad to have a baby looking like you. You hear all the time how people worry about these things, whose genes they're dealing with.' Not a skerrick of remorse in those words.

Tom was gobsmacked. There might be a child walking around who'd turn up on his doorstep in fifteen years and say 'Hello Dad'. My God. It was an earth-shattering thought.

'And you never thought that this might mean that years later I might have to deal with a child I never knew I had?'

'No, I have to confess, I didn't actually think, or care, about you.' Catherine began to sound the teeniest bit penitent.

And then the penny dropped. Tom's brain shifted gear. Dramatically. Thea! Was it possible? How could he be so lucky? But he'd keep up the heat being applied to Catherine. The woman deserved it. This was a major crime.

'So how exactly did you give my permission when I was on the other side of the world and knew nothing about the letter?'

'The letter needed to be returned with both our signatures, so … ,' Catherine paused, then rushed on, 'I signed for both of us.'

'You mean you forged my signature.'

'Oh well, you know, you'd gone overseas, I wanted to get rid of all those nasty loose ends. Couldn't be bothered to track you down and go through all of this baby stuff again with you. Clean slate and all that. I was embarrassed anyway. I knew it'd upset you.'

'Do you know what, Catherine, you truly are unbelievable. You and Paul deserve each other. You should both be heading for gaol.'

'But you won't do anything about this, will you,' she wheedled, 'because I know you. You wouldn't want the world to know about this. It will stay as our little secret.'

'You're right, Catherine, I'm not going to have you charged with fraud for forging my signature. But not for the reasons you imagine. You've actually done me a good turn. A great turn. An *excellent* turn.' He could almost kiss this treacherous creature, he felt so excited. 'And quite possibly a good turn for someone else I know.'

'What on earth do you mean by that?' She sounded suspicious.

He grinned. Couldn't stop grinning. The Cheshire cat had nothing on him. This was bloody marvellous. The grin resounded in the tone of his voice. Catherine must think he'd gone mad.

Let her. He wasn't going to tell her anything, no sirree. He wasn't going to tell her about that gorgeous little girl who might, just might, be his. Or anything at all about her gorgeous mother. Let her find out through the grapevine that he'd chosen a Catherine-opposite type of woman for his second wife. Nicola hadn't said yes. Hell, he hadn't even asked her ... yet. But he fully intended to do so.

'Have to rush Catherine. Something I must do. Sorry you jumped out of my frying pan into the fire with Paul, but you did, and you released me from a miserable future.

Thanks. Out of gratitude I wish you all the best from now on, I most sincerely do.'

Catherine had finally cleared the decks. Still grinning, he clanged down the phone.

Twenty minutes later, Tom was rummaging at the back of his personal filing cabinet. Hang the office. He'd broken all speed limits on the Bridge to rush home and rifle through his old files. 'Shit. Where's that number gone?' His stomach knots untied themselves when he finally located the card for the doctor he'd consulted with Catherine. Grabbing his phone, he rang the number, and got the receptionist.

'It's Tom Forrester here. I attended your clinic about three and a half years ago with my then wife, Catherine.'

'What's your patient reference number?'

Tom flicked through his paperwork, found the reference number and passed it on to the receptionist.

'Thank you. Please hold for a minute while I check our computer records.' Tom drummed his fingers, impatient with her administrative slowness. 'Ah yes, I've located your file notes. How can I help you?'

'Does Dr Stephen Roberts still work at your clinic?'

'He does.' The receptionist spoke cautiously.

'I'd like to make an urgent appointment to discuss something of a delicate nature with him.'

'Urgent? Hmm. Delicate, you say. Just about everything we see here is delicate. I don't think there'll be any problem. I'll put you on hold for a minute.'

Tom sat through a few minutes of the calming Mozart soundtrack he badly needed, before the receptionist came back on the line. 'Dr Roberts can see you this coming Friday afternoon, around 3.30. Does that suit you?'

'I'll be there. Thank you. Please ask him to have my file available for the meeting, and the file for Ms Nicola Pearson, former wife of David Pearson.'

'I don't know if Dr Roberts will oblige your request but I'll certainly pass on the message. Goodbye.' The phone line went dead. But Tom sizzled with excitement. He was going to pull every available string to get to the bottom of this serendipitous story.

CHAPTER THIRTY-TWO

Walking through the doors of the fertility clinic brought back a host of memories Tom had been trying to suppress. They took him back to a time when he still trusted his ex-wife and would have given anything to hear her say 'I'm pregnant, darling'. A cloud of melancholy settled over him, snuffing out his normal optimism. It took determined willpower for Tom to reset his mood. Black clouds could hold silver linings.

When Tom was ushered into the relevant consulting room, Stephen Roberts greeted him cautiously. 'I received your message, Tom, but you must realise I can't divulge anything about other patients, whoever they might be.' A worried frown creased his face.

'Are you trying to deflate any expectations I might have? Understood, Stephen, understood.' Tom shrugged off the black cloud and focused on the silver lining. 'First,

I want to tell you my story. Then I'm going to ask you to do something I know is within your authority.'

'Go ahead, I'm all ears.' Stephen relaxed his posture and shuffled back in his seat.

'Your file should say that my wife Catherine and I were patients here, and I provided a sperm donation as part of the assessment procedures.' Roberts glanced down at the file, nodded his agreement and Tom continued. 'Then we ... er ... abandoned the treatment options because our marriage failed.'

'Sorry to hear that. We find that infertility problems often cause such acute stress that many marriages fail.'

'Well, infertility as such wasn't our problem, as your file may or may not tell you. I'm here to talk about what she did next.'

'What who did next?'

'Catherine. My ex-wife.'

'What *did* she do?' The worried frown reappeared.

'When we began as patients I specified that the donation was for us. When we split, I rang the clinic and requested that my sperm sample be destroyed.'

Roberts consulted his file. 'We don't have a record of that call.' He bit his lip as he rechecked the paperwork. 'Nothing here.'

Tom quirked an eyebrow. 'So much for your systems.' The doctor flicked the file closed and squinted uneasily at Tom.

'Don't worry, I'm not here to sue you.'

Roberts cocked his head to the side, as if puzzled that

Tom had let his clinic's administrative bungling drop with barely a word of complaint.

Tom shrugged and continued. 'By the time the final papers were sent to us my overseas posting was in place and Catherine, er … Catherine forged my signature and gave permission for the donation to be part of your sperm bank.'

Roberts gasped and reeled back in his seat. 'Oh my God, these are serious allegations.'

'They would be under normal circumstances.' Tom's stern voice made that point clear. 'But fortunately for you and your systems, my visit concerns abnormal circumstances.' Tom drummed his fingers on the doctor's desk.

'What do you mean?' Roberts stared warily at Tom.

'Well, it's like this. I suspect that you used my sperm sample to treat an infertile couple named David and Nicola Pearson.' There, he'd said it out loud. It had to be right. He knew it.

'And what makes you suspect this?' Roberts played a poker face.

'By coincidence, a few months ago Nicola Pearson came to work for the bank where I work. By another sheer coincidence, I found out through a mutual friend that her husband was sterile and she used AID to get her baby.'

The doctor turned up his nose. 'Even if that were true, it could have been any one of a number of donors at a number of clinics.' Roberts relaxed his posture, signalling an *is-that-all-you've-got* sense of relief that he could ward off this man with easy excuses.

Tom pointed triumphantly at the paperwork on the desk. 'Well I know at least part of my story is true, because Nicola's file's sitting there. Sure, it's upside down, but I can read the surname from where I'm sitting.'

Roberts tried to slide the Pearson file under the Forrester file.

'Too late to hide it, Doc. Your file records prove that the Pearsons came to this particular clinic and you must know both sides of the story.' *Let Roberts get out of that Gotcha moment.*

Tom watched as a few cogs turned wheels inside the head of the man squirming in his seat across the desk, before Roberts ruefully conceded the point. 'You're right, I do.'

A few seconds later he turned on his best efforts at counselling for a troubled patient. 'Might this be a case of wishful thinking on your part, Tom?'

'You mean, am I just looking for a novel chat-up line for a good-looking woman?'

'I've never met her. She wasn't my patient. Is she?'

Tom let out an appreciative sigh. 'Well, yes she is,' he admitted.

'Any man might like to imagine himself with a connection to her.'

'Let me tell you, Doc, the reason why I think it's true is because I've met her little daughter. Her age fits the timeline for being my child, and her eyes are the exact same colour as mine.' Tom's voice rose in triumph as he played his ace.

The doctor stared at Tom's eyes from across the desk. 'Which are a distinctive shade of blue, I see. A deep midnight blue.'

'I'm glad you agree.' Tom reached for the inside pocket his jacket and extracted its contents. 'Here are two photos.' He handed the first across to Roberts with a flourish. 'This is me as a baby.' He slid the second photo across the table. 'This is a recent photo of Thea Pearson. Line them up, side by side. Flick back and forth between the two.' His voice rang with confidence. 'My evidence.' To him it was irrefutable.

The doctor studied the photos closely. 'Hmm, I see what you mean. But there's something else you need to consider. We do have a record of another donor possessing eyes with a colour like yours. Maybe he is the father of Thea Pearson.'

Tom's jaw dropped, his hopes dashed. 'That hardly seems possible.'

'Don't forget this is a big city, with a large pool of potential donors. Our data base keeps track of physical features, often the highest priority for many would-be parents. I took the precaution of checking for physical matches before you arrived today. Do you have a brother, or male cousins with eyes like yours?'

'No brothers, no. I do have a couple of male cousins, on Mum's side, but they live on the other side of the country, in Perth. I can't see them dropping by to provide a sperm donation.'

'Alright, so you might be able to rule out close family, but someone in Sydney with eyes like yours has been a donor here, and baby photos are not always reliable. Many young babies look alike.' Roberts was not going to give up easily on the task of deflecting Tom.

Tom snorted in scorn. 'Thea is the spitting image of me when I was two. I'm still convinced that she's my biological child.' He'd bet his life on it.

'Why haven't you organised a paternity test? DNA testing for this purpose is beginning to take off.'

'I wouldn't do that without Nicola's permission but, if I ask her permission, I have to raise her hopes unnecessarily and I might be wrong. This seems a more discreet pathway towards a potential truth.'

Roberts stared at Tom across the desk. 'If your hypothesis is correct, what do you want me to do about it?'

'I want to see you making a note on your file that if my assumptions are true, I give you permission, as of now, to divulge my identity as the donor.' Tom spoke as if he would brook no argument.

'A file note is inadequate. Can't be too careful these days. We live in a litigious world. Wait here, I'll get hold of our standard permission form and you can sign it.' The doctor rose from his chair and left the office for a few moments, returning with a wad of forms.

He handed them across to Tom, saying 'Please add the rider that your approval to disclose this information to Nicola Pearson dates from today, so there'll be no doubt of your intentions. You understand that in any case, if a pregnancy arose from your donation, which I'm not at liberty to confirm or deny, then the child might have the right to be told at the age of eighteen. There are people working to change the laws concerning the rights of children.'

'I understand.' Tom scanned the forms, added his instructions and hastily signed on the dotted line.

'Satisfied? Is that all?' queried Roberts.

'No. There's something else. I want you to give me your mobile phone number, and to promise that if Nicola Pearson rings, you'll tell her the identity of the donor, if it's me of course, as I fully believe it to be.' Tom stared hard at the noncommittal expression on the doctor's face and issued a defiant challenge. 'Despite what you've said about another possible candidate.'

'This is highly irregular. What do you hope to gain?'

'Well, Stephen, I'm hoping above all that Nicola will become my wife. I won't divulge your number to her unless she's already indicated a willingness to be my wife. But I don't want her to agree without her being in full possession of the facts.'

'And what if she says *No* to becoming your wife?'

'Regardless, since Nicola and I have now met, and we have a trusting professional relationship at work, and she's a single parent, as I'm sure your file tells you, I could help her raise her daughter. My daughter, I hope. In which case, our daughter.'

'She's managed well enough to date, without any input from you.'

'I know she worries about not knowing the identity of Thea's father.' He'd deduced that from conversations with Birko. 'Nicola has definitely noticed my eye colour match to her daughter, but she hasn't said anything. She doesn't know that I suspect Thea is an AID baby. There's no reason for her even to imagine that I ever came near this clinic. I've only discovered myself, this week, that I was an inadvertent sperm donor.' Noticing the scepticism on the face across the desk, he finished with, 'Regardless of the current laws, children deserve to know the identity of their father.' He'd saved until last the most compelling part of his argument.

Roberts inclined his head in agreement. 'You've got it all worked out, haven't you! Are you sure you could remain at arm's length?'

'Give me credit for having a few brains in my head. If it's true, and I am Thea's father but Nicola prefers to stay on her own, our ongoing relationship could be no different from any number of other separated families sharing the upbringing of a child.'

'Fair enough. That's the Family Court's business. But tell me, why exactly do you want my mobile number? Why can't she ring the clinic herself, during office hours?'

'Come off it, Stephen. She came here to see someone named George recently. I was in her office when she took that call. You know damn well she has a high-powered full-time job. When exactly can she make such a call? Your office hours coincide with hers. Is this the kind of phone call you want half the office to overhear, or gossip about when your emotions boil over at news like this?'

Roberts frowned. 'I see what you mean.'

'I want to give her your number when I'm with her, when I judge the timing is right for her to receive such an important piece of news.'

'Don't like the sound of that.' Roberts pursed his lips in disapproval. 'Sounds very controlling …,' he began.

Tom interrupted. 'Just being practical. What I mean is, when she's not distracted because she's in the middle of cooking dinner or calming Thea after a fall, that type of thing.' *How could this doctor have misunderstood his intentions?* 'Let me make myself clear. I want to give her your number *after* I've asked her to marry me, and *before* she gives her answer. I think she has a right to know, one way or the other, before any commitment is made.'

'Fair enough.'

'There's another reason for me wanting to be present when she calls you. From my perspective, I want to be able to tell, by watching her, if she's happy or horrified should she discover that I'm Thea's father.' Tom prayed the reaction would be happy.

The doctor sat silently for a few moments, giving Tom the once over. 'And such a call will come out of the blue, as far as I'm concerned?'

'No problem. It won't take long. Just tell her that you

have some special news that you've been authorised to tell her, something of interest about the identity of Thea's father. Does she want to hear it? I'm sure she'll say *Yes please*. And you can either say that Tom Forrester is the man, or rule him out. I accept that you can't divulge the name if it's your *other* donor, that *other* man with eyes my exact shade of blue.' Tom's ironic tone indicated that he believed no such donor existed, that the doctor was telling a deliberate porky to protect the clinic.

Roberts countered with 'What if the call comes at a time which is inconvenient to me?'

'Then ask her to ring you back at a specified time, out of business hours. I'll make sure I'm there with her.' Tom engaged the doctor in steady eye contact, doing his best to project the image of a reliable player in this drama.

Roberts stared pensively back at Tom. 'I remember you coming in with your ex-wife. You seem like a decent bloke. Well-intentioned. Intelligent. Emotionally stable. I'll have to mull over your request. And discuss the ethics with my colleagues.' He collected his papers and stood up to walk Tom to the door. 'I won't promise anything right now, but I'll give you a call next week. If my colleagues and I agree, I'll give you my mobile number then. But that in itself won't mean anything, one way or the other.' As he shook Tom's hand he said, 'The first person who's going to know whether you are, or are not, Thea Pearson's father is going to be Nicola Pearson.'

CHAPTER THIRTY-THREE

'Nicola, are you free tonight? Will you be at home?'

'I will. I'll be heading off home around five today.' The sound of Tom's voice on the phone drenched her in a thrill of anticipation, even as she wondered why he might think she'd be anywhere else tonight but at home. 'Are you angling for a formal invitation?' God it felt wonderful to tease someone other than Thea.

'Sure am.'

'You know you don't need one.' Her seductive tone sounded just like all the other women who flirted with their boyfriends over the phone each day on her train commutes. She suppressed a happy giggle.

'I have a few things to tidy up here first. I'll be there as soon as I can. I've postponed my dinner engagement with the lawyers who handled that last big deal of mine.'

'Dinner at my place, then?' Let those within hearing

distance of her conversation wonder if she had a new man in her life, at last.

'That sounds good. An omelette will do.'

'Right.' She wanted to say, 'You don't qualify as a guest, you feel like family, part of my life,' but she restrained herself. This was the office, after all. 'Thea and I will carry on with our normal evening routine and I'll rustle up something once you arrive.'

'Sounds good. See you soon.'

Nicola packed up on the dot of five and flew home on wings of joyful eagerness. Thank God this was Friday. Thea received her mother's biggest hug and broadest smile ever. 'Tom's coming to see us again in a little while, darling. Mummy's happy, happy, happy.' She grabbed Thea's hands and did a little jig around the kitchen.

Thea squealed with joy. 'Appy, Mummy 'appy. Me 'appy too.'

They were in the middle of story time by the time Tom arrived. Nicola rushed to let him in when the buzzer sounded. His fervent kiss as he came through the front door held many promises. 'First things first, Tom. Sorry, but a rhyming nonsense story about green eggs and ham awaits.'

'Then lead on. I'm glad Thea's still awake.'

Tom sat on the end of Thea's bed as Nicola acted out Sam-I-Am's dialogue, prompting Thea's round eyes and giggles. Those special blue eyes. Then came the *Time for Bed* book and a good night kiss from Nicola. Thea snuggled down with her Blanky. Tom knelt down beside the sleepy head resting on the pillow and kissed both her cheeks. 'Good night, beautiful baby.'

'I think you two have got a thing going on,' laughed Nicola.

'But of course. How could I resist her? She's her mother's daughter.' Their eyes met.

Nicola closed Thea's bedroom door and led the way towards the kitchen. She turned to face Tom. 'Hungry?'

'Hungry for you. That omelette will have to wait.' His strong arms enveloped her as he pressed his over-heated rock-like body against her soft curves. Nicola melted into his embrace.

Later, exhausted, they lay entwined on her bed.

'I know this has been a whirlwind romance, but …'

'But what?'

'And I know I should be asking you this in some romantic setting, but …'

'There's that but again.'

'I love you to bits. Pretty much since the day we met. Will you marry me?'

Nicola stared at him. Her old fears and worries suddenly hit her again and she wailed, 'But I'm not a slinky blonde bombshell.'

'So? You're a brunette curly-headed bombshell.'

Nicola remained nervously unconvinced. 'Have you asked me because you've taken such a fancy to Thea?'

'Now that's silly. What do you think?'

'I can't believe you mean it.'

'I do. You know I do.'

Panic-stricken, she blurted out her core fear. 'But it's too soon. You don't know everything about my background, my history.' She trailed off, distressed. He didn't know the full story about Thea. How could he rush her like this?

'Nicola, look at me. Like recognises like. You and I are two of a kind. We feel as if we've always known each other. We're on the same wave length mentally. Just one look and our bodies are on fire. Don't you feel it?'

'I feel it. You've been calling to me at the back of my mind from the day I met you. I need you. You need me. We need each other.'

'Agreed. You're the woman I never thought I'd meet. The woman I can't wait to marry.' He put a finger to her lips to hush her. 'But I don't want your answer straight away. I want you to think about what this might mean. For you. For us. For Thea. For your career.'

'Oh Tom, all my instincts tell me yes. But there's stuff you need to know.'

'Stuff?'

'Yes, stuff. My full story.'

'Darling Nicola, I told you, I'm not going to hold you to an answer just yet. There's plenty of time for your story before you make any final commitment to me. I don't think there's anything you could possibly tell me that would surprise or shock me.'

'How can you be so sure?'

'Because I know you.'

'It's strange how you can know someone so well in

such a short time.'

'Nature and instincts are wonderful guides. But there's something I want you to do before you give me my answer. Because there's stuff you need to know too.'

'Is there something *you* haven't been telling *me* Tom? Is there some dark secret in your past, something dreadful?'

'Not at all, darling.' He quickly smoothed her fears away. 'Nothing dreadful, nothing scandalous, nothing to be ashamed about. I think you pretty well know who I am and the relevant bits of my past.'

'What then?'

'There *is* a secret—I hope a good one. It's something important for your future happiness and peace of mind, but not something you can know about right now. The right time for its revelation will come soon enough. We'll deal with it then.'

'This all sounds highly mysterious and intriguing.'

'Perhaps, but you can relax for now.' He nibbled her earlobe.

'Impossible, when you're around. Too much sensory stimulation.' Her hand caressed his bare chest. 'Right now it's entirely possible for me to stop thinking about your mysterious secret. I have other things on my mind. Will you take me back to that magical place you took me to an hour ago?'

'With pleasure, my little temptress. I've been holding back, waiting for this exact moment—your explicit invitation.'

CHAPTER THIRTY-FOUR

Nicola's smile was dreamy, if drowsy, as she lay cradled against Tom's body, warmed by his radiant heat. She'd had no sleep, but the world was a marvellous place. Her body was a little stiff and sore in places she'd never dreamt would be so tender but a great weight had lifted from her mind. During that long night of love she'd told Tom her story, and it hadn't worried him in the slightest. How could it have loomed so large, for so long, as a stumbling block for her?

'Good morning, darling. Are you awake?' She angled her head to kiss Tom's stubbled chin. He was too sleepy and exhausted to do more than increase the pressure of his arms as his response.

'I've been lying here, thinking. Are you going to tell me any more about this secret of yours?'

'Not today.' Is that what he'd mumbled? He was barely half awake.

She pressed him again. 'I'm dying to know what this is all about.'

'I know you are. Soon. Hopefully next week. Be patient.'

It was plain he wasn't going to be tempted into talking about it. Perhaps he could be provoked into life in other more physical ways. Her hand did a little exploring. 'Nicola, for pity's sake, let me recover my strength for a few minutes. You've worn me out.'

Thea toddled into the bedroom, rubbing the sleep from her eyes with one fist and dragging her Blanky. Quite unfazed to find Tom snuggled up beside her mummy, she scrambled up onto the bed with them.

'Hello baby, my precious little bundle.' Nicola cuddled the warm little body, but kept the sheet drawn up so Thea didn't realise that her mother was naked. Now they were the Three Bears, all lined up together, Tom cuddling Nicola and Nicola with an arm round Thea. Tom shifted his arm to wrap it round both of his girls.

Nicola added a bit more to last night's stories. 'Tom, did you know why I picked her name? Why I picked Thea?'

'Tell me.'

'She's named after my grandmother Thea, whose full name Dorothea means gift of God. A perfect choice, don't you think? Thea was my miracle gift.'

'Getting her meant everything to you, didn't it?'

'Everything. Before you came into my life, of course.

Except for not knowing where she came from. It still worries me.'

'It doesn't worry me. Almost as much as I love you to bits, I love her to bits. She's a lovely little girl. Takes after her mother.' Tom was coming to physical life again. He nuzzled the back of Nicola's neck. Under the sheet, things were happening.

Nicola squeezed Thea. 'Why don't you go and play with your toys in your room for a few minutes, darling, while Mummy gets dressed. Then we'll have some breakfast.'

'Kay.' Thea slid to the floor and toddled off again, sucking on her Blanky.

'See, like I told you last night, even Thea can tell we're right for each other.' Tom reached for her again.

'Sorry darling. You'll have to wait. The demands of parenthood sometimes come first. You're in for a dramatic change in routine.'

'It won't take long, the way I feel,' he grumbled in her ear.

'Hold that thought.' She stroked her hand along his erect and throbbing shaft. 'I really have to attend to Thea at present.'

Thea was having her afternoon nap. Nicola and Tom were back on her bed, snuggled together, sated from their recent exertions.

'That was wonderful, Tom. Last night too. Thank you for being such a wonderful guide through foreign territory. Now I understand Catherine's reason for bragging to her friends.'

'You've re-energised me. You're one of those 'looks like an angel, but a devil in disguise' type of girls.'

'Am I? It goes to show what a quick learner you can be when you love someone.'

'For a long time I feared I'd never hear you admit it.'

'Admit what?'

'Your feelings. That you love me.'

'I know I'm a bottler—but I do feel things deeply.'

'That day at Manly taught me that. I was watching you all the time. How you were with Thea. How you were with me. How you went with the whole flow of the day. You react instinctively. You can't react like that without a great deal of intuition.'

'I loved every moment of that day. It made me so happy, so free to be myself.'

'You're one of those people who don't need to talk about your feelings and emotions all the time. They show via your behaviour and body language. And I can read you. But sometimes—like right now—I need you to verbalise your feelings more directly. Keeping me in suspense the way you've done has been agony.'

'I was highly suspicious of you at the start.'

'That was obvious. Do I have two heads, or something?'

'Your reputation precedes you. As does the image of men who do jobs like yours.'

'Sometimes the image doesn't match the reality.'

'So I've discovered. Your macho man image successfully hides a family man at heart. And for all your obvious sexuality, you don't try to flaunt it, or pressure me into something I'm not ready for.'

'Correct. I like the challenge of the hunt, what man doesn't, but I'm discerning with my targets. And I'm not interested in an unwilling partner.'

'Have there been many? Targets, I mean.'

'Not on my part. Quite the reverse. Maybe when I was young and stupid. Not in recent years. Men in my role are often the target of women looking for a good catch. Like Catherine. I can't claim to have been celibate, but I haven't had to work too hard in the past. Whereas with you—my God, it's been tough trying to win you.'

'Sorry darling, but you did scare me at first.'

'Why?'

'I could sense the power of your attraction, yet at the same time I didn't want to trust any more men in my life.'

'Don't judge everyone by David's standards and treatment of you.'

'You're so different from him. I count my blessings that I came back from PNG. I'd never have met my perfect match there. You.'

'You're right. My job has never taken me to PNG. Nor is it ever likely to.'

'You've even got that romantic streak. The roses, I mean.'

'Nicola, you deserved them. You're such a rarity among women today. Refreshing to my spirits you are. Without an ounce of crassness. A top-class lady in every way.'

'Look out, I might get a swollen head.'

'It took me a bare ten days to work out that you're a rare prize. I did enjoy giving you that surprise, that little bit of cosseting. It made me happy for the whole weekend.'

'But how ever did you get my address?'

'Pure luck. You now realise that I live in the general area. I happened to be driving by as you walked home. You were with Thea and a young woman.'

'That must have been Stephanie, my babysitter.'

'Stephanie? Oh yes, that girl I met the other day. I only saw her back view as you three walked together. Anyhow, sorry to have to admit the next bit, but I stalked you, in effect. I waited to see which building you entered, to obtain your street address. All I needed to do then was take a squiz at the tenant panel inside the front door, where the security buzzers are located, to obtain your apartment number. The rest was easy.'

'Why didn't you stop and say hello to us?'

'I knew next day was Valentine's Day. It was my idea of a bit of fun. You looked tired and unappreciated. I hoped it would add something special to your day.'

'You know it did. You saw me in the lift the following Monday.'

'I'm glad you remember. This is what I was burning to do that day.' He tipped her nose with his finger and brushed his lips across hers. 'In fact, every day since I first met you.' He deepened his kiss. 'You, my darling, have been my irresistible temptation since the day we met. I fought against the temptation, because I was prejudiced against a woman with a child, but I lost the battle.'

CHAPTER THIRTY-FIVE

Tom's phone had rung non-stop all morning. Darn, another call, and he was in the middle of a difficult interview. He grabbed the hand piece and barked 'Forrester'.

'Good. Stephen Roberts. I'm glad I got you.'

'Oh.' Tom quickly marshalled his thoughts. 'It's been a week now. I hope you've got good news for me.'

'It depends. We've been through our records. We did make a mistake over your phone call three years ago. We found a rough note saying you'd called to make sure your sperm sample was to be destroyed. There was a scribble to say you'd changed your mind about proceeding with treatment. The record of the call was misfiled and has just come to light. We've been conducting a review, working systematically through all our files to update our computer records before archiving them. We offer our sincere apologies for that serious error.'

'Apology accepted.' Tom spoke abruptly, but needed to be circumspect, as John Wrigley was sitting across the desk from him. Roberts knew he was calling a work number and Tom hoped he would twig.

'Tell me more, please.' Tom's bland words and neutral tone should alert Roberts to the reasons for this one-sided conversation.

'We accept that these are unique circumstances.' Roberts must have guessed, because he spoke more quietly. 'We are able to tell you that one child was conceived and has been born from your sperm sample, but we can't tell you anything more.'

'At least I know that much. One, you say.' Damn, he should have told Wrigley to leave. Too late now.

'Yes, one. The law might one day allow that child to seek you out, if the child so desires.'

'I understand. But what about … um … my specific request?'

'In this particular instance, my colleagues and I have agreed to your request.'

'You mean I can proceed, on the terms we agreed.'

'You can.'

'And you're not giving me any indication at this stage?'

'No, as I said, Nicola Pearson is the person we'll be speaking to about the matter you raised.'

'Understood. Thanks for letting me know. I'll pass on the number. The contact will be made soon. Can't talk further right now, sorry, I'm in a meeting.'

Tom hung up. He stared down Wrigley's openly

curious gaze. Had he been careful enough not to give away any clues about the nature of that particular conversation? Had Wrigley overheard the mention of Nicola's name?

Perhaps he had because Wrigley said, 'You do receive fascinating phone calls, Tom. I wonder what that one was all about.'

'None of your business, John. Let's get back to what *is* your business—your recent performance. I've got to sign off on this bond market report. You've got some explaining to do.'

Dinner was over, Thea was finally asleep and all was quiet. Tom temporarily resisted the call of Nicola's bedroom. This was the perfect time, private uninterrupted time, for Nicola to call Dr Roberts.

For more than eight hours he'd been on tenterhooks, knowing she could make the call, waiting for the verdict. He was convinced he knew the answer already, and in any case he'd gone well past the point of no return. His commitment was absolute, regardless, but he must be sure that Nicola was under no illusions.

'Nicola. Remember what we talked about last Friday night—about secrets? That there was something important that you needed to know? I'd like you to ring this number.' Tom reached into the breast pocket of his jacket, slung over the back of a chair, extricated his preciously-guarded business card with a mobile number carefully written on the back, and pressed it into her hands.

Nicola looked at the card, bemused. 'What's this all about, Tom?'

'It's a phone number, for a doctor named Stephen Roberts who works at the fertility clinic you attended. Not the doctor you mentioned to me in bed, that night when you told me how Thea came into your life. A different doctor.'

'Why do I need to ring him?' She looked mystified. 'I don't get it. How come you're involved?'

'You'll find out as soon as you make that phone call. Dr Roberts has something to tell you.'

'What? I don't understand. What do you mean? The clinic? Why not my old doctor–or George Woodard?' Nicola's eyes grew wide with apprehension.

He gave her a reassuring squeeze. 'It's about Thea. You should give him a call.'

Nicola's face drained of all colour. 'Thea! Oh my God. Not again!'

'Calm down, no need for concern, Nicola, don't panic, just call him.'

She looked at him. She looked at her watch. 'Right now? Interrupt his dinner time on a Friday night?' She ran fingers through her hair, a puzzled frown on her face, perplexed.

Tom soothed her as best he could. 'Yes, right now, he won't mind. He'll tell you if it's inconvenient.' He knew his calming words were contradicted by a certain tension in his demeanour.

She stared at Tom. 'I don't see how you got involved

in all of this. You didn't know anything about it until a week ago. What's going on here?'

'We're trading secrets. You've told me yours. I'm about to reveal mine. Fair exchange. Please ring him.' He handed the telephone to her.

Hands shaking, Nicola dialled the number. 'Hello, it's Nicola Pearson speaking. Is that Dr Stephen Roberts?'

After pausing for his answer Nicola said, 'I know it's an awkward time to ring. I hope you're not in the middle of dinner.'

Tom watched as the lines creasing her forehead on her face betrayed her curiosity. Anchoring her gaze on Tom, she rocked from one jittery foot to the other. He was anxious too. His mouth was dry. Tight bands wrapped round his chest.

'Tom Forrester has just told me that you have a message for me. Some information about my daughter Thea Pearson. Please, I need to know. Whatever it is.'

A few seconds later Nicola nodded her head, eagerly and vigorously. 'The donor? Yes, yes, of course I would.' She began pacing the room, the phone jammed against her ear.

'Yes, Tom's here with me,' she said. She looked at him, bewildered.

Tom wished he could hear the other end of this conversation.

A few minutes of silence ensued. Tom studied Nicola's face intently as she listened to the doctor's words. Her face crumpled as her eyes overflowed with tears. Tears of joy, streaming down her face. Still clutching the phone to one ear, she collapsed against him, gazing up at him in wondrous ecstasy. At last he knew the answer. Thea was his daughter too.

He took the phone from her. 'Thanks Stephen. All's right with the world.'

The refrain of Jimmy Durante's old song flooded their minds and swelled their hearts. The lyrics were so true—the rich reward of personal happiness went hand-in-hand with the effort of making someone else happy.

'I love that song, Tom. I'm glad you chose that CD of mine.'

'Me too. It's one of my favourites, when I'm in the mood. We've made each other over-the-moon happy.' He kissed her again. 'So now you know my little secret, Nicola. Not such a bad secret, huh? Our secret love child, definitely the product of two loving people, of love, in that sense.'

'The best secret there could possibly be. You've answered all my prayers, my worries, about Thea's origins. Why on earth didn't you tell me a week ago about your visits to that same clinic with Catherine?'

'Because my eyes are such a perfect match to hers. I didn't want you to marry me, thinking or hoping that I might be Thea's father, and then have you find out years later that I wasn't. That's why I didn't want you to make any commitments until we both knew.'

'Oh Tom, I'm so happy. I've never been happier. My dreams have all come true. We belong together. It was our fate. How else would you explain that chain of coincidences that led to this point?'

'Do I take it that the answer to my formal proposal of marriage is definitely *Yes*?'

'Yes, yes, yes! How could you doubt it? Absolutely all of my worries and insecurities, holding me back for these past three years, have disappeared. Someone loves me after all, a wonderful, exciting, caring, handsome superman.' She kissed the tip of his nose. 'And I know where the other half of Thea comes from. I love you, darling.'

Hours later, after a lot of loving, and excited plans for giving Thea a brother or a sister as soon as possible, conceived the way nature intended, Nicola's drowsy question came out of the darkness. 'What about Thea's birth certificate?'

'What about it, sweetheart?'

'It says father unknown. I could have put David as the father, but under the circumstances I didn't. I simply couldn't bring myself to commit that lie to paper.'

'Fair enough. It's good you told the truth.'

'Legally she was a child of the marriage but he'd turned his back on her and his access rights. That's why she was registered with the surname of Pearson, my married name and the name I was using for myself. Old habits die hard, don't they! I've been Pearson for so long.'

'But soon you'll be Forrester. Or will you keep your current name?'

'Hmm, Nicola Forrester. It has a certain cachet to it. I rather like it. It'd be strange to continue using my first husband's name when married to my second husband.'

'There's always your maiden name,' he teased.

'That's ancient history.' They were spooned together on the bed. She twisted her head around and planted a playful peck on his nose. 'It could have been worse. You could have been a Higginbottom or a Slaughter.'

'Don't be cheeky. Cheeky girls can get into a lot of trouble.' His free hand began a slow dance across her breasts. His erection pressed against her bottom.

'You're insatiable, Tom Forrester.'

'But manfully biding my time, for the moment. I want to hear the rest of your story about Thea's birth certificate.'

'Really? I salute your self-control! I'll be quick then. I didn't name David as the father because I didn't want to complicate Thea's life any further with a lie which could never be undone. You can hardly name one man as the father at birth and then nominate a different man later. What's more, David's words and actions forfeited his right to any claim on her.'

'I agree. It would have been impossible to keep up the

pretence throughout her childhood unless he was playing a positive active role in her life, which he wasn't.'

'Then again, it broke my heart to saddle her for life with the slur of illegitimacy and an apparently immoral mother.'

'Now you're harking back to the past. In a few years we'll be in the twenty-first century. Community attitudes are freeing up.'

Tom's hand fluttered down over her stomach and made unhurried circles on her hip and thigh, trying to ambush her negative train of thought, while keeping his positive. 'You know, I've been thinking about Thea's legal status too. Once I became besotted with you, and then her, and before I knew about the AID issues, I thought seriously about a formal adoption. You didn't realise that, did you?'

'No, darling, I certainly did not. You're a man of generous spirit, however hard you try to hide it in that tough world at the office.' She snuggled even closer against his rock-hard body.

Tom made a superhuman effort to dampen his response, knowing he must be strong enough to resist her for another few minutes. 'Now there's an even better solution. We'll apply to have my name entered as the father on her birth certificate. The 'unknown' father has now been identified. I'm pretty sure that clinic will issue some paperwork which will satisfy the Registrar of Births, Deaths and Marriages. Or we could organise a paternity test.'

'That's true. He has been identified.' Nicola sighed with gratification and wiggled her bottom against his thrusting heat.

Her provocative move was more than any man could normally withstand, but continue he must. 'And if you approve, we can also apply for an official change of name for Thea. After all, Pearson is not *her* family name, is it? Because she doesn't yet identify herself by that name, she won't suffer an identity crisis by losing the surname Pearson to become a Forrester. Little Miss-Midnight-Blue-Eyes is going to be part of our Forrester family.' He turned her fully towards him and planted a triumphant kiss on her forehead.

Nicola almost purred with contentment. 'It's the perfect ending.'

ACKNOWLEDGMENTS

Trading Secrets is a work of fiction which happens to be based on various real-life experiences, scrambled up and re-arranged to become a genuine product of the author's imagination. The story is not intended to reflect on any actual person, living or dead, except that the name of my much-loved daughter Thea inspired this tale.

I am grateful to my friends Stephanie Lee in Sydney and Lady Brown (Pam) in Yorkshire and writing colleagues Rachael Thomas in Wales, Serena Sandrin and Deb Tait, both in Melbourne, for their helpful comments on earlier drafts of this book under its various titles. It took me a while to settle on the current title.

Special thanks are due to my writing buddy Eliza Renton. Without her constant encouragement, patient re-reads and insightful, detailed feedback, this book would never have reached the hands of the reading public.

Once *Trading Secrets* was ready for readers, the amazingly tech-savvy Melbourne author Ebony McKenna taught me how to join the digital publishing world—as she has cheerfully helped other authors to do. The business of writing these days has become a rewarding communal effort.

ABOUT THE AUTHOR

Louisa Valentine, an Australian author, has long-since waved goodbye to her multi-faceted career in finance & economics and returned to her teenage passion for history, mystery and romance.

Her first novel 'Retreat into Paradise', an Australian rural romance of the old-fashioned variety, was published as an e-book in December 2019.

'Trading Secrets', her second novel, introduces a little mystery into her women's fiction titles.

Louisa Valentine lives a double life as an author. Her former married name of Valentine became the perfect pen-name for an author of women's fiction. As Louise Wilson she has also published nine non-fiction books. These bring previously untold aspects of Australia's fascinating history to life in well-researched and award-winning historical biographies and family histories.

She lives a double life in the real world too. One minute she's home alone, writing at her desk in Melbourne. The next she's driving up the Hume Highway to Sydney where she helps her daughter to run a busy household containing four teenage grandchildren ... two sets of twins born 14 months apart.

https://www.louisewilson.com.au

Thank you for reading *Trading Secrets*. If you liked the story, you should enjoy my earlier book *Retreat into Paradise*. Here's a brief introduction:

City girl Hannah Stockton writes histories as her day-job and family histories in her spare time. Needing a temporary escape from a violent boyfriend, she takes up an advertised position as a live-in caretaker 'with light duties' at a country retreat outside Melbourne. The owner, Philip Boulton, is a hunky high-flying banker who visits on weekends to attend to his small herd of cattle. Hannah is dismayed to discover that Philip has been taught all he knows about farming by his next-door neighbour, who lusts after Philip and resents Hannah's presence. Hannah can't tell whether Philip is 'more than friends' with his guru.

Philip has recently discovered a family secret. Given his profession, he's sensitive about this fact becoming public. Fearing Hannah's skills as a family history researcher, he keeps her at a distance while he processes his secret.

Meanwhile, as her 'boss', he helps Hannah to overcome her fear of cattle and she learns to love country life … and Philip.

If you'd like to hear about future stories by Louisa Valentine, please 'Like' me on
www.facebook.com/LouisaValentineAuthor.

Or visit www.louisewilson.com.au

Remember, authors spend countless hours conceiving, drafting and perfecting stories in order to provide readers with a few hours of reading pleasure. Authors appreciate all the assistance they can get with spreading the word about their book. So please help in one or more of the following ways …
What is your rating for this book?
Share or Tweet that you finished it.
Tell friends & family if you enjoyed it.
Leave a review on your online sales outlet.
Leave a review on Goodreads.

Thank you for every bit of reader feedback.

www.ingramcontent.com/pod-product-compliance
Lightning Source LLC
Chambersburg PA
CBHW032002130726
47903CB00012B/448